A Most Dangerous Affair
By
Christy Gissendaner

Triskelion Publishing
www.triskelionpublishing.net

Triskelion Publishing
15327 W. Becker Lane
Surprise, AZ 85379 USA

Printing History
First e Published by Triskelion Publishing
First e publishing February 2006
ISBN 1-933471-81-6
First printing by Triskelion Publishing
First paperback printing September 2006
ISBN 1-933874-32-5

Cover design by Triskelion Publishing
Lady in Mask and titling by Michelle Rouillard

Publisher's Note. This is a work of fiction. Names, characters, and places and incidents are a product of the author's imagination. Any resemblance to a person or persons, living or dead, business establishments, events or locales is purely coincidental.

5 Angels from Fallen Angel Reviews Viola Haversham and Marcus Kingsley were on the verge of being married when Marcus is found in a compromising position with another lady. Viola's heart was broken as Marcus left England with his new bride. Fate has now brought Marcus back as a widower; can he persuade Viola to take him back?

Viola pretends she has recovered from the pain of her broken romance. She has built a nice sturdy wall around her heart and refuses to be hurt again. Viola has matured since Marcus left and she is a much wiser person. Marcus has never forgotten Viola. He made a horrible mistake one night and paid for it by losing the woman he loved. Although he did come to care for his wife, he never loved her like he did Viola. Viola is like the immovable mountain and Marcus is constantly trying to move it. He wants her to believe in him, to trust him and to love him again. It is an uphill battle as Viola has never forgotten the anguish and the shame of what happened. Since she remained in England, she was the center of gossip and pity. The reader can identify with Viola's feelings since the incident is fully delineated and well-expressed within the story. In Marcus, this reader was quite ambivalent about him as he found some semblance of happiness with the woman he married while Viola was going through hell. Marcus and Viola do have a sizzling sexual chemistry together and this is reflected in the storyline.

A Most Dangerous Affair is a heart-wrenching tale that can bring tears to the reader's eyes. It has two very strong lead characters that readers won't forget easily. The storyline is nicely paced and it is a first-rate page-turner. It pulls the reader in and doesn't let go until the last page. Susan T. from **Fallen Angel Reviews**

Mystery, mayhem and intrigue with a hefty dose of romance are the ingredients in this tale creating a very exciting read. From the first you will be engrossed in the love between Marcus and Viola and understand the pain and bitterness in Viola as she faces betrayal. But you never lose the chance to cheer Marcus for his love and his determination to have Viola. All of this with steamy hot sex scenes makes for one exceptional read.

Wateena
Reviewer for **Coffee Time Romance**

A Most Dangerous Affair by Christy Gissendaner is a thrilling sensual romance filled with intrigue. The handsome and seductive Marcus goes about winning Viola's heart. Whenever they are together the chemistry is exciting. Viola melts in Marcus's strong arms. Their stimulating encounters are described in explicit details that are easily visualized and will speed the pulse of the reader.

The settings are described in such a way as to bring the story to life. The dialogue is well written and conveys the thoughts and emotions of the characters. The mystery behind the betrayal and then the danger that enters the story later is exciting and intriguing. The ending result is quite surprising.

Filled wit suspense and intrigue A most Dangerous Affair is an extremely sensual romance that is sure to thrill the readers. Anita from **The Romance Studio**

Dedication

"This book is dedicated to my parents, Robert and Cindy Gissendaner, and my grandparents, Edward and Mildred Dasinger.

And for my cousin, Amy Phillips, who kept pushing me to finish Marcus and Viola's story. Hope you like how it turns out!"

Chapter One

June 1823

Viola Haversham had never been one for idle gossip, but this afternoon proved to be an exception. She had just arrived for tea at the home of her cousin, the Countess of Buckley, when she overheard the most devastating news.   Viola paused in the entranceway and strained to hear the conversation between two young debutantes standing closest to her. Their voices were muted by the potted palm they stood behind and she could not make out the entire exchange.   The two girls stopped their frantic whispering when Viola's name was announced and they covered their giggles behind gloved hands. Viola gave them a quelling look and they turned from her so quickly their pastel skirts swirled up to reveal a glimpse of ankle.

Viola, dressed somberly in dark blue, commanded the respect usually reserved for the elder matrons of society and she was easily able to fluster the younger girls with just a look. Although she was only twenty-one, Viola projected the aura of an old soul, which made her seem far older than her years. The carefree days of her youth were behind her and she had relegated herself to the distinct possibility of entering the most dreaded situation, spinsterhood. The connotations of the word itself was almost sinister and guaranteed to strike fear in the hearts of all the young ladies of the *ton* except Viola, who took pride in the fact her life was her own and no man had control over her.   Even Viola's friends, whom she considered quite forward thinking, would endure marriage to hideously awful men rather than face the rest of their life in spinsterhood.

Viola studied the debutantes again, taking note of their fashionable dress and artfully arranged hairstyles. The care they took with their appearance indicated they were on the hunt to catch a husband. She did not doubt she was pitied, maybe even ridiculed, by the girls for her apparent lack of suitors. What they did not understand was Viola preferred to be alone. Society thought her lack of suitors was an indication of something unworthy in Viola and she had long ago accustomed herself to the whispers whenever she entered a ballroom or tea. She would have misinterpreted their calculating looks now if she had not overheard tidbits of their conversation.

Sometimes these giddy debutantes served a purpose, Viola admitted to herself as she digested the information she had overheard. From what she had been able to discern of their excited babble, the Marquess of Kingsley was rumored to have returned from India after a three-year absence. Simply because the two girls knew of the rumor of Viola's involvement with the marquess was testimony to the fact that gossip was the favorite pastime in London since they were too young to have witnessed firsthand the year of Viola's debut. Viola thought the gossip would have died down by now, but she could see she had been wrong.

Viola casually removed her bonnet and shawl and handed them to the footman waiting at her elbow. The debutantes eyed her speculatively and Viola pretended she did not have the slightest interest in their conversation. Moving into the room with an unhurried pace, she joined her cousin at the center of the room.

"Have you heard the news, Viola?" Margaret gave her a subtle warning look as she reached her side. She put a restraining hand on Viola's elbow as she proclaimed gaily for the benefit of those close enough to overhear. "Your reclusive neighbor has finally returned to English soil."

"Has he? When did he arrive in England?" Viola asked in what she hoped was a normal tone. Her voice was carefully modulated so only a hint of interest was conveyed. She was aware of the attention she and Margaret were being given and she acted accordingly.

"Shortly after dawn." Margaret linked arms with Viola and began to lead her across the elegantly appointed drawing room. Margaret was a few inches shorter than she, so Viola bent her head forward attentively. To the curious onlooker it would seem as if she bent her head out of respect for Margaret's shorter stature, but in truth it was a move calculated to give them a few moments of privacy.

"Taylor was coming back from a ride in the Park when he noticed Kingsley's carriage parked in Pall Mall. Taylor was lucky enough to catch him just as the marquess was heading inside his house."

The question that sprang to Viola's lips went unasked as a new voice insinuated itself into their conversation. Viola's and Margaret's heads turned simultaneously to see who had spoken.

"Did your husband have a chance to speak with the marquess?"

The Dowager Duchess of Bradford joined Viola's and Margaret's private conversation by expertly placing herself between them, forcing them to include her or else appear unbearably rude. Viola almost applauded the ancient matron's smooth insinuation into their group. The dowager was several inches under five feet tall and she was easily able to slip in undetected. Viola hadn't been aware of another's presence until she had spoken. Margaret's perturbed look indicated her own amazement at the stealthy maneuvering of the tiny lady.

The dowager linked her arms between the two of them and smiled up at them benignly. When they did not immediately speak, the dowager's pale eyebrows drew together in a frown and she poked her finger in Margaret's direction. "Well? Come on, girl. Speak up. I asked you a question, did I not?"

Margaret cleared her throat as a pale blush lit her cheeks. She recovered quickly and fumbled to answer the dowager's query. "Yes, he did. It was only for a moment, but Buckley assured me Kingsley was well."

Margaret bent her head forward in a similar manner to Viola's. Next to the dowager, she noted even petite Margaret looked like an Amazon. She quickly hid her grin of amusement behind a pair of dark gloves and coughed delicately.

"Excellent news!" The dowager clapped her hands together gleefully. The excited motion of her hands nearly overbalanced the lady and Margaret reached out to steady her. Once she was balanced, the dowager continued excitedly. "He was always such a rascally scamp. London has been dreadfully dull without his presence. It is about time this dreary place is livened up a bit."

"Surely there are others who could keep you entertained?"

The dowager made a huffing noise and waved her hands dismissively at the small gathering in Margaret's drawing room. "Does this look like an entertaining crowd to you? Of course, no party is complete without a male present."

Margaret attempted to keep a straight face at the dowager's enthusiasm and failed miserably. The tell tale signs of a smile began to tilt up the edges of her small mouth. "So you are telling me in the past three years you have not encountered the tiniest bit of excitement?"

The dowager smoothed a hand, covered in an array of dazzling rings, over her still bright red hair and winked cunningly. "Maybe just a little bit of excitement. I may not be so young anymore, but many men still find me attractive. Let me assure you I am not quite dead yet."

Viola hastily coughed into her hand to hide a horrified laugh. The dowager could not possibly be any younger than eighty! She immediately snapped to attention when the dowager turned her calculating gaze to hers. Viola did not even want to imagine what the old bird was thinking. Sadly, the dowager had no compunction about saying exactly what was on her mind.

"Needless to say, I am getting far more satisfaction than you, young lady. If you are not careful, you are going to end up firmly on the shelf. You need to get yourself a husband and soon. Good looks do not last forever, you know. What are you now? Twenty-three?"

"Barely twenty-one," Viola managed to answer though her face flamed bright red. She could not believe the dowager was comparing romantic escapades. And what was even more embarrassing was the fact the dowager was the victor even though her husband had been dead for almost two decades.

"Still much too old to remain unmarried," the dowager continued blithely on with a wave of her hand. The rings on her fingers caught the light and Viola winced at the sudden glare. "When I was your age I was already married and the mother of two children. Of course, I married a complete wastrel, but at least I have my children to comfort me in my old age."

The reference to her children gave Margaret the excuse she needed to make an effort to turn the conversation away from her beleaguered cousin. "And how are your sons, Your Grace? I have not seen the duke in ages."

The dowager pinned Margaret with a sly look and shook a finger at her. "Do not attempt to change the subject. You and I both know it is past time for your cousin to wed. Now that Kingsley is back in town maybe we can end all this nonsense once and for all. It would be the match of the season."

"Surely you are not suggesting I pursue the marquess?" Viola's heart dropped into her stomach, but she kept a neutral tone.

"I most certainly am! Everyone knows his marriage to the Weatherington chit was a sham. I had great hopes you and Kingsley would make a match of it when you debuted. I am very disappointed you let him slip through your fingers. If I were thirty years younger, I would pursue him myself. As it is, I truly hope you will make it quite obvious to him you would be his ideal bride."

"I have not seen him in three years. Surely you cannot believe an attachment still exists between us?"

The dowager put a hand to her forehead and sighed dramatically. "Ah, the folly of youth." She used the same hand to poke a finger at Margaret's side, which caused the younger woman to wince in pain. "How long do you think they will keep denying what is right before their noses?"

Margaret's gaze flicked to Viola over the dowager's head and she tilted her chin to indicate for Viola to make good her escape. Viola nodded to indicate she understood as she began to carefully ease away from the dowager.

"Maybe we should leave them to their own pursuits. Surely they know better than anyone if they are compatible? By the way, have I shown you my new pianoforte?"

Margaret managed to divert the dowager's attention long enough for Viola to flee across the room. Though Viola detested to take the cowardly way out, she knew she was no match for the crafty dowager. If she stayed in her presence any longer, she would either strangle the old biddy or scream in frustration. Since neither option was advisable, she had to resort to underhanded tactics.

Viola let out a sigh of relief as Margaret's ploy successfully rescued her from the clutches of the dowager. Viola obediently perched herself on a small sofa and clasped her hands together in her lap. Now that she was safe from the inquisitive old woman, she had time to contemplate her reaction to the fact Marcus was returned. The frantic beat of her heart gave her the worry she would embarrass herself by falling into a dead faint.

He had finally returning after a three-year absence.

The *ton* would be over her like flies to honey now they'd found out he was back in England. She wondered if she would be able to make it out of London before anyone knew he was back. She groaned as she remembered where she was. It was highly unlikely she would escape in time.

A quick look around the room confirmed that nearly every eye in the room was fixed on her. No doubt they were waiting for her to beat her breast or demonstrate an equally hideous reaction. It really was unlucky on the very afternoon Marcus returned, Viola would be forced to have tea with some of the most notorious gossips in London. Viola noticed the most obnoxious of all the gossips seated directly across the room and she resigned herself for the snide remark she knew was coming.

When Viola did not oblige the crowd by showing a visible reaction, Amelia Gray sniffed and lifted her nose in the air. "It is terribly rude of him to return when the season is almost over."

"You are still just put out because he refused to attend your coming out ball," Margaret answered curtly. She ignored the shocked looks on some of the women's faces. Margaret was renowned for her easygoing nature and it was highly unusual for her to voice her opinion in so forceful a manner.

Naturally, the dowager duchess beamed at Margaret's show of spirit. She even went so far as to clap Margaret on the back with gleeful pride.

"I, for one, am quite happy he is finally returned." Margaret continued in a firm tone which the dowager emphatically echoed with a nod of her head.

Amelia tossed her head defiantly and rudely ignored her hostess. Her dark eyes turned to pin Viola with a sly look. "What about you, dearest Viola? All of society once thought Kingsley would offer for you. Surely you were as surprised as the rest of us when he offered for Agnes Weatherington?"

Viola managed to smile convincingly even though she felt like gnashing her teeth together. "The match was not at all surprising to me considering Agnes confided her feelings for Kingsley at an earlier date."

"I never knew you and Agnes were on such friendly terms," Amelia pointed out with a challenging lift of her chin. "I do not recall witnessing you two together."

"We were barely more than acquaintances, but Agnes was aware Kingsley considered me his closest friend. As such, she felt I would be trustworthy."

Amelia's green eyes flashed with irritation she had not been able to rile Viola. With another toss of her black curls, Amelia ignored Viola's comment and sauntered to a different part of the room. Viola knew without a doubt Amelia had moved to spread her malicious gossip. Since reaching the advanced age of twenty-two without a proposal of marriage, Amelia had become very hostile to the ladies she looked upon as competition. Viola would have been tempted to pity the girl had Amelia not possessed such a patent dislike for her ever since her debut. Amelia had once claimed a *tendre* for Marcus and she had resented Viola for her close friendship with him.

Amelia and her cronies were deep in conversation and Viola caught their telling glances as they smirked at her over their shoulders. It was obvious she was the subject of their ridicule and she was on the verge of standing and wishing all of them to the devil. She would have done so too if she had not been surrounded by nearly two dozen ladies of the *ton*. Viola was already too much of an enigma to them and she had no wish to make such a spectacle of herself.

Instead, she turned her head to one side and cast Margaret a pleading look. Margaret nodded discreetly to indicate she understood her plea. She detached herself from the dowager and came forward to join Viola on the sofa. She offered to pour Viola a cup of tea before quietly whispering, "Please try to ignore Amelia. Your anger would only increase her spitefulness."

"She has actually been bearable the past few months, if you can believe it. Her claws suddenly appear now that Marcus is back in London. If she wants him, she is more than welcome to him." Viola forced a laugh. Her attempt at lightheartedness did not pass muster with Margaret, who looked at her with concern.

"Was it really such a surprise to hear Kingsley is back? You must have suspected it would happen, especially since his father has taken ill."

Viola's spirits plunged even lower as she recalled the present duke's illness. The Duke of Kingsley was like a second father to her and she had continued her relationship with him even though she was no longer in contact with his son. His health was rapidly failing and she found it hard to think of him without sadness.

"I did not expect him to return to the city. I would have imagined he would go to Kingsley Hall."

The Hall was located in the heart of Kent and bordered Haversham, Viola's own ancestral home. Viola felt a pang of homesickness at the thought of her beautiful home with its rolling hills and endless acres of wildflowers. After the season, her father had been forced to remain in the city on business and she had been unable to travel to her home. She had been in London for several months now and she longed to see the beautiful countryside again. It would be a welcome sight after suffering the crowded atmosphere of the city.

"Taylor mentioned Kingsley had an important meeting with his barrister. He is planning to ride on to the Hall within a couple of days."

"Marcus is very close to his father. I cannot imagine what would be so important it would keep him from his ailing father." The last was said in a vaguely disapproving tone.

"You know better than anyone how much he loves his father. Do not let your feelings for Marcus distort your judgment of his character." When Viola

would have made to argue, Margaret's perceptive
eyes halted her with a look. "Can you not put the
past behind you and find it in your heart to forgive
him?"

Viola looked at her cousin with a pained
expression. Viola's heart had been broken by him and
she could not fathom her cousin's easy dismissal of
that fact. "How can you say you want me to forgive
him? Do you not remember what he did?"

"I only know Kingsley suffered as much as
you by those unfortunate events. Do not hold him
responsible for circumstances beyond his control."
Margaret's stern tone brooked no arguments.
Although Margaret appeared calm and docile to the
rest of the *ton*, Viola was well aware of her cousin's
willful nature and she knew better than to argue with
her. Viola had yet to win an argument with her
cousin and she doubted she ever would.

Sensing Viola's reluctance to continue the
conversation, Margaret stood up and shook out her
full skirts. "Now, if you will excuse me, I must see to
my other guests." She leaned down to whisper a
warning. "Do not let the others see your distress.
You know how hurtful these vultures can be if they
sense you are upset by Kingsley's return. And for
God's sake, smile once in a while. It is unnatural for
someone to frown as often as you do."

Margaret's advice held some merit, so Viola
purposefully schooled her expression to mask her
emotions. She allowed a small tilt to her lips, but she
could not manage to form an actual smile. She was
painfully aware her expression probably more closely
resembled a grimace.

Although she had spent four years living under the scrutiny of the *ton*, Viola still found it difficult to not let her emotions become evident. Her face easily mirrored her thoughts, which Viola considered her greatest weakness. London society was based on appearances and anything resembling an honest emotion was ridiculed. The strict adherence to proper behavior was a crutch Viola still had to come to terms with. And proper behavior dictated that Viola must not show her dismay at the return of the one person she never wanted to see again, no matter how badly she wanted to.

A distraction was what she needed to divert her attention from her current predicament. Perhaps if she had something to occupy her hands, she would not focus so on Marcus's return. With that thought in mind, she leaned forward to reach for the cup of tea Margaret had placed on the table beside her.

The steam caressed her face as she lifted the cup to her lips and took a dainty sip. She idly wished the cup could contain a liquid more fortifying than tea. A good splash of brandy might do much to settle her nerves. As she lowered the cup, she kept her gaze firmly fixed on a spot of the wall across the room.

Roses and trailing vines decorated the wall of the morning room. Her eyes became unfocused as she gazed unseeingly at the rose patterned paper. The flowers reminded her of the gardens at home and inevitably brought to mind a moment that had occurred only five years earlier, although it seemed much longer since she had been so young and happy.

Chapter Two

Five years before

Fifteen year old Viola Haversham crept down the stairs of her family's country estate and rushed across the hall. Thick carpeting muffled her footsteps until she reached the point where the floors were uncovered. There she slowed her pace to tread more carefully as she cautiously edged forward. Her bare feet nimbly stepped over the floorboards that she knew from experience were prone to squeakiness. Just a few more feet and she could reach out and wrap her slender hand around the doorknob. She was just about to ease the door open when softly spoken words suddenly halted her mid-stride.

"Where are you stealing off to at this time of night?" a mocking voice called from the darkened shadows of her father's study. Viola let out a small squeak and pressed her back against the wooden door. Her hair swung into her face and she quickly brushed it out of her eyes. Who could be up so late at night?

Viola knew the voice did not belong to her father since he had gone up to bed hours ago. It also sounded much too young to be her father's. She squinted, trying to detect the identity of the person.

All she was able to make out was the figure of someone sprawled in her father's overstuffed armchair. He was obviously tall considering the length of the leg casually swung over the chair's arm. His boot was well made and appeared to be of the finest quality. His tone was cultured and hinted at an aristocratic background.

"Who are you?" She nervously stepped back a few feet. Her eyes darted to the right as she judged the distance to the stairs. It was not too far, so she had no doubt she could elude the stranger if he meant to harm her.

"You do not recognize me?" The male figure shifted in the chair to an upright position, but his face remained in the shadows. The question was tinged with amusement.

The soft voice was strangely familiar, so Viola inched forward to the open doorway of the study. "I am afraid I cannot see you well enough to identify you." Mayhap he was one of her male cousins who had stopped by for a visit, but she could not remember her father mentioning such.

"Then come a little closer." He lifted his hand and crooked a finger at her. "You do not have to stay out there in the hall like a frightened rabbit."

Viola glanced over her shoulder nervously and chewed her bottom lip. Indecision was evident on her face, but her eyes held a flicker of curiosity. She was intrigued by the soft, hypnotic voice of the stranger. She moved a step closer and paused in the doorway with one foot extended into the study. Her bare toes curled into the lush carpet of her father's study as she debated whether or not to move closer.

"There is no reason to be afraid, Viola. I can assure you I will never hurt you."

"How do you know my name?" Viola asked with a bit of trepidation. Perhaps she had been too hasty in trusting her instincts. She quickly drew her foot back from the room. "Does my father know you are here?"

"He invited me, so I assume he is aware of my presence." A soft chuckle echoed in the room and Viola's mind whirled with recognition. She would recognize that laugh anywhere. A bright smile lit her face with the realization.

Viola moved further into the library until she was standing next to the armchair and its occupant. A shaft of moonlight spilled through the open window and fell across a leg encased in superfine trousers. As she stared at his leg, a hand passed into the beam of light and rested on his left knee. His long, tapered fingers flexed as he rubbed his knee gently. Viola's eyes followed the movement as a suspicion began in her mind.

"Does your knee pain you?"

"Why do you ask?" His answering chuckle confirmed her suspicions of his identity.

"I have a friend who complains of an ache in his knee often. He fell out of a tree when he was eight and injured it."

"How did this hapless lad fall out of a tree?" he asked with an amused tone.

"He always was terribly clumsy," Viola teased with tongue in cheek. "He was forever stumbling over his large feet."

"Or maybe it was because a five year old hoyden pushed him out of that tree?" He leaned into the light and Viola could see she had correctly confirmed his identity.

"Marcus, it's really you!" Viola exclaimed as she threw herself at him. He caught her as she tumbled into his lap and wrapped his arms around her loosely. He pressed a kiss on the top of her head and laughed at her exuberant greeting. Viola hugged him tightly before attempting to get back to her feet.

The brief contact made her aware of how hard his body had become and a faint fluttering started in her lower belly. She quickly moved away from him at the unfamiliar sensation and her gown tangled around her legs at the sudden movement. Marcus had to help her free herself. He let out a soft chuckle at her predicament and Viola's feelings of embarrassment faded as she remembered how much she had missed her best friend the past few months.

"When did you return? How long are you staying?" Viola questioned as Marcus assisted her back to a standing position. The hands at her waist steadied her and she felt the strong flex of his fingers as he waited for her to get her balance. His hands could easily encircle her waist and she felt a tiny thrill at the thought. "Have you finished at Eton?"

"One question at a time please." Marcus got to his feet and walked toward the window. A slightly noticeable limp drew Viola's eyes and concern flashed across her face. The humid weather caused his knee to ache and he often said that walking helped the pain abate.

"Does your knee truly pain you still?" Viola crept up behind him and spoke over his right shoulder. She felt a twinge of guilt for being the one to cause him such pain. Marcus had been teasing her unmercifully that afternoon and she had only reacted out of frustration. She hadn't really meant to push him hard enough to make him fall out of the tree. He'd been bedridden for weeks and Viola apologized countless times for her mean spirited action. Marcus was forgiving and claimed not to blame her, but she it didn't stop her from feeling responsible.

"It does not hurt often. It is only the damp weather that has made the pain flare."

He turned to face her and the moonlight shone fully on his smiling face. Viola sucked in a breath as she stared at her dearest friend in the world. Marcus was absolutely breathtaking. His thick chestnut hair gleamed in the moonlight and was brushed back from his forehead. It curled slightly at the ends and lent him a rakish look. His brown eyes were deep set and looked at her warmly from beneath dark, arching eyebrows. His wide grin cut a slash across his tanned face and revealed straight, even white teeth. For a moment, all Viola could do was stare mutely at his stunning features. When he had left for Eton, he'd been a lanky boy of fourteen with skinny arms and legs. He'd barely been much larger than Viola. Now he easily topped six feet and his body had developed the lean muscles of an athlete. Although he visited often in the past four years and she had witnessed the differing stages of his maturity, Viola had not fully realized how handsome he had truly become. Suddenly she felt warm, but oddly wrapped her arms around herself as if to ward off a chill. How could she feel hot and cold at the same time? She tried to move her eyes away from him, but she could not help giving him a second look.

"What is the matter?" Marcus leaned back against the window and crossed his arms across his chest. He shifted to put most of his weight on his uninjured right leg. He crossed his left leg at the ankles and allowed a slight grimace of pain.

"Nothing." Viola quickly shook her head. She was embarrassed to be caught staring at him. "I was just so surprised to see you. You have to tell me all about Eton. I want to know everything."

" I wrote to you nearly every week and told you all about it in my letters," Marcus reminded her.

She had greedily absorbed the knowledge contained in his weekly letters. His life in London had seemed terribly exciting to a young, sheltered girl stuck in the country. She had read of his experiences and had longed to be there to share them with him. It was desperately unfair that Marcus was able to obtain an excellent education while she was forced to stay at home with tutors. Her father had hired the very best tutors in England, but Viola still wished she'd been born a boy so she could go off to school with him.

Although Marcus's letters succeeded at entertaining her, she suspected he had carefully edited the contents. He had regaled her of the sights and sounds of London, but failed to mention any naughty deeds. Viola knew Marcus's nature better than her own and there was no way he had not been in any mischief the entire time he had been gone.

"I know you wrote, but hearing it is infinitely much better than reading about it. Promise me you will tell me *everything*."

"Later. First you must answer my original question." Marcus strode forward to stare down at her in mock seriousness. He was half a foot taller and his greater height forced Viola to tip her head back to look at him properly. "Where were you off to at this time of night? Am I interrupting a midnight rendezvous with you and a young lord?"

"Of course not." Viola blushed and lowered her head. She was not really embarrassed, she just didn't want Marcus to suspect she had no suitors. All the other girls her age had already developed womanly curves and Viola still looked the same as she did at twelve. While all of her peers were sneaking kisses with the local lads, Viola lived in near solitude with only her horses for company. Now Marcus was back, she would finally have someone to confide in.

Her unbound hair fell into her face and she peeked up at him through the thick curls. Marcus reached out a lean, tanned hand to gently push back her hair and force her gaze to his. His palm was warm against her cheek and she tilted her head against the caress. He waited patiently for her to explain where she was heading.

"You will think I am such a ninny," she admitted softly.

"I would never do that," Marcus assured her. His eyes mirrored his promise. As far as she could remember, Marcus had never broken a promise he had made to her. It was one of the reasons she considered him a great friend. She knew she could always rely on him and that was comforting to someone who had no companions. There were few children near Haversham who could be considered a suitable friend for the only daughter of an earl. Marcus, the son of a duke, was the only young aristocrat in the area to be considered a proper playmate for Viola by her protective father. When they were children, Marcus encouraged her adventurous spirit and had accompanied her on many harebrained schemes. Surely Marcus would understand why she was sneaking out of the house at night?

Viola took a deep breath and squared her shoulders. She supposed she would have to tell him since it was obvious he would not let her out of his sight until she did. "I am going to check on Isabella."

"Your mare?" Marcus was visibly surprise as he moved his hand away from her cheek. "Whatever for?"

"She's afraid of the dark."

Marcus's lips began to twitch as he tried to hold in his laughter. "She's what?"

Viola tilted her head and looked at him haughtily. "Isabella is afraid of the dark."

"That is the most ridiculous thing I have ever heard of, Vi! A horse cannot be afraid of the dark."

"What makes you so certain?" Viola felt the beginnings of anger. "Do you claim to be an expert?"

"My father raises horses and I have never heard of such a situation before."

"That does not mean Isabella is not afraid."

"Surely you are imagining things, Viola."

"If you doubt me, come and see for yourself." Viola challenged him with a lift of her chin. No matter what he said, she knew Isabella was afraid of the dark and she would prove it to him.

"It is the middle of the night!"

"Is Isabella not the only one afraid? I never knew you were frightened of the dark," Viola mocked. She had learned early in childhood the quickest way to get Marcus to do what she wanted was to offend his sense of pride. She smiled when her ploy worked. The indecision on his face was swiftly replaced by resignation.

Marcus looked at the mutinous set of her face and sighed heavily. "Lead the way then."

*****

It was good to be home.

It was even better to see Viola again. Even if she sometimes had the tendency to make him commit foolish acts. Just like tonight. The stables were no place to be at this time, but if going there made Viola happy, he'd suffer through it.

He unbuttoned his greatcoat and followed his young friend out the door of her home. When she stepped into the light of the full moon, Marcus belatedly realized she was only wearing a night rail with a robe draped loosely around her slender body. As she walked across the lawn, a slight breeze caused the hem of her gown to twist about her ankles and bare feet. Her toes sunk into the damp grass and he repressed a sympathetic shiver.

"Where are your shoes? You will freeze out here wearing next to nothing." Marcus waved his hand at her inadequately clothed body.

Viola glanced down at herself and shook her head. "I am quite comfortable. My robe has always been enough to keep me warm when I come out here. And you know better than anyone I detest footwear."

"You come out dressed like that often?" His eyes moved from her thinly clothed body to her bare feet and he grimaced. "What if someone sees you?"

"The only people who ever see me are the groomsmen." Viola dismissively shook her head as if his fears were foolish. "I highly doubt I will run into anybody of great importance in the stables. Important personages seldom visit stables in the dead of night."

She spoke to him as if she were explaining things to a simple-minded child. Marcus stared at her retreating back with a growing sense of unease. It was inconceivable that Viola paraded around the stables half dressed with only stable boys for company. Casting another quick glance at her body, he was grateful that at least she was still undeveloped. Even so, she still possessed the face of an angel and he knew she would attract attention even with a lack of curves. He hated to think of what might happen to her when she acquired a more womanly figure.

All in all, though, it was unacceptable for a nobleman's daughter to walk about in her nightclothes. Though Viola often flaunted convention, he couldn't allow her to act in such a brazen matter. Marcus began to worry her father's overindulgence of her as a child might lead to serious repercussions. Guiltily he remembered how he himself had catered to Viola's every whim since she was a child. If he were honest with himself, he had to admit he had done his fair share of spoiling also. Since her rebellious nature was partly his fault, Marcus supposed it should be left up to him to make sure she became properly attired.

"Put on my greatcoat," Marcus ordered as he swung the heavy fabric across her thin shoulders. She made a sound of disapproval when the heavy fabric dropped around her and she turned to look at him with baleful eyes, but remained blessedly quiet. He reached for the buttons and closed them when she made no move to do so. As he did, his fingers brushed against the silky skin of her throat. He felt the pounding of her heart beneath the fragile skin and almost pressed his thumb to the spot, but caught himself in time and returned his attention to fastening the coat.

His fingers quickly completed the task and stepped away. Viola tossed her curls over one shoulder and continued on to the stables. The fabric dragged on the ground behind her much smaller frame and Marcus had to suppress a groan. He had just purchased the coat last week on Bond Street and it had cost a small fortune. Viola grabbed handfuls of the wool in her hands and held it high above her knees so it would not hamper her hoydenish stride. It wasn't the most maidenly of actions, but at least it got his cape off the wet ground.

Viola pulled up short as she reached the door to the stables. She wrapped her small hands around the handle and tugged. Marcus saw it was too heavy for her and quickly jumped in front of her.

"Let me do that for you."

She stepped back and smiled at him as if he'd just offered her the moon. "Thank you, Marcus."

Once inside they were enveloped in darkness and Marcus stretched his hands out in front of him to feel the way. He heard the scratch of flint and he turned to see Viola held a candle in her hand. She caught his eye and motioned for him to follow her.

As they neared the back of the stables, Marcus could hear the thrashing and neighing of a horse. He watched as Viola wriggled over the gate and approached her mare cautiously. He was about to call out a warning, but she reached out a hand to stroke Isabella and the horse calmed and stood placidly in an instant. Viola murmured soothing sounds as she stroked the horse's flank. She glanced over her shoulder at Marcus as he swung his long legs over the gate and dropped to the other side effortlessly. He came to her side and patted Isabella's neck in a distracted manner.

"How long have you been sneaking out here?"

Viola shrugged her small shoulders, causing one side of her night rail to drop alarmingly. "Almost a year now. We had a small fire in the stables in June and since then Isabella has been afraid of the dark."

Although Marcus still sincerely doubted a horse could suffer from such an affliction, he nodded in agreement. He knew better than to argue with Viola once she got some maggot in her head. She was the most stubborn child he'd ever encountered and he did not intend to spend all night in the stables debating with her.

"Obviously something has her unsettled," he grudgingly agreed. He watched as Viola threaded her fingers through the fine hairs on the back of her horse's neck. Her hands moved leisurely across the horse's back and an unbidden image came to him of Viola's fingers lightly caressing his naked back. Horrified Marcus shook off the image and blamed his lapse on the fact it had been weeks since he'd a woman. His celibacy had to be the reason such a thought regarding his young friend had occurred to him.

"I told you!" Viola stopped stroking Isabella long enough to shoot Marcus a questioning look. "Why did Father not tell me you were coming?"

"I told him not to. I wanted to surprise you in the morning at breakfast."

"When did you arrive? Why did I not hear a carriage?"

"I arrived at the Hall late this evening, but Father had gone to London. I got lonely, so I rode over to Haversham a few hours ago."

"Is Father yet not aware of your arrival?"

Marcus shook his head. "I told the servants not to wake him. He will know soon enough in the morning. There was no point in disturbing him."

"So I am the first to know you are back?" Viola moved around her horse to stand beside him. She threw her arms around him and hugged him tightly. "I cannot wait to tell everyone you are home!"

"Haversham has always felt more like home to me than Kingsley Hall," Marcus agreed. He gently disengaged her arms from his waist. He didn't trust himself to hug her when it was so obvious she was no longer the child he remembered. "Perhaps because I spent more time here since my father was always in London."

As a close neighbor and godson of Viola's father, he'd been given free rein to the Haversham estate. Robert Haversham, Earl Chatham, clearly had aspirations of a marriage between Marcus and Viola. As a result, Marcus had been encouraged to visit often. His own father, the Duke of Kingsley, also made it apparent he wished for his son to marry his closest friend's only daughter. Marcus was not averse to the idea, but he and Viola still had a few more years until they could seriously consider marriage. Although judging from the heated thoughts he was now having of Viola, it would not be many more years until they were suitable.

Marcus reached out to pat the top of her head, his fingers tangling in the hair she always wore unbound. When Viola's mother was alive, Marcus would sit by and watch as Lady Haversham brushed Viola's waist length hair until it gleamed. No matter how her mother pleaded, Viola preferred her hair to remain unbraided. Now he noticed she had cut off most of her locks and it barely reached her shoulders. The short length framed her face, coming to a point below her chin, and he found it suited her although it definitely was not the customary style for a young lady. The mahogany curls felt silky smooth under his fingers as he stroked them gently.

"So pretty," he murmured as he wound a curl around his finger. "When did you cut it?"

Viola's nose wrinkled and she looked at him in distaste. "Nearly a month ago and it has grown back too fast. I hate my hair. It is too curly and much too brown."

"It is the color of mahogany and curls are all the rage," Marcus pointed out helpfully as he released the curl he had been touching.

Viola ran her fingers through her hair and tucked it behind her ears. "I suppose everyone could not be blessed with straight blonde hair. Some of us are destined to suffer a brown, curly fate."

Marcus, whose own hair was almost as brown and curly, grinned at her. "At least we are in the same company."

Viola clapped a hand over her mouth to keep from giggling. Tears of mirth gathered in the corners of her eyes and her dimples appeared. "I did not mean to insult you, Marcus. On you brown hair is quite becoming."

"Is it really?" Marcus pointed to his hair and waggled his eyebrows. "You do not imagine me blonde?"

At the mental picture of a blonde Marcus, Viola could no longer hold in her laughter. She laughed heartily and wiped the tears from her eyes. "I have missed you so much the past four years."

"As I have you," Marcus honestly answered. Viola had been like a little sister to him whenever he was at home in Kent. The two had been almost inseparable during their childhood and he felt closer to her than he did any other female.

"Come." Marcus put an arm around Viola's shoulders. "Let us go back to the house and I will tell you all about my adventures at Eton."

"All of them?" Viola asked with a suggestive wink. Her green eyes brightened with the thought that he would divulge all of his secrets. Rumor had it Marcus had gained an extensive knowledge in London, not all of it pertaining to books.

"Maybe not all of them," Marcus answered quickly as he remembered some of his racier activities while at school. The past four years had taught him much about the life of a young, titled lord. His education had been exceptionally edifying in the last two years as he had matured and began gathering the attention of older women. The first woman he had bedded had been the older sister of a school chum. He had been sixteen and the nineteen year old temptress had taught him much about women.

In the years that followed, he was amazed at how easily women would grant him sexual favors. He supposed it had more to do with the fact he was the sole heir of a dukedom rather than any personal attribute of his. Nevertheless, he always treated them with the utmost respect and when their relationship ended, he ensured they parted ways amiably. He'd enjoyed the time he'd spent between their legs, but the interludes left him longing for something meaningful. Not even his best friend Taylor, who had the makings of a true rake, knew of Marcus's dissatisfaction.

"Do not fear you will offend me," Viola stated in a matter of fact tone. "I know all about the reputation you have acquired. I was especially enlightened to learn of your recent popularity with the ladies."

Marcus sputtered and he looked at her in surprise. "Who would tell you such things?"

"Margaret has just returned from London and she relayed all the gossip." Viola's eyes widened with feigned innocence. "I wonder how you actually had time to study!" She began to count off on her fingers. "Let's see. There was an actress, the daughter of a Russian count, and…"

"Vi, you must learn not to listen to everything you hear," Marcus interrupted admonishingly as he led her back toward her house. Though he was irritated she'd heard rumors of him, it was the fact she might be ashamed of him that worried him the most. "This is a subject you should know nothing about. You are barely fifteen."

"Fifteen and seven months," Viola corrected him. "More than old enough to know all there is to know."

"Ohhh!" Marcus drew the word out for emphasis. "Pardon me. Seven months does make all the difference, but are you speaking from past experience?"

"What if I was?" Viola answered cheekily. "What could you do about it?"

"I could tell your father for a start." Marcus felt the beginnings of real irritation. Surely little Viola had not done something so rash? His irritation led him to speak a little harsher than necessary. "And then I could hunt down your gentleman and make him see the error of his ways."

"That is so unfair," Viola huffed. "You get to have all the fun while I have to protect my virtue as if it is priceless."

"What makes you think it is fun?" Marcus knew it was not an appropriate subject to discuss but he liked sparring with her. Viola never failed to keep him entertained with her unusual view of how the world should be. And if Viola were to be his wife, it would be helpful to know her opinion on such things.

"Why would you do it so often if it was not fun?" She shrugged her slim shoulders. "Come to think of it, the entire *ton* does it quite regularly according to Margaret."

"Perhaps you are right," Marcus answered with a choked laugh. "But I must demand the opportunity to repair the damage done to my reputation. You make me out to be the veriest rake."

"You do not have to deny it." Viola grinned up at him. "I think it makes you much more exciting than those other stuffy young lords. They are only concerned with what is proper. Your impropriety is what is so wonderful about you, Marcus. You do as you feel and damn the consequences." She peeked up at him from beneath lowered lashes and a wicked gleam flashed in her eyes. "Besides if you are to be my husband, I'm grateful you're getting so much practice."

Marcus nearly choked on horrified laughter. He did not know which was more astonishing, Viola had guessed their fathers' wishes or the fact that she was alluding to sharing a marriage bed. In the end, he decided to pursue the safest line of questioning. "What makes you think I am to be your husband?"

He knew their fathers wanted them to marry, but he wondered how Viola had picked up on the fact. He was obviously mistaken by thinking their parents' blatant ploys were only directed at him.

Viola rolled her eyes and gave a huff of indignation. "Piffle! Don't think you are the only one who has suffered their underhanded attempts at matchmaking. Just the other day my father made me commission three blue dresses solely because it is your favorite color. He said it made my eyes sparkle and then reminded me of the fact it was the exact shade of the toy boat you had when you were younger."

Marcus stroked a finger across his upper lip to hide the fact that he was grinning like a fool. The disgusted face Viola had made reminded him of the time he had put a frog in her shoe. It had taken her days to forgive him for the deed and he did not think it would be in his best interest to bring it up now.

"It is true that blue is my favorite color. Do you suppose your father will insist on a blue gown for our wedding?"

"Without a doubt and I thoroughly plan on wearing pink just to spite him." All trace of levity left her face and she peered up at him seriously. "Do you really think we will marry?" A frown marred the skin of her forehead as she tilted her head back and studied his face.

Marcus lifted a shoulder and shrugged with forced nonchalance. "I am not sure. Why do you ask? Do you not want to marry me?" A spurt of unexplainable concern appeared as he waited for her answer. When he'd envisioned Viola becoming his wife, he'd never given a moment's thought to her wishes. It may be conceited of him, but he'd always assumed she would never refuse him.

"I believe you would make an excellent husband. I just hope they allow me to have a debut before they leg-shackle us."

Viola smiled impishly and Marcus let out the breath he had been holding. So she was not refusing him after all. If time was all she needed, he would be more than happy to give it to her provided it was him she chose to marry in the end. He did not know why that thought gave him such comfort, but he couldn't envision marrying anyone else. He supposed it was because he was comfortable with Viola and it would so much easier than actively pursuing another wife, one he could never be sure wanted him for him or just because of the title he would someday inherit.

"So you are looking forward to a London debut? Why do I find that hard to believe?"

If she did indeed have a season, it would put off their wedding for at least another three years. It suddenly seemed an inordinate amount of time. By then he would be almost twenty-two and she nearly eighteen. The thought of what Viola would be like at eighteen nearly knocked him back on his heels. He found himself hesitant to agree to her plan, which was odd since he had never been able to deny Viola anything. He glanced down at her youthful face, with its promise of beauty already apparent, and knew it would be hell watching her develop into a woman over the next few years.

Viola, unaware of the direction his thoughts were heading, put her hands on his chest and gave a slight push. "I want a season more than anything. Margaret says it is such great fun, especially all the balls. I have been taking dancing and flirting lessons all year and I cannot wait to practice all I have learned."

"Flirting lessons?" Marcus rubbed a fist against the spot on his chest she had touched. Damn him if his skin was not actually tingling.

"Yes. Flirting lessons." Viola fluttered her eyelashes and peeked up at him coyly. She reached out to swat his arm with an imaginary fan and giggled softly.

A chill went through Marcus's body at the

thought she would be practicing her wiles on all the young bucks in London.   Her husky voice and laughter was enough to raise the hairs on the back of his neck so he knew others would be equally affected. He could only hope they demonstrated as much control as he did when faced with the temptation of a flirting Viola.

"Am I not doing it properly?" Viola stopped her eyelash fluttering and planted her fists on her hips.

"You are doing fine," Marcus reassured her.

"Then why are you frowning as if I am doing it all wrong?"

"I'm sorry, Vi. I'm a little tired and not the best of company." He hated lying to her, but he'd to get away from her now before he did something he would regret, like exhibiting jealousy just because she planned to flirt with other men. He knew it was expected of her when she debuted, but damned if it made it any easier to swallow.

Viola nodded in understanding and reached out to wrap her arm around his as they headed back to the house. At the top of the stairs, they turned to go their separate ways and he mumbled goodnight to her. Viola looked over her shoulder and flashed him a brilliant smile from the doorway to her room. Marcus knew he would curse himself for it in the morning, but he had to touch her one last time.

"Viola?" He hastily cleared his throat when it came out as a muffled croak.

"Yes, Marcus?" She watched him with vague amusement on her face as he strode forward and pressed a light kiss against her forehead.

"It has been good seeing you again," he mumbled as he stepped away. The words he'd wanted to say refused to leave his mouth.

"Same here." A bright smile lit her face before she disappeared into her room. Marcus slumped against the wall and willed himself under control. Three years was not really too long to wait, was it? He groaned even as he thought it.

Marcus remembered her animated face while talking about a London season and bit back a curse. Viola would definitely be a handful when she debuted and he knew the duty would be fall to him to keep her in line. Her father seldom attended society events and someone would have to watch out for Viola when she went to London. Her penchant for trouble was well known in these parts, but her cheerful nature was infectious and everyone said she was a joy to be around. She would definitely make an enlivening companion and he had no doubt she would take society by storm. He only hoped he would be the suitor she chose in the end. And that he could keep his hands off of her until she was eighteen.

Chapter Three

"Viola? Would you care for more tea?"

Viola turned her attention back to the present and looked up to see Margaret gazing at her in expectation. "No, thank you."

"Are you sure you do not want to join the others?" Margaret indicated the rest of the party gathered on the opposite side of the room. Viola glanced at the crowd and barely managed to suppress a shiver of revulsion. With the exception of a few, the room was mostly crowded with the women who'd made it plain to Viola that she was an oddity because of her unusual views on how women should act and be treated. Her knowledge of politics (it was a known fact she wrote many of the speeches her father gave in the House of Lords), and her disinterest in marriage caused them to label her a radical. If Viola had not been the daughter of an earl and close friend of the powerful Duke of Kingsley, she had no doubt she would be shunned from all of polite society. Her social standing was precarious. Though she was invited to all of the events, she was never made to feel welcome by anyone except her closest friends.

"Not particularly. They are probably gossiping about me and I would hate to spoil their fun."

"Regrettably you are more than likely right." Margaret's lips twisted wryly. "They only say such hurtful things because you intimidate them. Sometimes I wish…" Margaret's voice trailed off and she shrugged with regret at her cousin's plight. "I know you say you never want to marry, but I cannot understand your desire to spend your life alone."

"Margaret," Viola began in a warning voice as she rehashed the long standing argument between them. "I tried love once and look where it led. I'm not going to leave myself open to such pain again."

"You should not let one bad experience ruin it forever."

Viola gave Margaret a knowing look. "If things had not ended well between you and Buckley, would you want to fall in love again?"

"I like to think I would be open to the possibility. Three years is more than enough time for you to get over the marquess."

"My heart has healed," Viola interjected stridently. "I just do not care to find someone new."

Instead of arguing, Margaret sighed and balanced the tea tray she was holding. "I'd better be off again. I must attend to my hostess duties."

Margaret moved away to see to her guests and Viola stood to take a stroll around the room. She stopped at a window overlooking Grosvenor Square and pushed aside the curtain to watch the passers-by. Fashionable ladies and gentlemen strolled the wide street. Carriages rolled past and Viola occupied herself with identifying to which family the crest belonged. It was a game Marcus had taught her when she had been nine years old. Their families were both in London for the season and she had often been left with Marcus while their parents attended all the social gatherings. They would sit at the window in the parlor of the Kingsley townhouse and try to guess the crest on each passing carriage. Marcus was abominable at the game while Viola could name almost every crest. As they grew older and Marcus entered society himself, Viola often played the game to pass the time. Though she tried to stop it, she was not able to prevent her thoughts from returning to Marcus. Closing her eyes, Viola recalled one afternoon in particular she had spent playing the game with Marcus. The day she realized her feelings for Marcus were no longer those of a child.

*****

Three years earlier

"I bet you ten shillings you cannot name crest."

Viola shielded her eyes from the glare the setting sun made on the window and squinted at the carriage Marcus indicated. It bore a crest of a serpent on a blue and white background

She grinned triumphantly. "Yes I can. It is the crest of the Earl of Esterday."

She held out her hand for her forfeit and Marcus reached into his pocket to pull out the required amount. Her coins clinked against several others she'd already taken from him that afternoon. When she added her new winnings to her collection at home, she will have amassed quite a profit. "When are you going to learn you cannot stump me?"

He shook his head in amazement. "How can you know all of them?"

Viola smirked at him and shook out her pink skirts. "It is quite simple really. When peerage has been drilled into your memory since you were a little girl, you have no choice but to use it to your advantage. Otherwise it would be a worthless pile of knowledge to have."

"It will come in handy when you debut. Maybe then you will be too busy to dig a hole in my pocket."

Marcus leaned back on his elbows and turned his face toward the sun. His dark coat strained across his chest and Viola appreciated the view of blatant masculinity as he lounged on a sofa. At twenty, Marcus was the toast of all society. He'd entered the social scene nearly two years ago and his popularity had grown so much that merely his attendance at a social function made it an instant success. Hostesses clamored to have him attend their parties and ambitious mamas strove to have him introduced to their daughters. As the only heir to a dukedom, Marcus had been guaranteed popularity, but it was his unfailing charm had caused one matron of society to describe him as "smooth as cream and no doubt just as tasty."

Viola had nearly laughed herself silly when she had heard that scandalous description of Marcus. He had shrugged it off, but anyone could see Marcus was comfortable with his newfound fame. His father had been so proud of Marcus's success at Oxford he had already handed most of the control of his estate over to his son. Marcus had a bright future in front of him and could want for nothing. He had all of society wrapped around his finger, especially the female population, and control of a very wealthy estate.

Viola leaned back on her own elbows and watched Marcus from the corner of her eyes. He turned to face her fully and Viola once again found herself struck dumb by the sheer attractiveness of his features. He was quite possibly the handsomest man she had ever seen. The evidence of his mother's Italian ancestry was apparent in his dark eyes and strong features. His tall, leanly muscled frame had been inherited from his father along with his deadly charm. Marcus had always been considered fine looking, but lately he was being termed a heartbreaker. Almost every one of Viola's friends claimed to be in love with him and Viola could well understand their feelings. She was almost halfway in love with him herself.

Since his return from Oxford, Viola hid her burgeoning feelings for fear it would ruin their friendship. She would be seventeen in a month and would soon make her own bow to society. She supposed it was only a matter of time before Marcus would make an offer for her. Their families were friendly and she knew it was the hope of both of their fathers that she and Marcus would one day marry. Marcus would propose eventually, but Viola was unsure if a loveless marriage was preferable to a life alone. It was her dearest hope Marcus would realize she was no longer a child and begin to look at her as more than a friend. Until he could see beyond his duty to his father, she would not accept an offer of marriage from him.

"What are you thinking about so fiercely?" Marcus ran a finger over her nose. She made a face and he grinned before placing his hand on the step between them. She'd always loved his hands. Unlike the pale smooth hands of a dandy, Marcus's were strong and capable. His tapered fingers were well groomed, but not in a feminine manner. The back of his hand, lightly dusted with dark hair, proclaimed his masculinity. He tapped against the stone and she looked up to see him watching her.

"I hesitate to ask what is going on in that mind of yours."

"I was thinking how splendid you look in your evening attire." Viola hedged with a conspiratorial wink. "All the girls are sure to trip over their tongues tonight at the ball."

"If they trip over anything, it will probably be their own self-importance. I have not met one eligible female this season who has a thought in her head besides those of gowns and hair ribbons."

"It is considered unattractive for females to claim to have thoughts much beyond those." Viola grimaced as she remembered the countless hours she had been drilled on proper etiquette at the expensive finishing school her father had forced her to attend. "Our lives are dedicated to finding a husband, preferably one with a wealthy title, and having dozens of heirs."

"Then you will be sunk before you even sail since you seldom refrain from speaking whatever is on your mind. The poor lads will not know what to do with you. I almost feel sorry for them."

"Do not feel sorry for them. I have no intention of marrying anyone. Besides you are a fine one to talk. You are just as outspoken as I am and you have had ladies dangling after you for two years. Am I to now pity them in return?"

"No you shouldn't pity them either. It is only my title they are interested in. Not me."

Viola highly doubted it. One only had to look at Marcus to be interested in him. The title would just be considered a bonus to most debutantes. "But that is how it works. Girls are born and raised to believe an advantageous marriage is all they should aspire to in life. Can you blame them for wanting to capture the only heir of a dukedom? A duchess is the highest title they can achieve unless they marry into royalty which we all know is very unusual."

"No more talk of the vicious marriage mart, I beg of you." Marcus heaved a great sigh, which expanded his chest to impressive size. "Truly it is not so much the young ladies I fear, but their mothers. You can't imagine how badly I wish you could be there to save me from the matchmaking mamas."

Viola wished exactly the same thing, but she bit her tongue. "It is only one more month and then I can be your savior at every single social event. For now you will have to make do with Margaret and Taylor."

Viola's cousin and Marcus's best friend had recently become a match and Viola suspected they would marry before the season was finished. At first Viola had been unsure of Taylor's interest in Margaret since he was a true rakehell, but she soon realized he'd indeed reformed and was obviously in love with her dear cousin.

Marcus shuddered with disgust as he stood. "I am tired of playing chaperone to those two. It is enough to make a person blush at the way they carry on."

"I doubt they could make *you* blush." Viola tried not to salivate at the tempting bottom at her eye level. If she reached out, she could find out if it was as firm as it looked. Could she possibly do it and make it seem an accident?

"I am not quite the rakehell you make me out to be." Marcus glanced down at her just as she was about to grab hold of his bottom.

She snatched her hand back and smiled innocently up at him. *So close*, she thought wistfully. One more inch and she could have gotten in a good pinch.

Fortunately, Marcus seemed oblivious to Viola's reaction. "I suppose I had better get going. It would not do to offend the ladies at Almack's. They might revoke my membership."

"For you, I think they would overlook murder," Viola teased as he helped her to her feet. Her head barely reached his shoulders, so she had to tilt her chin back to meet his eyes. She brushed at a speck of lint on his coat and straightened his cravat. "You are the only heir to an extremely wealthy dukedom. No hostess in her right mind would deny you entrance."

She followed him out the door, reluctant to lose the precious time she spent with him.

"Thank you for putting my qualifications in the proper perspective." Marcus laughed as he leaned down to kiss her cheek. His breath feathered across her smooth skin a second before she felt his lips. He lingered for a moment before pulling away and straightening to his full height.

"I will see you tomorrow at supper," he called over his shoulder as he hurried down the steps and disappeared into his waiting carriage.

Viola watched as the carriage headed down the street and she pressed a hand against her chest to stop the furious pounding of her heart. She had always considered herself to be made of firmer stuff than the rest of the female population. She'd never imagined herself as a wife in every sense of the word, but in the last year she'd developed the oddest sensations whenever she was in Marcus's company. Her hands grew clammy and her knees turned all wobbly. A fluttering in her stomach happened whenever he looked at her. The most casual touch was enough to make her pulse race. She knew enough about life to realize her feelings stemmed from desire. Unfortunately, she also knew enough to recognize Marcus was not exhibiting any similar signs.

They were thrown together so often she feared Marcus would soon learn of her feelings. She could imagine no greater embarrassment than unrequited love. Viola hoped her infatuation would soon fade because Marcus's growing reputation as a rake, despite his avowals to the contrary, clearly indicated he did not return her feelings. Until she was convinced Marcus truly wanted her as a wife, she would remain unattached. Her debut was only a month away and maybe if Marcus saw her flirting with other men, he might shape up and begin to realize what was right under his nose.

*****

June 1823

In Margaret's drawing room, Viola's perusal of the street soon bored her. Clearing her head of memories of Marcus, she made her way back to the sofa. She'd just sat down when there was a commotion in the hallway. The door to the drawing room flew open and Catherine, Margaret's three year old daughter, burst into the room. She was quickly followed by a flushed governess.

Spotting her mother, Catherine exclaimed loud enough for the entire room to hear. "Momma! I need to tell you something!" In a flurry, Catherine rushed across the room to her mother. She came to a halt and her exuberant smiled revealed every single one of her teeth. Her blonde curls were disheveled and a ribbon drooped under one ear.

Margaret ignored her daughter's disorderliness and bent down to hear the news her daughter was obviously anxious to impart. "What is it, Cat?"

"Papa is here and he brought a visitor. He told me I could call him Uncle Marcus and that he was an old friend of Papa's," Catherine informed her mother happily. "He also gave me a peppermint. Look!" Catherine held up the sticky candy for her mother to see.

Several gasps and excited murmurs followed Catherine's news. Margaret's green eyes widened and her gaze searched out Viola's across the room. Viola's face paled and she dropped against the sofa limply. Her heart began to pound and she feared she really would faint. Marcus was now not only in the same town as she, but in the same house! The confrontation Viola had dreaded for years suddenly seemed imminent. Margaret made her way calmly to Viola's side and stood so she was hidden from the view of the room. Catherine followed her mother and promptly clambered onto Viola's lap. Viola was so distracted she did not notice the sticky handprints Catherine left on her skirts until it was too late.

"Oh dear, your skirt!" Margaret put a hand to her flushed cheeks as she noticed the red stains on the delicate fabric. She lifted her eyes and only had to look at Viola to see she was about to panic. "Viola, I will go and greet Taylor and Kingsley. You must act as hostess while I am gone. I will devise some reason to send them on their way and I will hurry right back."

Viola looked up at her cousin in alarm. "I don't want to see him."

"You will not have to," Margaret answered simply as she scooped up her daughter and put her on the floor. "Just put on a happy smile and I will take care of everything."

Viola took several deep, calming breaths and nodded. Three years ago, her hopes had been dashed and her heart broken when Marcus had jilted her for another lady. After his new bride's untimely death in childbirth, Marcus fled the country for India. He'd not visited England once in the past three years. Viola began to think she could face him calmly if he ever returned. She could see now she'd been wrong.

"This should be interesting."

A cackle alerted Viola to the Dowager Duchess of Bradford's presence. Viola turned her head and lifted an eyebrow as the tiny lady seated herself. Margaret's daughter mimicked the lady and perched on the left side of Viola.

"I fail to see the humor in the situation," Viola

remarked nonchalantly and took a sip of tea. The dowager leaned in close so their conversation could not be overheard.

"If Kingsley learns of your presence here, do you have any doubt he will make a scene?" The old lady's eyes positively shone with excitement. Viola would not be surprised if the dowager pulled out her opera glasses to view the upcoming confrontation. She probably carried them around in her reticule for just such an occurrence.

"Not much." She had refused to see Marcus all those years ago and she knew he would take advantage of the fact she would be at his mercy with so many witnesses present. "You're correct. He will barge in here and make a scene. With such a volatile situation at hand, perhaps it would be best if I left." Viola made a move to stand up but the dowager placed a surprisingly strong hand over her knee.

"I forbid you to run away. You are made of sterner stuff. It is not in your nature to avoid conflict and I cannot allow you to act so out of character."

"And how would you know of my character?" Since her debut, Viola doubted she'd exchanged more than a handful of words with the dowager.

The dowager winked at her knowingly. "I've watched you these past years and come to the conclusion you remind me of someone."

"And who would that be?" Viola asked with feigned interest. Her mind was still focusing on the fact that Marcus was in the same house with her.

Dear lord and she was a mess!

Viola looked down at her stained skirt and

reached for a napkin. She moistened it with her tongue and began to viciously scrub at the peppermint.

"You remind me of myself," the dowager answered. Viola swung her head to look at her in amazement. "You act just like I did when I debuted. You flaunt convention, but never do anything too scandalous. You are not opposed to speaking your mind and unlike these other fluffs," the dowager paused to wave her hand dramatically at the other ladies in the room. "You actually use your head for something more than to perch a bonnet upon."

"Thank you, I think." She put the napkin aside as she gave up a hopeless cause. The peppermint stains would never come out of her silk dress. "But I fail to see why I should not leave. If I am as intelligent as you say, wouldn't leaving be the wisest course?"

"It would only delay, not prevent, your confrontation. Chin up, Viola. You are about to brave the dragon and I have no doubt you will emerge unscathed."

The dowager patted Viola's hand comfortingly before taking her leave. Catherine did the same and hurried after the older lady. It appeared the child had fixed her attentions on a new idol. God help Taylor and Margaret if Catherine began to idolize the dowager duchess! Viola was left alone on the sofa and she eyed the door with a mixture of trepidation and urgency. In the likely event Marcus did come through the door, she must be prepared to face him rationally. She must not seem upset, else it would be all over London by evening.

Chapter Four

"How was India?" Taylor Gilbert, the Earl of Buckley, asked as he poured two glasses of sherry. He handed one to Marcus and took a sip from his own glass.

Taylor was a slender man with dark blond hair and piercing blue eyes. He'd run wild with Marcus in their younger years, partying and whoring excessively, until he met Margaret and became a devoted husband and loving father. He'd given up his rakehell lifestyle for the comforts of family life and had never regretted the change.

In his naïve youth, Taylor had truly enjoyed the many delights the city had to offer, but he'd sensed that Marcus was never comfortable with the habits of a rake. Taylor had found it odd and had questioned his friend about it. Though Marcus denied any such reticence from taking place, Taylor believed Marcus would much prefer a staid, sedate lifestyle in the country. Marcus had been raised in the country and though he had taken society by storm, Marcus would never truly adapt to city life. The same was true for his wife's cousin.

Marcus propped a lean hip against Taylor's desk and regarded him thoughtfully. "It was uneventful. My business dealings are being handled efficiently by my manager. I saw no reason to prolong my stay."

"It took you three years to work that out?" Taylor arched a pale eyebrow. "Seems an extreme amount of time to do something as simple as review your manager. I'd begun to think you were running away from something. Or *someone*."

"I am warning you, Taylor. I don't want to talk about it." Marcus' voice was steely. His fingers tightened around his glass as he tossed back the rest of the contents. He set the glass down with a little more force than necessary.

Taylor remained silent as he studied Marcus' controlled anger. He suspected he knew the cause for Marcus's abrupt trip to India and his present ill mood. One night three years ago, Marcus had confided the entire truth of what happened with Viola and Taylor wished there was some way he could help his obviously suffering friend. To someone who did not know him as well, Marcus appeared to be at ease, but Taylor's critical eye could detect that Marcus's entire body radiated tension and his eyes were shadowed by grief.

It was highly unfair for one man to have so much to deal with in his life. The loss of his wife and child had damaged Marcus, but it was the loss of Viola that had almost destroyed his friend. Marcus's cheerful, easygoing nature had been replaced by the sullenness of a brooding stranger even before Agnes's and the baby's death. It was as if someone had extinguished the flame which had once burned so brightly in him and left only a shell of the man he'd once been.

Taylor's dark thoughts were interrupted by the arrival of his wife. After four years of marriage, his heart still gave a little jump whenever he saw her. He only wished his friend would someday have what he'd found.

Margaret breezed into the room and cheerfully greeted the occupants. "Kingsley, how wonderful to see you again!"

"You look well, Margaret." Marcus leisurely got to his feet. Taylor studied Marcus as he glanced at his wife with a speculative eye. Margaret was a petite, reserved blonde and the complete opposite of her younger cousin. The only common feature between the cousins was a pair of vivid green eyes which seemed to look right through a man. Viola's eyes always held an inner light, which Marcus had confessed long ago made him ache to discover all her thoughts. Marcus winced and Taylor intuitively knew that the Margaret's similarities to her cousin brought back painful memories for his friend.

It was inconceivable to believe after so many years just thinking about Viola would cause him pain, but the letter Taylor had received before Marcus' return told him all was not well. The thought of Viola lingered in his consciousness no matter what he did to get over her. He'd fled England and thrown himself into a flurry of activity. He'd pushed himself to work extraordinarily long hours in his foreign office. He seduced countless women, but none were able to satisfy his urges. He had decided, even before his father fell ill, to return to England since it was obvious he would never completely wash his hands of Viola.

"Thank you. You are looking fine yourself."

His years in India had hardened Marcus' lean muscles to an impressive degree. He was used to Marcus gaining the attention of females, but Taylor was relieved when Margaret's gaze remained honest, rather than openly sexual. When their daughter entered the room and tugged on her mother's skirts, Taylor experienced a pang of sympathy. If Marcus' daughter had lived, she would have been just about Catherine's age.

Catherine cupped her hands around her mouth spoke in a mock whisper. "Mama, Cousin Viola doesn't feel well. She told me not to interrupt you, but I think she needs your attention."

Marcus came to immediate attention at the mention of Viola. His negligently indolent air disappeared to be replaced with one of fierce determination. "Viola? She is here?" He shot Taylor a sharp glance before pinning Margaret with a questioning look.

Margaret's horrified green eyes turned up to his. "I was having tea when you arrived. Viola was naturally invited."

Marcus' surprise clearly shown on his face. He hadn't been this close to Viola in years and it was apparent he was not about to let the opportunity to speak with her pass him by. "I must talk to her."

"Marcus, maybe you should wait and see her in private." Taylor nimbly stepped in front of his taller, heavier friend to block the door. "Viola is certain to be unprepared for your visit."

"I can vouch for that." Margaret lifted Catherine and balanced her on a hip. "She doesn't want to see you."

"She's refused to see me for three years. She cannot run away forever." An emotion resembling pain flitted across his face before Marcus hastily hid it.

"I agree with you. She cannot keep running,"

Taylor placated him. "But now is not the time. She is surrounded by thirty women who would like nothing better than to have something to gossip about. Surely you do not want to embarrass her in that way?"

"I would not care if the bloody queen was in there. She brought this upon herself by refusing to see me. I will see her now and unless you would like me to physically remove you, you will step aside." Marcus's frown cut grooves in his lean cheeks.

"Can you not wait until a more opportune moment?" Taylor held his ground stubbornly until Marcus forced him aside.

"I have waited three years to see her again and I am not wasting another moment."

Margaret shared a worried look with her husband. "Are you not going to try to stop him?"

Taylor held up his hands helplessly. "I, for one, do not want to cross Marcus. He's been in a foul mood all day. Not to mention he outweighs me by nearly two stones."

"So you will sacrifice my cousin to save yourself?" Margaret shot her husband an aggravated look and handed Catherine to him before turning to rush after Marcus. Taylor sighed in resignation and followed after his wife. He knew Viola would inevitably have to face Marcus and perhaps it would be better to get it over and done with. Then maybe the two of them could move on with their lives. Hopefully a life together.

*****

Viola looked up expectantly when the door to the morning room opened. Her false bravado fled when the possibility of encountering Marcus became imminent. She prayed Margaret had been able to send Marcus and Taylor on some type of errand so she could make her escape unscathed. Her teacup rattled against its saucer when a pair of broad shoulders filled the doorway. Those certainly did not belong to her cousin, Viola thought with a sinking feeling and hurriedly set her teacup down. A hush fell over the room when a familiar figure appeared. Viola clamped her lips together to keep from gaping and her hands trembled violently. She clutched her skirts tightly in her hand as she came to her feet.

Marcus's face relaxed into an easy smile as he gave a quick look at the ladies in the room. They seemed to bask in his presence and returned his smile one by one. He acknowledged a few of the ladies by name before turning his head and finally pinning her with a heated gaze. His mouth widened in a wicked smile as he headed across the room toward her. Anyone watching would have believed he was happy to see her, but Viola could see the emotion brewing in his dark eyes.

She retreated until she could feel the wall at her back. She felt the interested looks of the other ladies in the room and her face flushed with embarrassment. Marcus stopped within inches of her and stared down at her silently. Viola's entire body gave an involuntary shiver as he calmly studied her. She noticed he was tanned from his travels and appeared larger, more menacing. He was no longer the boy she had fallen in love with. Before her stood a healthy, virile male who looked at her as if she were an insect best studied under a magnifying glass.

His well-formed lips tightened and drew her

attention to the tiny lines at the corner of his mouth. The planes of his face appeared harsher, but it only gave him a vital handsomeness. His hair had grown longer and the tousled disarray made one imagine he had just risen from bed. A shadow of a beard darkened his jaw and made him appear almost savage. Three years ago, Marcus had always been immaculately groomed. Yet his slightly unkempt appearance now did little to distract from his good looks. If anything, they only enhanced his attraction.

Viola's treacherous heart leapt at his nearness and she had to suppress the urge to reach out and touch him. Her palms itched to touch his whiskered jaw just to see if he was really there and not a figment of her imagination. She clutched at the folds of her skirt and surreptitiously wiped her sweating palms against the cool silk. Only the memory of his betrayal kept her in her seat and not in his arms. Marcus's dark eyes bored into hers and she managed to return his gaze unflinchingly.

Marcus looked away long enough to turn and face the other ladies. He flashed the famous grin which had captivated them so many years ago. From their dazed looks, it was obvious his effect on women remained unchanged.

"Forgive me ladies, but I fear I must steal Lady Viola from you for a few moments."

Twitters and nervous giggles met his statement as he wrapped his lean fingers around her wrist and turned to escort her from the room. She heard several envious sighs and she wanted nothing more than to offer her place to someone else. Viola felt herself being dragged out of the room and she dug her heels in mutinously. Marcus tossed a warning glance at her over his shoulder and tugged harder on her wrist. Viola knew she was no match for his strength so she reluctantly followed him instead of making the scene worse by incurring his wrath. In the hall, they encountered the shocked faces of Taylor and Margaret. Marcus clamped an arm around Viola when she would have made a move to hide behind Taylor.

"Kingsley! What are you doing?" Margaret made an attempt to rescue Viola. "Let go of my cousin at once!"

Marcus pinned Margaret with a fierce glare and tightened his grip on Viola's shoulder. She must have made a sound of pain, because his gaze moved to her face and he relaxed his hold on her. "I have some unfinished business with Viola. Now if you will excuse me, I plan to have a private word with her."

"You cannot force her to talk to you." Margaret continued to argue, but her husband put a calming hand on her shoulder and shushed her. Margaret jerked away from Taylor with a hiss and marched right up to Marcus.

"I am horribly ashamed of your behavior, Kingsley."

Margaret jabbed him in the chest with her forefinger and Marcus shot Taylor an aggrieved frown. Taylor handed Catherine to her governess and hurried to intervene.

If she were not so outraged with Marcus, Viola would've been amused at the way Margaret had finally found her tongue around the one man who'd always flustered her.

"This really is not well done of you, Marcus," Taylor commented as he struggled to keep a grip on his wife, who was trying to twist out of his arms.

"I apologize for my rudeness."   Marcus reached for the door of the study. "But I fully intend to speak with Viola with or without your approval." Marcus ignored the Buckley's stunned looks as he pushed Viola through the doorway of the study and closed it behind him. He rested his back against the door and crossed his arms across his chest negligently. "Alone at last."

*****

Alone?

If she hadn't promised to herself she would act like a lady, she'd slap him. As it was, she used words to display her anger. "You are the most insufferable person I have ever had the misfortune to lay eyes on."

From the moment she had seen him, she had been too overcome to speak. Now that she'd found her voice, there was a multitude things she wanted to say. "How dare you waltz in and embarrass me in front of half of the *ton*?"

"Come now, Viola. You have never cared what the *ton* thought of you and we both know it."

"You beast! It was you who never gave a fig what the ton thought of me. You jilted me and it was my reputation left to be swept over the coals."

"Ours was only a harmless flirtation in their eyes. No one knew we'd progressed into a serious relationship. My marriage to Agnes hardly reflected on you at all."

Viola stared at him in disgust. "I can assure

you the *ton* did not think of our relationship as a mere flirtation. I was so young and stupid I didn't care who noticed I wore my heart on my sleeve for you. Your quick marriage to Agnes indicated quite clearly what had happened. I was ridiculed for months after you married."

Marcus stared at her silently. He was probably trying to reconcile the image of the girl he had once known into the virago standing before him. Not much had changed since she'd been eighteen. Her hair was still the same vibrant reddish brown and her green eyes sparked with fire. Why did he look at her as if he'd never seen her before? It unsettled her and made her wish he would speak

Her lips tightened into a thin line. Her tiny nostrils flared with every breath she took. So many memories threatened to overwhelm her, but the way he looked at her now brought a specific one to the forefront of her mind.

It had been her debut into society and Marcus stood at the bottom of the stairs waiting for her to appear. He smiled up at her with brotherly affection when she appeared at the top of the stairs. The moment she saw him, her world tilted on its axis and his heart literally skipped a beat. She was dressed in a white organza dress which floated around her like a cloud before settling to cling to her developing curves. For once, her hair was tamed into an elegant chignon instead of loose around her shoulders. She smiled shyly at him when she reached the bottom of the stairs and held out a slim, ungloved hand.

Ladies never appeared in public without

gloves.

Marcus had smiled at her refusal to adhere to the strict rules of attire for young ladies. He bowed over her hand and pressed a kiss to her smooth skin. It was something he had done a hundred times before, but never had it caused her pulse to race. Her fingers fluttered in his and he gave her a wolfish grin, one she'd seen him give other women but never her. She lifted the hem of her skirts and proudly showed him her satin dancing slippers. She had teased him that she would attend her first ball barefoot and he was relieved to see it was not true. They shared a laugh and, at that exact moment, she realized he was head over heels in love and wanted him forever.

"I missed you," Marcus admitted to the present-day Viola. "More than you could ever imagine."

Viola huffed and tried to reach around him to open the door. He shifted to the side to block her way, shamelessly using his larger body to prevent her from leaving. She snatched her hand away hurriedly when his motion brought it into contact with his hip.

"We need to talk, Vi. There is much to explain. So many reasons I could not have married you then."

Viola laughed coldly as she wiped the hand that had touched him against her skirt, but it could not remove the remembered sensation of taut muscle and warm skin that had burned her even through her gloves.

"It is quite obvious why we could not marry. I caught you with her, remember? I do not care to hear your excuses."

"It's not an excuse I want to tell you. Just the bloody truth."

She turned back to face him and arched an eyebrow. "You broke my heart when you chose Agnes instead of me. There is nothing left to say."

"You know there was more to it. I never would've done anything to intentionally hurt you."

"Nevertheless you did hurt me. Nothing you can say will change that fact."

"Can you not even attempt to hear me out?" His dark eyes flashed with annoyance.

"What good would it do, Marcus? You can't erase the past."

Marcus could not believe it was Viola speaking. She sounded like a completely different person. The Viola he knew had always been cheerfully optimistic. Just being with her had been enough to make him feel the world was a decent place.

"When did you become such a cynic?"

"When I witnessed the boy I loved, the one who claimed to love me in return, making love to another. My view on life changed dramatically at that moment."

"There are so many things you don't understand. If I could change what happened, I would. Believe me I would, but you're right. I can't erase the past." He ran his hand through his hair in frustration. "It's been three years, Viola. When are you going to forgive me?"

"A lifetime would not be enough. You were everything to me. When I lost you, I had nothing. You cannot expect me to welcome you back with open arms."

"I am not expecting you to, but I would appreciate it if we could hold a decent conversation. Do you forget what we once meant to each other?"

"Obviously I did not mean as much to you as you did to me. If I had, you never would've mistaken Agnes for me."

"You are being unfair. It was a misunderstanding that night. You know very well I would never have chosen Agnes over you."

"And how am I supposed to know that? As I remember it, you and Agnes were quite familiar with each other. After all, you kissed her before you ever kissed me. For all I know, she could've been the one you wanted all along."

Viola crossed her arms over her chest and Marcus's eyes instinctively followed the movement. Suddenly she wished she had not brought up the topic of kissing. The room seemed much smaller as Marcus's gaze moved to her lips. They felt oddly dry, but she refused to give him the satisfaction of moistening them. Viola turned away from him angrily and Marcus stared at her slim, unrelenting back with mounting frustration. He waited for her to speak, but the silence grew between them.

"You cannot ignore me forever, Viola. Three years is more than enough time for you to give me a chance to explain."

Viola's shoulders stiffened even further as she stubbornly kept her gaze away from his. She remained mute.

"Have it your way, Viola. We will delay our discussion for now. Even though it is long overdue and I fully intend to have my say."

She passed him with her head held high, impatient for him to move away from the door so she could leave. He put a restraining hand on her elbow. "You know where to find me in case you decide you want to talk."

"It will surely be a cold day in Hades before I do." She shook off his hand and escaped the study.

She heard him curse violently as she slammed the door closed. Brushing past Margaret and Taylor, she ran upstairs and locked herself in the first room she came to. Instead of throwing herself across the bed in a fit of anger, she perched on the edge of a chair and closed her eyes. As they had nearly every day of the past three years, memories of Marcus flooded her mind and she was helpless to stop them from coming.

Chapter Five

Three years before

"I believe this dance belongs to me."

Viola smiled and looked coyly at the young Viscount Greenley. He was handsome and debonair and surely her favorite of all the young bucks. He was almost as tall as Marcus, with broad shoulders and a pleasant face, and he was an excellent dancer. Besides Marcus and her father, there was no man she was more comfortable with. She'd met the viscount earlier in the season and they'd hit it off immediately. There were few events where she did not encounter him and she enjoyed the time they spent together.

"Why, yes it is!" she said cheerfully as he led her toward the dance floor. "I always save the first dance for you." They took their places and waited for the first strains of music. The musicians struck a discordant note and Viola winced at the screech.

"And the last for Kingsley," the viscount said with a tight smile as he bent at the waist and she sank into a curtsy.

"He is my oldest, dearest friend."

The music began and Greenley swept her up into his arms. They twirled around the room gracefully and Viola was soon absorbed in the rhythm of the dance. Surely her favorite part about having a season was being allowed to dance until dawn.

"I do not know why you hold him in such esteem." Greenley, as he'd insisted she call him when they were alone, tightened his arms around her. Viola knew he was embracing her far too closely, but when she made no move to object, he grinned wolfishly. "He is a veritable rake."

Viola, who was more than aware of Marcus's activities, could only nod her head in agreement. "As can be said of at least a dozen other gentlemen here tonight. Present company included." She gave a pointed glance at the hands holding her improperly close.

He looked at her in approval. His eyes filled with mirth and he threw back his head to laugh heartily. "You never cease to amaze me, Lady Viola. You can insult someone to their face and make it seem like a mere observation."

"It is a rare talent. It is a pity that more young ladies do not possess it."

His face brightened at her wit. Viola flushed with pride. As they spun around the room, Viola's gaze caught Marcus's and he bowed gallantly to her. He was devastatingly handsome in complete black and stood out against the paler clad suits of the other gentlemen. She smiled at him and gave a quick wave before returning her attention back to her dance partner. The viscount also eschewed pale colors and sported a dark blue coat just a tad lighter than Marcus's. Not for the first time, Viola wondered if the main reason she enjoyed Greenley's company was purely the fact he reminded her so much of Marcus.

Viola was startled out of her guilty thoughts when she noticed t Greenley looked at her oddly. Do I have something in my teeth, she wondered. She was almost tempted to run her tongue along her teeth when he suddenly spoke.

"I wonder if he knows you are in love with

him?"

Viola stumbled and looked up at his knowing expression. She did not pretend to not know whom he referred to. Greenley was far too clever and would know if she was being dishonest. "Surely you are not serious?"

"Do not look so worried. I will not tell anyone your secret. I only wonder why he has not made an advance toward you in all these years."

He asked what Viola herself had frustratingly wondered many times over the past year. She feared Marcus would never look at her as anything but a good friend. Since her debut, he continued to actively seek her company but he never indicated a level of feeling higher than that of a cherished family friend. He flirted shamelessly with the other young ladies, yet he always treated Viola with the utmost respect. She wished just once he would forget who she was and treat her the same as the other girls, the girls she'd seen return from the terrace with Marcus with stars in their eyes and flushed cheeks.

"I am afraid he still considers me the same as he did at eight. He has yet to realize I've grown up."

Greenley raised a doubting brow. "Looking at you, no one can doubt you've matured. He must be wearing blinders not to notice the devastating woman you've become."

Viola blushed under his frank appraisal, but she smiled at him in amusement. "You flatter me, my lord."

Viola could not doubt his words as she looked at his serious expression. The way he stared at her made her feel desirable but she did not feel an overwhelming need to be with the viscount. With Marcus, she felt she was incomplete until she was with him. She longed for Marcus to just once look at her the way Greenley was right then. It would make things so much easier.

"I only speak the truth," he replied blithely but his face assured her it was so. As the dance ended, the viscount swept into an elegant bow and she sank into a deep curtsy. He led her from the dance floor and back to her cousin. They'd barely reached the edge of the dance floor before they were intercepted.

"I can escort her." Marcus materialized at their side to offer. He put a restraining hand on Viola's other elbow and she tingled at the possessive gesture. "Save you the trouble, Greenley."

"It is no trouble," the viscount said through clenched teeth. His light brown eyes flashed a warning that went unheeded. While of similar height, Marcus easily exuded a powerful presence the other man would be a fool to ignore.

"Oh, but I insist." Marcus said and held out his arm for Viola. "May I?"

His gaze dared Greenley to defy him. When he looked as if he wanted to argue, Viola hurried to accept Marcus's escort and thus avoided a potential confrontation. Marcus was extremely protective to begin with, but he was especially so when it concerned the viscount.

"I would be honored, Marcus. Thank you for the dance." Viola wrapped her arm through Marcus's. Noticing her gesture, Greenley quickly disappeared into the crowd. Viola clucked her tongue at Marcus.

"That was not well done of you. You have insulted my friend."

"Greenley is a toad," Marcus said as they attempted to squeeze through the massive crush at Almack's. "I would not worry overmuch about his opinion of you."

"But his aunt is a notorious gossip. It would not do to be in her poor graces."

"Viola, no one who really knows you will ever doubt you are a model of propriety. You have always done what was expected of you since the moment you could wear long skirts. At least in the public eye."

Viola wondered why she could not take it as a compliment. She pinched Marcus's forearm lightly and she turned to face forward as he led her back to Margaret. "Not everyone is as fortunate as you, Marcus. You can do whatever you fancy and no one will scold you. If I do not obey by society's rules, I will be an outcast."

"Sometimes I miss the hoyden you once were."

To be honest, Viola did also. Since her debut, she felt smothered. She longed for the clear, crisp air of Haversham and the freedom to do as she pleased. "I had to grow up sometime, Marcus."

"I'm well aware you're no longer a girl."

Viola wanted to pursue the conversation further, but they drew close to her cousin, which effectively ended their private moment.

"There you are, Viola! There is someone you absolutely must be introduced to. You will excuse us, will you not, Kingsley?"

"Certainly." Marcus lifted Viola's hand and kissed her knuckles. His dark eyes sparked with humor when Viola made a face at him and he deliberately kissed her hand a moment longer than respectable. Was it her imagination or did Marcus actually *lick* her hand? Her palm tingled and her cheeks pinkened when Margaret made a sound of disapproval and snatched Viola's hand out of his grasp. Marcus lifted his head slowly and winked at Viola before turning his attention to Margaret.

"Forgive me for detaining you, Lady Margaret." A teasing glint entered his eye. "Have I mentioned how devastatingly beautiful you look tonight? I will never forgive myself for letting Taylor claim you first."

Viola amusedly looked at her cousin's bashful expression and had to fight the urge to chuckle. Though Margaret was completely faithful to Taylor, she'd never been able to hide her reaction to Marcus's good looks. When he turned on the charm and actually flirted with her, Margaret was reduced to mute embarrassment.

Margaret hid her fluster by looking away from Marcus with the pretense of waving at someone. "There she is now. Come along, Viola." Margaret latched arms with Viola and led her across the room. When she was safely out of the earshot of Marcus, she confided, "I do not know how you can carry on an intelligent conversation with that man! When he looks at me, I positively turn to jelly."

"You say Taylor makes you feel the same way, yet you manage to speak sensibly to him. Do you not find it odd that Marcus can affect you in such a way?"

Margaret let out a hearty laugh and her eyes cut to her cousin. "You know very well while he is attractive, Taylor can never claim to be heart-stoppingly handsome I am comfortable with Taylor. Your marquess puts everyone else to shame. I feel like a dolt next to him."

"He is not my marquess," Viola pointed out as they circled the room with apparent aimlessness.

"He is much more yours than any other young lady's. He does not speak to anyone half as much as you." Margaret eyed her cousin suspiciously. "When he could have his pick of any lady in the room, I wonder why he spends so much time with you?"

"We are old friends. It is expected that he would talk to me far more often than to complete strangers, especially since the other ladies are desperate to drag him to the altar. I am considered safe company."

"Not in this crowd." Margaret motioned to the members of the ton surrounding them. She cautiously lowered her voice as she continued. "If Marcus continues to single you out, it is bound to be remarked upon. No matter if it is true or not, a flirtation will be suspected."

Viola raised an eyebrow in challenge. "Marcus and I are friends and we should be able to do as we please. I care not one whit what these people think of my relationship with Marcus."

Viola laughed at Margaret's perturbed expression before glancing over her shoulder to search for Marcus. He was leaving the room, but caught her eye and smiled at her before leaving to seek his own entertainment.

Viola watched as he disappeared from the room with disappointment. Since her debut over a year ago, she'd spent less and less time in Marcus's company. As a young debutante, she was forever fending off unwanted suitors or being dragged from one event to another. The few times she had been in Marcus's company, she'd been surrounded by the rest of society and been unable to have a private conversation with him for months. She had thought of suggesting a private outing, but she feared it would be too forward. She was no longer of an age where she could claim Marcus's attention without it being commented on. Though she felt she should be able to speak freely with him, she knew it would be highly improper for her to seek his company in private. It was beginning to seem she was destined to be denied his company for the rest of the season.

"Who is it you are so desperate for me to meet?" Viola asked as Margaret led her through the crowd. Viola did not think there could possibly be someone she had yet to be introduced. She had spent the last few months engaged in endless rounds of introductions until she began to think she would have to meet every person in England.

"The Countess of Weatherington." Margaret craned her neck to peer across the room. "She throws an annual country party and she wants to meet you before extending an invitation."

Viola raised an eyebrow questioningly at the odd request.

"Do not worry. She did the same to me the season of my debut. She is very selective and insists on knowing the guests beforehand."

Viola met the Countess and must've passed muster because she received a coveted invitation to the party. They were introduced to the countess's daughter, Agnes, whom Viola recognized from several other balls as one of the wallflowers. Agnes was timid and when she spoke, it was in such a quiet whisper Viola had to lean forward to hear her.

After taking their leave, Margaret and Viola strolled around the room and engaged in casual conversation with their acquaintances. Viola hated the meaningless chatter. Her eyes caught sight of Marcus as he returned to the ballroom and she wished once again she could be alone with him. Marcus had always encouraged her to speak her mind. She never had to mince her words for fear she would be considered forward.

Marcus saluted her with his glass and she raised a pointed eyebrow at the amber liquid. He had absolutely no tolerance for alcohol and if he consumed even one glass of brandy, he would be intoxicated. She watched as Marcus took a tiny sip from the glass and winced. He claimed all men were supposed to like brandy and it was just like him to try to increase his tolerance by drinking the stuff even though he detested it. He'd once done the same with tea, but had given up after weeks of claiming he'd never tasted a worse drink. Viola hid a giggle behind her hand when he casually set down his brandy glass and proceeded to ignore it.

The evening seemed to drag interminably

until finally the clock struck eleven. Almost as if by magic, Marcus appeared at her elbow to escort her in to supper. As his fingers curled around her upper arm, Viola heaved a sigh of relief. "Thank God it is you."

Marcus's face quickly turned cold and forbidding. "Has some gentleman acted inappropriately with you?"

"Do not be ridiculous, Marcus. Of course not."

Marcus's face cleared suddenly and he smiled. "So no duels to defend your honor?"

"Not at present." She stepped forward and waited for Marcus to pull out her chair. She seated herself and looked up at him teasingly. "Has some lady been too forward with you?"

Marcus's teeth appeared as he flashed her a wolfish grin. "Quite probably, but I would hesitate to tell you about it. You would rush in to defend my honor, which is unfortunately beyond repair."

"Tarnished beyond all hope." Viola clasped her hand to her chest. "I fear nothing can save you now."

"Not to mention how would it look to have a mere girl defending my honor. I would be laughed out of all the clubs."

"Which we all know is a fate worse than death. Even worse than not being able to drink a glass of brandy without losing the ability to walk."

He winked at her before moving away to take his own seat farther down the table. He was unfortunately seated next to Amelia Gray. Viola hid a smile behind her hand at his look of resignation.

Amelia had brazenly flirted with him the entire season and Marcus could hardly bide the chit. Whenever he was trapped in conversation with Amelia, he would make a signal to Viola and she would attempt to rescue him. He would do the same for her if she were approached by a distasteful suitor. Unfortunately, at the dinner table there was little she could do to save him. She and Marcus were seldom seated near each other. All the hostesses inevitably had a single son or daughter that they designed to place next to society's darlings. Which was the reason Viola was pleasantly surprised when Viscount Greenley took the seat next to hers. He was infinitely much better company than a stuttering third son or poor relation. She began to think dinner could be quite entertaining after all as the handsome viscount smiled charmingly at her. He claimed her attention so completely throughout the meal that she missed the dark look on Marcus's face as he noticed the pair of them in animated conversation.

*****

Marcus was unusually quiet on the ride back to her father's townhouse. For once, Margaret and Taylor had left in a separate carriage so Viola was alone with Marcus. Viola suspected Taylor had a question of the utmost importance to ask her cousin and she was overjoyed. Viola had barely settled into the coach before noticing Marcus's foul temper. Her own buoyant spirits deflated a little at his sullenness. He sat across from her rigidly and stared out of the window. Viola attempted a conversation, but he stubbornly refused to answer except in monosyllables. Viola leaned back against the seat and tapped her foot, impatiently wishing the ride was over and she could escape the enforced quiet inside the carriage. She began to hum quietly and swayed with the tune in her head.

"Can you stop that infernal noise?" Marcus asked sharply.

Viola's eyes widened. Marcus had never raised his voice once to her in all the years she had known him. Perhaps it was an after effect of the glasses of brandy she had seen him consume. He'd finished off one at supper and Viola could hardly fault him for his indulgence. She would've been tempted to do the same had she been seated next to Amelia Gray. Even so, it was unlike Marcus to be in such a foul humor regardless of the situation.

"Pardon?"

Marcus's eyes bored into hers with an intensity she had never seen. Instinctively she recognized his current mood was the result of something much more than alcohol. "Must you encourage him so?" His fingers tapped a staccato rhythm against his knee.

"Encourage whom?" Viola's mind whirled in confusion. It was unlike Marcus to switch topics so suddenly. Could he possibly be jealous? Viola disregarded the notion and blamed it on the brandy once again. "Do you mean the viscount?"

"Of course I mean that blackguard," Marcus answered with a curl of his lip. "I do not like the way he looks at you."

"You have said that of at least a dozen men since I debuted. Why is Greenley so different?"

"Because he is the first one whose company

you seem to enjoy. I fear you may be hurt."

"Do not be ridiculous. I am not a child anymore, Marcus."

"I am aware of that. Do you not think I would notice you are old enough to begin garnering the attention of men? If I imagined you were still a child, it wouldn't be necessary for me to warn you. Greenley is not someone you should toy with. Unlike your others, he will not take your refusal lightly."

"What makes you think I would refuse him?" Viola lifted her chin and answered recklessly. She hoped to goad him into making some sort of declaration regarding their own betrothal. Her first season was almost finished and he'd not spoken of their assumed marriage in over two years.

"If you possess even half of the intelligence I believe you do, you would never consider a romantic attachment to him. He is older than you and entirely unsuitable."

Viola clenched her hands together to hide her dismay. Perhaps Marcus no longer wanted to marry her. To hide the hurt his words had caused, she acted as if she were truly considering the viscount.

"He is only a year older than you are now. Husbands are generally much older than their wives anyway." Viola looked away. "Your disapproval is ridiculous if it is based on nothing more than his age."

In the past months, Marcus had become increasingly protective of her. He was almost like her shadow. Once she'd reveled in his attention, but his constant hovering was growing tiresome. If she stepped outside for a breath of air, Marcus inevitably followed. When a young man began to show a marked interest in her, Marcus would frighten him away before he could declare his intentions. Her one and only kiss from an overeager suitor had resulted in Marcus nearly coming to blows with the unfortunate gentleman. Only Viola's desperate pleas had prevented Marcus from beating him into a bloody pulp. Though she had hardly wanted to be kissed by the gentleman, she didn't think it warranted bloodshed. One look into Marcus's eyes was enough to scare even the most dedicated gentleman away from her.

He must be upset because Greenley was the first to ignore his less than subtle warnings. Content she had discerned the reason for his bad temper, Viola's spirits fell. She'd always known Marcus looked upon her as a sister. He was certainly acting the part of an older brother now. What would it take to make him act like a suitor?

"You are a bully. Why the sudden concern for my welfare."

"Your father trusts me to protect you from unwanted suitors."

"What if I do not need protection? What if I like the attention I receive from him? At least he realizes I have grown up and thinks I am beautiful."

Marcus leaned forward until Viola was pinned by his long legs and arms. "If you fancy yourself in love with him, then you are a fool."

She straightened her spine and lifted her chin at a haughty angle. "I said nothing of the sort. I am not in love with anyone." *Except you*, she longed to say.

She pushed against his chest and he leaned

away from her. She did not like it when he tried to overwhelm her with his closeness. He seemed to know his touch was enough to turn her mind into a jumbled mush. "Do not presume to think because you are stronger than me I will not put up a fight."

"Viola, I would not dare to use my strength against you, but I warn you now. Greenley is not someone you should trust."

*****

Margaret proudly flashed her ring as Viola came into the drawing room.

"Taylor asked you to marry him?" Viola jumped to her feet to greet her cousin. She'd been thumbing through the Times when her cousin was announced. The paper lay forgotten as Margaret relayed her joyous news.

"He did." Margaret reached for her hand and squeezed it. "It was so romantic, Vi. I never imagined he would insist on taking separate carriages home so he could propose."

"What did he say? I want to know everything!"

"He told me he couldn't live without me and insisted I marry him at the earliest opportunity." Margaret's face beamed with happiness and Viola was surprised at the ebullience of spirit in her normally reserved cousin. Perhaps some of Viola's own nature was beginning to rub off on her. Whatever the reason, Margaret positively glowed and Viola was ecstatic for her.

Viola hugged her cousin and beamed. "I'm so happy for you. Taylor is lucky to realize that you would make a perfect wife."

"Yes he is. But what about you?" Margaret primly seated herself on the couch. "Has the handsome lord declared his intentions?"

"Greenley is only a close friend." Viola took the seat opposite Margaret. She reached for a biscuit and bit into it daintily. Crumbs still managed to fall onto the bodice of her dress and she swiped at them briskly.

Margaret shook her head and frowned. "I meant the handsome Marquess of Kingsley."

"Marcus?" The biscuit dropped from Viola's fingers to land on her skirts forgotten. "He is like an older brother."

"He is a devastatingly gorgeous man and he most certainly is not your brother. Before Taylor, I might've been tempted to set my cap for Kingsley, but any fool can see he only has eyes for you. Last night it was all he could do not to leap across the room and gobble you up."

"You are mistaken." Viola emphatically shook her head. "Any feelings Marcus has for me are of the friendly persuasion. Marcus only thinks of me as his neighbor's daughter. That is all."

"Deny it all you want," Margaret warned. "But I recognize the signs quite easily now. He is quite possibly head over heels. Even Taylor remarked on Kingsley's obsession with you and you know how dense he is when it comes to noticing such things! He said all Marcus seemed to talk about was you. And any fool can see why he is so enamored. You are positively beautiful and his best friend to boot. What more could he ask for?"

"Your happiness is clouding your judgment.

Not everyone can be as fortunate as you and find their perfect mate."

"The trick to finding the perfect mate is to open your eyes and realize he has been right in front of you all along. Shame on you, Viola. How can you deny it? You two would be perfect together."

Viola thought so too, but damned if she was going to embarrass herself by revealing her feelings to Margaret. "Even if Marcus did look upon me as something more, I'm hardly ready to settle down. I am looking forward to a second, possibly a third, season before I even begin to seriously look for a husband."

"You say so now, but what about when the right man makes his proposal?" Margaret accepted the cup of tea Viola poured for her. "Will you deny him then?"

Viola pondered the statement for a moment. She had yet to find a man worthy enough for her to even consider marriage. Every suitor came up lacking because none could possibly compare to...Marcus. Viola had been unconsciously using Marcus as a measurement for a potential husband. In the last few years, their fathers had stopped trying to push them to marry so she figured they were giving her a chance to meet someone she might want to marry more than Marcus. Since his return from Eton, Marcus hadn't brought up the subject of marriage. She assumed it meant he no longer had an interest in marrying her. It'd forced her to give her girlhood dream and try to find someone new. Only trouble was she could not find anyone she wanted more for a husband.

"I guess if the right man does happen along, I

will think about it then," she answered her cousin evasively. If Marcus truly was the right man, Viola predicted she would die an old maid because he certainly showed no signs of falling in love with her. Although she would adore to marry her dearest friend, she would not do it for any reason other than love. She'd long protested she would never marry, but the thought of marriage to Marcus was enough to alter her opinion of the wedded state. He would never try to assert control over her which was integral to someone as fiercely independent as she. Marcus valued her willful nature, even rejoiced in it. In truth, Marcus would be the best husband she could ask for.

"Lady Viola, young Kingsley is here."

Viola was startled when the object of her thoughts suddenly walked into the room after being announced by Harris, her butler.

"Marcus!   I wasn't expecting you this morning." Viola got to her feet and hastily brushed at the biscuit crumbs still clinging to her clothing. Margaret made a knowing sound under her breath and Viola nudged her with a foot to shush her. Her chest tightened as she watched him approach. If only he wasn't so damned attractive, she might have a chance at forgetting him.

"I stopped by to see if you would like to go for a ride in the Park. It is a too lovely a day to stay inside." He bent at the waist and bowed gallantly to Margaret. "How are you, Margaret?"

"Quite well. Viola was just remarking on the lovely weather. She said it would be a delightful day for a ride."

"Did I?" Viola questioned just as Marcus did

the same.

"Did she?" Marcus grinned as he settled in the chair next to Viola. He was dressed for the ride in fawn breeches and a deep blue jacket. He looked very appealing that morning and Viola's eyes naturally strayed to him. He lounged in the chair and propped his head against the padded back. The green of the chair's upholstery lent a golden shade to his eyes, which cut in Viola's direction. She had the uneasy feeling he knew what Margaret was up to. Instead of looking irritated, he seemed vastly amused at Margaret's underhanded attempt at matchmaking.

"She did," Margaret blatantly lied. "Did you not just tell me you would dearly love a ride?" She lifted her hand to touch Viola's shoulder and her ring reflected the light. Marcus lifted an eyebrow at the sight of the diamond on her finger.

"So Taylor finally found the nerve. Congratulations."

"Thank you." Margaret pinkened becomingly. "It was quite a surprise he asked me. I never imagined he felt such strong feelings for me."

"He is thoroughly besotted. I am sure you two will be very happy together."

"I am sure we will," Margaret nodded in agreement and allowed a brief smile. She slid to the edge of her seat and began to get up. Viola put a restraining hand on Margaret's knee, but she casually brushed it aside. "I must be off. I promised to meet Taylor at his mother's so we could tell her the news together."

Viola gave her cousin a stern look, which Margaret answered with a grin. Viola could definitely recall Margaret mentioning earlier in the week that her future mother-in-law was in Italy for the remainder of the month.

Marcus got to his feet and bowed. "Do not leave on my account."

Margaret interrupted him with a shake of her head. "I really must be going. I would not like to leave Lady Buckley waiting. Have fun on your ride." She winked at Viola before dashing out the door. Viola shook her head at the antics of her cousin before turning to face Marcus. He was watching her with an amused expression. "What was all that about? Isn't Lady Buckley out of the country?"

"She is."

"Why did she say she was going to visit her then?" He switched seats and joined Viola on the couch. His thigh brushed against hers as he leaned forward to snatch a biscuit from Viola's plate and bite into it with relish.

Viola couldn't answer as she watched the motions of his lips as he chewed. The shape of his well-formed mouth mesmerized her. His bottom lip was slightly fuller than the top and looked very kissable. She wished she could stop her endless fascination with Marcus, but whenever she was with him she was overcome by a powerful need. It was shameful, but she often fantasized of the two of them together. She had little knowledge of sex, but her burgeoning curiosity sometimes overwhelmed her. She moved her eyes upward and ran her gaze across his strong features. She wanted to know what he looked like naked. What it felt like to press her skin against his.

Marcus lifted an eyebrow and she hurried to answer the question she'd forgotten he'd asked. "Margaret is so happy with her betrothal she has decided to play matchmaker. I believe she invented an excuse to leave just so we could be alone together." Why should she hide the truth? Margaret's machinations had hardly been less than obvious.

"Ah!" Marcus snapped the fingers of his left hand together. "And you and I would be her first victims then?" He took another bite of the biscuit and a crumb dropped onto his chin. Viola almost reached up to brush away the crumb, but Marcus wiped it away himself before she could make a move.

"Margaret has decided we would suit." Viola forced a laugh. "Could you imagine anything more ridiculous? You and I?"

Marcus expertly avoided her question by snitching another biscuit. He took an inordinately long time to chew it before speaking. "Would you really like to go for a ride? The weather is perfect."

Viola glanced out the window at the bright sun and cloudless sky. It was a perfect day without a hint of rain in the air. "Why not? Let me change into my riding habit and we will be off."

She left the room and it was not until several hours later that she realized Marcus had left her question unanswered.

Chapter Six

A couple of weeks after her cousin's engagement, Viola found herself at the Weatherington's country estate. She was beginning to doubt the sanity of attending.

"Are you sure you know the way out of the maze?" Viola asked for the third time in as many minutes.

Greenley looked back at her and smiled confidently. "Of course I do. Two lefts, a right and then another left."

His arms dramatically swung around to point out the direction. He moved briskly down the path and Viola hurried to follow him. The heel of her shoe caught in a root and she stumbled before righting herself. She managed to free her foot but a ripping sound indicated she'd torn the expensive satin of her slippers. She barely managed to prevent the curse that automatically sprung to her lips.

It seemed they had been walking around in circles for hours. Her feet hurt and she was starving. Viola glanced at the sky and was alarmed to see the sun was rapidly setting.

He took a turn and came to an abrupt halt. "Damn," he whispered beneath his breath. His shoulders dropped in defeat and he sighed heavily.

"What is it?" Viola peered over his shoulder. She groaned when she saw they had reached another wall. "A dead end?"

"Do not panic. We will just retrace our steps. We must've taken a wrong turn at the last fork."

"That is what you said the last five attempts to get us out of this blasted maze," Viola argued as she trailed along behind him. "It is getting late and it looks like rain." The words were barely out of her mouth when a fat raindrop plopped on her nose. She looked up at the sky. "Not funny," she mouthed to whichever greater power controlled the weather. He obviously took exception since several loud claps of thunder sounded right before the rain began to fall in earnest.

"Come, Viola! We will have to make a run for it." Greenley grabbed her hand and they took off at a run. After several twists and turns, they arrived at the gazebo in the middle of the maze which had been their original destination. They rushed under it and Viola looked down at herself. She was drenched from head to toe. Her hair hung in limp strands and her dress clung to her body like a second skin. A glance at the viscount confirmed he was no less damp. His short hair was plastered to his forehead and water ran off his shoulders in tiny rivulets.

"We look like drowned kittens," Viola said with a tired laugh. She twisted her skirts in both hands and water dripped to the floor of the gazebo. A puddle formed around her and she dropped her skirts dejectedly.

He exchanged a less than amused gaze with her. "I have a plan. I will go and find the exit, then come back for you. There is no sense in both of us trudging around in the rain."

Viola knew with his sense of direction he would end up getting hopelessly lost. She imagined someone would eventually notice they were missing and send out a search party. She wished she'd had the foresight to tell someone where they were heading before she'd agreed to enter the maze. Instead of convincing him to wait out the rain, she said a quick prayer he could find the exit and nodded.

"Good luck," she called after him as he dashed into the rain and hurried out of sight. She would probably die of starvation before he found his way back to her. She wondered how many days she could survive without food or water. Looking at the puddles forming around her, she disregarded the need for water. Acquiring water would obviously not be a problem she thought with a slight grin.

Viola sat down on the cushioned seat of the gazebo and tried once again to squeeze the excess water from her gown. The pretty silk would most likely have to be thrown in the rag pile. Abandoning her attempt to save the dress, she looked down and noticed her new slippers were also covered with mud and hopelessly ruined. All in all, it had turned into a horrible afternoon. She'd been invited to Lady Weatherington's annual party at her country estate and she'd looked forward to the weekend for weeks. Now it was all ruined. First Margaret had taken ill and been unable to accompany her on the three-hour trip to the country, so she'd been stuck with one of her father's elderly aunts. Then Marcus had snubbed her the entire afternoon to spend time with boring Agnes Weatherington. Now she was lost in the maze and soaked to boot. It all seemed very unfair.

She crossed her arms across her chest and huffed loudly. "What have I done to deserve this?" Have I committed some unforgivable sin that my weekend should be ruined so completely?"

"Are you having a tantrum?" an amused voice suddenly asked. "I would've imagined you had outgrown them by now."

Viola's head jerked up and she glared at Marcus. "Yes I most certainly am having a tantrum. I am cold, miserable and lost."

Marcus lounged against a column with indolent grace. Though he was just as soaked as she was, she noticed he retained a dignified appearance. He pushed away from the column and moved forward to stand above her. He gazed down at her and a drop of water beaded on his chin before dripping to land at her feet. His dark hair lay flat against his head and the ends dripped water onto his shoulders.

"You look like a drowned rat," he finally said with a slight grimace.

Viola ignored his less than satisfactory comment. He might have at least compared her to a kitten. Being compared to a rodent was simply unacceptable.

"Thank you for that extremely ungentlemanly remark." Her slippers squished as she got to her feet. "How did you find me?"

"I passed your viscount and he told me he left you here."

"Is Greenley far behind?" Viola turned to look behind her.

"I sent him back to the house to change into dry clothes. He was starting to look a little peaky. I believe he may be developing a fever."

"I suppose you must escort me out of this

blasted maze then." Her damp skirts caught in her slippers as she tried to walk and she stumbled. Marcus reached out a hand to steady her.

"Thank you," she said with dignity as she straightened to her full height. She held her skirts above her ankle and stepped forward without mishap. She tossed a victorious smile over her shoulder as she continued walking. Marcus grinned when she stepped into a puddle and let out a soft curse.

"Would you like my coat?" he offered, but Viola refused. She was already hopelessly drenched and the thick wool of his coat would only hamper her. She linked arms with him and bent her head against the chilling rain as they stepped out from beneath the gazebo. At each turn, they went to the right and Viola lifted an eyebrow at the seemingly easy design of the maze. She couldn't believe she and Viscount Greenley had spent nearly three hours wandering lost. Within minutes, they were out of the maze. Viola breathed a sigh of relief. One problem solved. Now if she could just get Marcus to show her a little more attention. She came to a halt, forcing Marcus to do the same.

"Where is Agnes? It is strange you have finally let her out of your sight when you have so determinedly stuck by her side the entire day." Viola's curiosity got the better of her and she blurted out the question. She bit her tongue and cursed its unruliness.

"I assume she is safe and dry inside her house. Where I might mention we should be."

"Do you think she is pretty?" She was on a

roll, so she might as well satisfy her curiosity.

Marcus laughed out loud. "I suppose one could say she was moderately attractive."

Viola thought that Agnes was horribly pig eyed and boring and she said so. Marcus ignored her comment and turned to head toward the house. Her mouth opened and closed soundlessly. Marcus had never turned his back on her the entire time she had known him. It was unbearably rude and she was just about to point it out to him when he spoke to her over his shoulder.

"It is still raining. Unless you want to catch pneumonia, I suggest you come inside."

"You probably can't wait to be with Agnes and her pig eyes," she muttered as she trailed after him. She did not know why she felt so threatened by her. Marcus had flirted with many girls and had yet to settle for one. In truth, he had yet to show an interest beyond a mere flirtation. Surely he would not become infatuated with a mousy chit who barely opened her mouth.

Viola followed him up to the house and stepped past him to enter first. Her slippers made horrible squishing noises as she crossed the marble hall and up the staircase. She glanced behind her once and saw that Marcus followed at a discreet pace. Once on the second floor, she turned and headed towards her room. It was the last door on the left and as far as she knew, the wing was fairly empty. Viola had personally requested a room that would guarantee a modicum of privacy. Lady Weatherington had assured her she would not be disturbed by the activities of other members of the party. She was surprised to see Marcus continued to follow her down the hall. He stopped at the door directly beside hers.

"Is that your room?" Viola asked with a wave of her hand.

"Yes." Marcus pushed the door open. Viola caught sight of a large bed and she looked away quickly. The thought of Marcus sleeping next to her was unsettling. "Does that bother you?"

"Of course not." Viola lifted her chin. Her damp curls were flattened against her forehead and she brushed them away. "I do not care where you sleep."

Marcus looked at her with a strange expression and his lips parted as if to reply. Viola waited with baited breath for him to speak. Finally, he just shook his head and reached for his door.

"Get inside and change into some dry clothes." Marcus disappeared into his room, leaving her alone in the hallway, after giving her the order.

"You are not my father!" she shouted and kicked his door. She marched into her own room and slammed the door behind her. It made a satisfying crash and she sincerely hoped Marcus had been able to hear it.

*****

Viola yanked on the bell pull one last time and gave an exasperated sigh. She'd been ringing for nearly an hour and received no answer. Then she remembered her maid had twisted her ankle and been given the rest of the day off. The clock on the mantel showed it was almost eight. If she didn't hurry, she would be late to supper. Normally she wouldn't mind, but she was famished. She'd missed luncheon to visit the maze with Greenley. Her stomach growled and she pressed a hand against it to stop the noise.

She would dress herself, but the gown she was currently wearing made it extremely difficult. She'd already tried to reach the buttons, but her arms couldn't reach. She gave it another try, her shoulder popping as she grimaced. This surely would not do. Viola paced her room for several moments before eyeing the door that connected Marcus's suite with her own. Dare she ask him to assist her? He was like family and no one need know.

Making a decision, she marched toward the connecting door and knocked sharply. When no answer came, she tried the door handle. It turned and she poked her head in the room.

"Marcus?"

She moved into the room. The shades were drawn and the room was enveloped in darkness save for a single candle burning at the bedside. Viola averted her eyes from the bed, but not before she noticed Marcus's dinner jacket tossed over the foot. He obviously could not have already gone down to supper.

"Marcus, are you in here?" she called out again. She turned to leave.

"Viola?" Marcus emerged from his dressing room. "What are you doing in here?"

Viola turned back and her mouth nearly watered at the sight of him in only his breeches and white dress shirt. His lean fingers finished fastening his shirt and she was disappointed she could no longer get a teasing glimpse of his chest. He reached for his jacket and pulled it on as he eyed her suspiciously.

"I've been ringing for assistance, but cannot get an answer. I wondered if you could possibly assist me for a moment."

"I take it you are no longer angry with me." Marcus straightened the cuffs of his jacket. He dropped his arms and looked at her. "What is it you need?"

She was still a bit upset about him ignoring her. "I know this is awkward, but can you unbutton my gown? My hands cannot reach the buttons."

Marcus looked at Viola askance. He must be getting ill, she thought to herself as she looked at his wan expression. "Is that the same dress you were wearing earlier?"

She ran a hand across the wrinkled, nearly dry fabric. "It is."

Marcus motioned for her to come closer. "You should've asked for my help sooner."

Viola crossed the room and presented Marcus with her back. Dozens of tiny cloth covered buttons lined her spine. Viola pulled her hair across one shoulder and bent her head to give him access to the topmost buttons. His fingers brushed her nape as he undid them. Cool air feathered against her skin as he proceeded down the row. At the small of her back, his fingers touched her bare back. She shivered in response as her nipples tightened.

"All done." Marcus's voice sounded strained.

"Thank you." Viola held her gown to her chest with both hands as she turned to face him. A muscle in his jaw ticked and she hoped it didn't mean he was still irritated at for making fun of Agnes. Perhaps he truly liked her and was offended by Viola's casual disregard.

She shuffled her feet nervously. "I want to apologize for those things I said about Agnes earlier. I was ill tempered and I didn't mean them."

"I know you didn't." Marcus moved to the window and turned his back to her. He bent to slip on his shoes and Viola stared at the back of his head silently. She wished he would turn around and talk to her. Instead he kept his back to her and remained silent.

"I will see myself out then." Viola waited to see if he would try to stop her. When he didn't, she headed for the door. "See you at supper."

He made a vague response. Back in her room, she stamped her foot and huffed. What did she have to do to get his attention? Strip nude and paint herself purple? She laughed at the mental image. Not a bad idea actually, but she'd much prefer if he were the one holding the brush and slathering the color on her. It was a totally inappropriate thought for her to have, but she'd never cursed with proper thoughts to begin with. Most people thought as a young debutante, she should be protected at all times. Little did they know, but the soul of a wanton lay beneath the surface, screaming to come out.

Since appearing purple and nude was out of the question, she moved to her armoire and surveyed the mass of gowns gathered there. What horrible luck for her maid to twist her ankle on the very afternoon Viola needed her the most. Not sparing a moment longer than necessary, she decided on a green gown trimmed in ivory lace. When she'd commissioned it last month, her dressmaker assured her the color was perfect for her complexion and it would match her eyes exactly. After she dressed, thankfully with no help required to fasten it, a glance in the mirror assured her the color suited her very well indeed.

She headed downstairs to join the rest of the party. She arrived just moments before the clock chimed nine and she stood off to one side to wait for her escort into supper. Most of the party was members of society Viola knew only barely. With the exception of Marcus and Greenley, she was with virtual strangers. Viola felt awkward standing off by herself so she sidled a few feet closer to a group of ladies standing near the door. She ceased her movements when she overheard some of their conversation.

"I hear Viscount Greenley had an urgent matter to attend to in London." One of the matrons said to her companion. "Something to do with his family I believe."

"I hope nothing serious?" the second matron remarked.

"I don't believe he gave a detailed explanation."

Greenley had left for London? Viola looked around the room in confusion. Surely he wouldn't have left without saying goodbye to her? Maybe he'd been too embarrassed after the situation he'd placed her in that afternoon. The ladies switched to another subject and Viola was frustrated she couldn't discover more.

As the guests lined up for supper, she noticed Marcus was still conspicuously absent. As she'd suspected earlier, he really must be taking ill. Her dinner partner was an elderly widower, who had a tendency to ramble on about nothing in particular. Several times she found herself losing track of the conversation. After saying "pardon" for the tenth time, she abandoned all attempt at listening.

The meal was interminable and she had to fight to keep from yawning. When it was finally over, she politely made her excuses to Lady Weatherington before retiring. She was exhausted and wanted nothing more to do than climb into bed for much needed rest. Her adventure in the rain seemed to have given her a slight head cold.

Her preparation for bed was halted by a knock on her door. She set aside her nightgown and headed for the door. She opened it and smothered a groan. The last person she wanted to entertain was Agnes Weatherington. Opening the door further, she hid her irritation and waved her unwanted guest into the room.

Agnes brushed past her, a light floral scent following in her wake. "I noticed you barely touched your meal and wondered if you were unwell."

Agnes was not really so unattractive, Viola admitted to herself. Her hair was a lovely shade of brown and she possessed a calm soothing demeanor.

"I'm just a bit tired from traveling," Viola lied. She managed a convincing yawn.

Agnes tutted and nodded sympathetically. "I understand. I hope you will forgive my intrusion in that case. I will leave you to your rest."

"Thank you for the concern. I am sorry I was not better company tonight."

Agnes paused in the doorway and turned back to face Viola. "I know it's really none of my business, but do you and Marcus have an understanding?" Her face carried an expectant expression. Viola wanted to lie, but she found she couldn't do it. "An understanding? I should say not. I've barely spoken to him in the past few weeks."

Agnes smiled brightly. "My mother has expectations we will make a match of it. I dare say I would not look unfavorably on him. He is the most sinfully handsome man I've ever encountered. I didn't mean to pry, but I wanted to make certain I would not be trespassing."

"I assure you Marcus has never entertained any thoughts of me beyond friendship." Viola told her a half truth. She may once have held hopes they would marry, but his recent behavior confirmed her wishes were unfounded.

"You and Viscount Greenley seem very friendly recently. Would it be presumptuous to think he will propose marriage?"

Viola wondered what point Agnes was trying to make. She decided to humor her. "He is a good friend. I imagine if he ever proposed, I would give it great thought."

"How wonderful!" Agnes appeared satisfied at Viola's answer. "I will leave you to your bed now. I hope you feel better in the morning. Mother has planned a grand picnic if it doesn't rain."

"A picnic sounds delightful." In truth, it sounded like another boring way to spend an afternoon, but Viola was much too well-mannered to say so.

As Agnes bide her farewell, Viola shut the door quietly and leaned her head against it. Agnes wasn't a bad sort of person. Viola just doubted she was the sort of woman Marcus needed in his life. He needed someone who wouldn't be overshadowed by his presence. Agnes was much too dull and staid to ever hold his attention for a great length of time. He needed someone full of passion. Someone who wouldn't bore him to tears. He needed...well, he needed Viola if the truth was to be told.

Viola readied herself for bed, determined to stop thinking of Marcus. She was able to unbutton her gown by stretching this way and that. As she sunk into the soft mattress, she wondered what she would do if he did intend on marrying Agnes. Smile and pretend to be happy for him, she supposed. Even if her heart was breaking.

*****

Viola woke to a day filled with sunshine and not a cloud in sight. *The perfect day for a picnic* as Lady Weatherington announced gleefully over the morning meal. Viola tried not to groan as the other members of the party began to excitedly plan the excursion. Their loud voices grated against the ache which formed in her head. Lady Weatherington assured everyone it was a short walk to the pond where the picnic would be held, but carriages would be available for those who would like to ride.

With the picnic planned to begin at noon, Viola still had three hours to occupy herself. Marcus had yet to make an appearance and Viola had just about resigned herself to a lonely morning when Agnes approached her. Agnes was in high spirits as she invited Viola to visit the library. It sounded better than spending the morning alone, so Viola accepted the invitation and was ushered into the most magnificent library she'd ever seen. She stood in the center of the room and gazed up at the endless rows of books stacked neatly into shelves that towered far above her head. Her own library at home was grand, but it couldn't begin to compare to the Weatherington library.

"My father loved books," Agnes explained as she moved into the room to stand beside Viola. "He collected them since he was nine years old."

"It is a very impressive collection." Viola turned to take in the whole view. "I could spend years in here and never grow bored."

Agnes was able to sense Viola's love of books from her expression and she sighed. "I wish I had your passion. I was never very good at my studies and I'm afraid my poor Papa despaired of my skills."

Viola felt a sudden surge of sympathy for the girl. "I am sure you had many others to atone for it."

"I am fairly skilled with the pianoforte." Agnes smile was full of pride. "Not to boast, but my instructor says I'm the best he's ever had."

"See there." Viola smiled in return. "I am hopeless with musical instruments. Dozens of instructors ran screaming from Haversham with their ears bleeding all on account of me."

Agnes let out a gusty laugh, which she hastily covered with one hand. "Oh my!" Her blue eyes twinkled merrily. "That is terrible."

"Exactly the words my instructors said before they fled." Viola affected a deep voice to mimic her instructors. "No musical aptitude whatsoever, I'm afraid. Perhaps she could take up embroidery?"

Viola giggled as she took Agnes's arm and led her further into the room. She suffered a moment's shock when she realized that she had just *giggled*, something she'd not done since she was a young girl. She turned her head and gazed at the multitude of books before her. "Which ones shall we pick to read?"

"I prefer works like these." Agnes ran a fingertip over the binding of a few books stuffed between two heavy tomes on crop rotation. "I have to hide these from Mother," Agnes said with a conspiratorial wink as she made her selection. "She forbids me to read anything but the society pages and the Bible. She believes reading novels will make me terribly choosy when it comes to picking a husband and we all know I cannot afford to be choosy."

Viola thought it horrible that Agnes was forbidden to read her choice of literature and even more horrible was her lack of self-esteem. Right then and there, she decided to befriend the poor girl. "I would like to borrow one of your books if you don't mind."

"Of course I don't mind. You're more than welcome to any of them." Agnes seated herself and flipped open her book to begin reading. Viola turned back to the shelves, perusing the titles thoughtfully. As she'd never read novels, she had no idea which to choose. In the end, she selected the one with the most wear on the cover. It must be entertaining to have been read so often.

She sat beside Agnes, who leaned over to peer at the title of the book in Viola's hands. "Oh, that's my favorite! It's all about this knight who rescues this lady from a tower…"

Viola hid a smile at Agnes's obvious enthusiasm for the novel. When her face brightened in excitement, Agnes was almost pretty and no one could deny she was very kind and caring. She would make an excellent bride for some lucky gentleman if any would take the time to get to know her. Viola began to understand what Marcus might see in his quiet companion. Though Viola wished she were the one to capture his attention, she couldn't fault Marcus's choice. If it had to be anyone else, she hoped it was Agnes.

*****

The day was indeed lovely as Viola and Agnes set off at a brisk walk to join the picnic. They'd lost track of the time as they immersed themselves in their books and it was nearly one in the afternoon before they made it to the pond. Agnes was quickly summoned by her mother to assist in the hostess duties. Viola stood by herself and surveyed the groups dotted along the shore of the pond.

There was no one she knew well enough to join. She aimlessly wandered to a large tree at the edge of the tiny pond. Looking at the large, inviting branches, Viola wished she was a girl again so she could climb up until she disappeared from sight. She was so lost in her daydream it took her several moments to realize someone else had the exact same idea and was already up in the tree.

She peered closer and caught a quick glimpse of a familiar clad leg before it moved out of sight. Viola put her hands on her hips and hissed up at the tree. "What do you think you are doing up there?"

"Exactly what you wished you could do," a voice returned. A limb shook and a few leaves drifted to her feet. Marcus's face appeared through the cover of branches. He held his finger to his mouth in warning. "But if you wish to know the truth, I'm hiding from Amelia Gray and her dreadful mother."

Viola held her hand to her mouth to smother a chuckle. "It's a sad situation when a peer of the realm must resort to hiding in trees to escape mere women. Shall I go join them and inform them of your whereabouts?"

"If you do, I will personally see to it you are forced to dance with every unsavory gentleman here tonight."

"You wouldn't dare!" Viola shook her finger at him. "This entire season you have made it virtually impossible for me to meet any disreputable man. There is no way you would change now by pushing me at them."

"Maybe I should just call the Grays over and we all can have a nice, long chat then." Marcus laughed at the face Viola made and reached out a hand. "Come join me."

Viola's mouth dropped. "You cannot expect me to climb a tree here!"

"Why not?" Marcus's grin was infuriating, causing her to roll her eyes at him. "You do remember how, don't you?"

"Of course I do." She glance to make sure no

one was looking before hitching up her skirts and hastily pulling herself onto the lowest branch. She stood and wrapped her arms around the second branch, where Marcus was sitting, and swung up beside him. She held onto the trunk for support and smiled at Marcus with satisfaction.

"Well done!" He saluted her before peering through the branches. "I don't think anyone saw you."

"I hope not." Viola bent her head to watch the members of the picnic. "The company at dinner last night was extremely tedious. Speaking of which, where were you last night? Were you ill?"

It took several moments before he answered. "I didn't feel like eating. I stayed in my room and read."

Viola thought that sounded strange since he'd been dressing for supper when she'd visited his room, but she didn't press the matter. It was entirely none of her concern how he spent his time. She noticed Marcus rubbing his knee and she grinned.

"I'm surprised you allowed me to come up. The last time we were in a tree together, I pushed you out of it."

"One would hope you'd matured a little since then." He stretched his leg and propped it on a branch in front of them. "Maybe I plan to get my revenge by pushing you?" He put his hands to her waist and playfully shoved. She swatted his hands away, nearly losing her balance as a result. Marcus grabbed her as she toppled.

Viola, recovered from her small fright, clung to his shoulders. Marcus didn't immediately release her. Still in his embrace, she took advantage of the situation and inhaled the scent of him. Her nose was pressed against his throat and her nostrils twitched at the bewitching smell of him. She lifted her head to look at him. Something flickered within the dark depths of his eyes a moment before he released her. He scrambled farther down the branch while Viola placed her hands on the tree trunk and took several deep breaths. They sat there, silent and unmoving, neither wanting to admit what had just happened. Intuitively Viola knew something had changed between them as a result of their short embrace.

Chapter Seven

"You are being unusually quiet today," Marcus observed.

They'd departed early that morning and Marcus had offered to carry Viola back to London from the Weatherington's country manor. Her maid was next to her, but she was sleeping off the effects of laudanum, which had been prescribed to ease the pain in her ankle. She and Marcus were basically alone for the first time in days.

"I was just reflecting on what could have happened to Greenley," Viola answered even though nothing could have been further from her mind.

Marcus visibly tensed and Viola pounced at his reaction. Here was her chance to satisfy her curiosity. "Why do you dislike him so much? You positively bristle whenever his name is mentioned."

"I attended Eton with him. Thankfully I had little contact with him, but he seemed callous and unfeeling."

"You are mistaken. He may be a little superficial, but he's never been anything less than amiable to me."

Marcus's dark eyes turned to her, seeming unsure whether he should say more. "He was a bully to the smaller boys. He was almost expelled for his harsh treatment."

"Really?" Viola's eyes widened. She supposed it was possible for him to have been a bully. He did have a tendency to disregard those he considered inferior.   For instance, Viola knew he refused to dance with the daughter of anyone whose father held a title less than an earl. She'd wondered on numerous occasions about his attitude regarding the lower classes.

"You may be correct.   He doesn't look favorably on people he considers less than worthy."

"He is undoubtedly the worst sort of snob," Marcus agreed.

Viola sighed and tilted her head to one side. "He is very handsome though. I suppose one could overlook his lesser flaws if you take that into consideration. It's too bad not everyone can possess both the looks and charm you have been blessed with."

"If you are trying to irritate me, you are doing an excellent job," Marcus warned.

Viola continued to tease him. "I can't help it if all of the young ladies are smitten with you. Everyone falls all over themselves to have your attention."

"Not everyone," Marcus interjected.   "You, for one, do not care a fig about my looks."

"You are like family to me. I know you too well to be struck mute by the sight of your handsome face."

"So you do admit I'm handsome?"

"Of course I admit it. I've never denied that you were attractive." Viola gave a cheeky grin. "But I am aware of all your bad habits therefore I have an advantage."

"And what would those bad habits be?" He leaned forward and watched her with an interested expression.

"You are insufferably domineering." Viola counted off on her fingers. "You detest tea and have no tolerance for alcohol. And you snore."

"How would you know?"

She was about to comment when the coach hit a large pothole. The coach swayed to the side and Marcus was tossed out of his seat directly into the floor at her feet. She laughed helplessly at the sight of him crumpled on the floor. A moment later, they hit a second pothole and Viola's knee dug into Marcus's ribs as she fought to stay upright.

"Ouch!" Marcus rubbed his side. "I think my ribs are broken."

"You are such a whiner." She reached out her hand and helped him to his seat, then carefully eased her maid to the position she'd been in before they were jostled.

He gave her an accusing look. "You have an extremely pointy knee."

"I do not!" She was outraged as she studied at the alleged body part. "My knee is perfectly symmetrical."

"Perfectly pointy." Marcus untucked his shirt from his breeches and lifted the edge to glance at his side. "I do believe I am bruised."

"A gentleman should never disrobe before a lady who is not his wife."

Marcus's amused eyes met hers. "I can recall being asked just last night to unbutton your gown. So let's not discuss proprieties." He touched his side and grimaced. "Damn! It really hurts."

"For goodness sake, then stop touching it!"

She pushed his hands away and leaned across the seat to have a look at his supposed injury. The skin of his abdomen was darkly tanned and she wondered briefly if he was the same color all over. Her cheeks flushed at her wicked thoughts as she reached out a hand to gingerly touch his side. She prodded the slightly blue area over his left rib cage.

Marcus jerked away from her with a hiss. "If you're trying to bruise me further, you're doing a fine job. Keep it up and you can toss a broken rib in the mix."

"Oh poor baby. Would you like me to kiss it and make it better?" She fluttered her eyelashes at him. She'd not practiced the art of simpering since the first week of her debut so she was a bit rusty. Watching the other girls do it made her realize how silly it made them look. She'd promptly forgotten all her lessons in flirting and proceeded to utilize her own brand of charm.

"Would you?" Marcus wriggled his eyebrows suggestively.

Viola rolled her eyes and turned away from him. "Don't be ridiculous."

Even though the thought of kissing him was tempting, she knew she was treading in unfamiliar waters. She couldn't deny she'd often stared at his well-shaped lips wondering what it would be like to kiss them. Would they be soft or firm? Warm or cold? Viola shivered at the thought.

"What is more ridiculous? The thought of kisses that heal or the thought of kissing me?" Marcus waited for her answer.

Viola caught her breath, wondering how the

conversation had turned from teasing to serious in just a matter of a few seconds. Surely he didn't mean he wanted to kiss her? "I know your reputation, Marcus. Your kiss is reputed to be any girl's fantasy."

"But is the thought of kissing me your fantasy?" Marcus asked pointedly.

"Why do you ask?" Viola gave him an odd look.

"Because I believe I am in danger of kissing you right now. In fact, I am quite sure of it."

She stared at him disbelief. "Here? Now?"

" Why not?" Marcus reached out with both hands to cradle her face. "Can you honestly say you've never wondered about it?" His thumb idly rubbed her chin while he waited for a response.

"Not a good idea, Marcus," Viola hedged. "Suppose my maid wakes up and tells our fathers. Surely they would not approve."

Marcus shook his head. "I think our fathers would be overjoyed at this moment. It is their dearest hope that we marry someday. They would overlook almost any indiscretion as long as it resulted in a marriage between you and me." Marcus brought his face closer to Viola's and his warm breath flowed over her skin. "Make your decision, Viola."

Viola's eyes locked with his. He should know she would be helpless to refuse him. She'd wanted him to kiss her since she was sixteen. "What do I do?"

"Come here." His expression dared her to move closer. As she did, she prayed his kiss would make her toes curl the way Margaret said hers did whenever she kissed Taylor. "Are you ready?"

She moved her face closer to his and gave a barely perceptible nod. Her eyes closed as his lips touched hers slowly. His mouth was warm and firm. She made a sound in the back of her throat as he angled his head. His fingers slid from her face and touched her neck. She wondered if he could feel the frantic pounding of her heart. Viola's toes tingled with feeling as she pressed closer to him. His hands moved to her waist to steady her as she arched her neck and clutched at his shoulders. Her nerve endings pulsed as he pressed fleeting kisses on the corner of her lips. When he pulled away to gaze at her, his eyes were impossibly dark. They regarded each other silently, waiting for the other to be the first to speak.

"Is that all?" Viola asked with disappointment. She'd expected more than a brief meeting of lips, earth shattering though it may have been. "A simple kiss is enough to make the other girls fall at your feet?"

Marcus's lips twisted into an amused smile. "It wasn't my intent to kiss you like I did them."

"Why not?" Viola asked in outrage.

"Because you are a close friend and still young."

"Agnes is the same age as me," Viola pointed out. "Did you kiss her?"

Marcus's shamed look confirmed her suspicions. "You did!" She threw her hands up with disgust. "You kiss her passionately and only think her moderately attractive."

"What do you know of passion?" He leaned forward until she was trapped against his chest. For once, she was not irritated that he was crowding her. This time it was a heady sensation which started in her stomach and expanded outwards. His dark eyes roamed over her face and she was strangely excited by the glimmer in his eyes. He wrapped his hands around her knees and pulled her to the edge of the seat. His hands remained on her knees and she felt the heat of his touch throughout her body. His eyes drifted to her lips before returning to her eyes.

"I know nothing of passion." She touched his cheek. Her fingers stroked across the slight stubble of his jaw before moving to his lips. "But I have no doubt you could show me."

Marcus covered her hand with his own and pressed a kiss in the center of her palm. His tongue licked the skin there and she shivered. A tingle started at her palm and traveled her arm. He gave her a wicked grin. "Are you quite positive I'm able to show you?"

"Quite," Viola whispered as he lowered his head back to hers. He hesitated for just a moment before covering her lips with his own. His mouth slanted across hers and he boldly touched his tongue to her lips. Viola's surprised gasp gave him access to her mouth and he swept in to touch his tongue to hers. The velvety sweep teased her senses and she melted. He continued to kiss her as he pulled her out of her seat and into his arms. She sprawled against his chest and pressed her body against his shamefully. Marcus's hands traveled down her back and grasped her bottom. He positioned her so that her knees straddled his hips. She felt the hard press of his arousal against her belly, which shocked her enough she let out a small gasp. She was out of her element and Marcus must have sensed her withdrawal because he tore his lips from hers.

"Is that a better demonstration?" he asked with a glint of satisfaction. Though he acted the part of a rake, his hands trembled against her knees. It was a sign he was just as affected as she.

It took a moment for Viola to catch her breath. She was still straddling him and found it difficult to think in such close proximity. Bracing her hands against his shoulders, she put a respectable distance between them. "Is that what you do with all the girls?"

Marcus shook his head. "Not all of them."

"Did you do it with Agnes?" Viola's eyes flashed with jealousy. He cradled her face and tugged her gaze back to his.

"I've never kissed Agnes the way I just kissed you." His serious expression assured her he was absolutely honest.

"Too bad for her." Viola leaned down to teasingly run her tongue across his lips. "You are quite accomplished. It's a shame she missed it."

"I will be sure to give her your condolences," he said just before she moved her lips to his. She traced the curve of his lower lip. He allowed her to experiment with the kiss before once again taking charge. Viola wriggled her hips to get closer and his hands moved to her waist to hold her still. She had an instinctive urge to move against him and she fought against the restriction of his hands. So suddenly she barely had time to protest, he turned her so she was lying flat on her back.

His lower body pinned her to the seat. She moaned when his hips flexed against hers and her eyes flew open to focus on his face. His face was flushed and he was breathing heavily. Viola could see his control was slipping away and she smiled in satisfaction. So this was what a man in desire looked like. Agnes's novel had alluded to this act, but reality was far better than imagination. Her eyes slid closed as she wrapped her arms around his neck and urged him back down. She could tell he wanted to resist, but he gave in and kissed her once more. The muscles in his arms bunched as he heaved himself away from her and she barely managed to suppress a sigh of regret.

He moved to sit on the opposite side of the carriage and Viola pushed herself to a sitting position. It took a moment to straighten her disheveled clothing before she could look at him. As he ran a hand through his mussed hair, his hands shook. Realizing that her own hands were trembling, she folded them tightly in her lap.

"This certainly changes everything." Marcus dropped his head against the seat and slanted a look at her. Her brows drew together in confusion as he clarified. "If you're old enough to kiss like we just did, then you're old enough for marriage."

She was old enough for much more than just kissing and she intended on making him see that. "Is this your idea of asking me to marry you?"

"We're home." His gaze was drawn away from her disgruntled expression as he motioned toward the window.

Viola saw they had indeed reached her

father's townhouse. Her mind was still whirling with thoughts of marriage to Marcus. Had he really been waiting for a sign she was grown up? If a kiss were the only sign he needed, she would've thrown herself at him months ago. She barely had time to catch her breath before the door was swung open and Marcus descended from the carriage. He turned to assist her and Viola put a nervous palm in his.

She stepped from the carriage on shaky knees and tried to ignore the fact that Marcus's eyes were on her the entire time. Their kiss in the carriage had shaken the foundation out from under her and she was unprepared for what would happen next. Marcus walked beside her up the narrow steps of her father's London home. He followed her inside and Viola grew tired of his ignoring her.

"What do we do now?"

"What do you want to do?" He tried to look unconcerned, but his tension was evident as he waited for her answer.

"I'm not sure." In a few short minutes, their relationship altered dramatically and she was still unsure of Marcus's feelings. She knew he often kissed ladies he had no serious interest in and she feared it might be a similar situation with her. What if he only suggested marriage because of a misplaced sense of honor? She moved to the sitting room and he followed. Closing the door behind them, he faced her. "You never should've kissed me. I knew it would harm our friendship. You do not have to feel obliged to marry me." She was giving him one last chance to change his mind.

"I may have kissed you first, but you

practically threw yourself at me after that. As to our friendship, we've hardly been on speaking terms the last few months. Did you not find it the least bit odd?"

"I had assumed you were busy. We've both had a hectic schedule this season." Viola pressed a hand to her temple. Her head had begun to pound furiously. "I do not expect you to spend every minute with me."

Marcus strode toward her until she was forced to angle her head up to see him. "I was so damned jealous of you I could not stand to be near you. Especially not while you were flirting with bloody Greenley."

A pulse visibly appeared on the side of his neck and Viola was entranced by it. She had the oddest urge to press her lips to the very tempting spot. She wondered what he would do if she leaned forward and tasted the skin of his neck. Reluctantly she forced her eyes away.

"You were jealous? Of me and the viscount?"

"Yes I was. I wanted to smash something every time the bastard touched you." Marcus took hold of her hand. "You've always been mine and I never intended to share you. I've been in agony waiting for you to realize you felt for me what I feel for you."

Viola's heart leapt at his confession. He'd just admitted he had feelings for her. Feelings Viola wholeheartedly returned. She rushed up to him and wrapped her arms around his neck to hug him fiercely. "I never wanted him. I only befriended him to make you jealous. I thought you were never going to offer for me."

Marcus's teasing voice tickled her ear. "But I thought you were not interested in marriage?"

"Maybe I was wrong."

He let out a deep breath and wrapped his arms around her waist. His chin rested on the top of her head as he breathed in the scent of her hair. "You can't know how long I've waited to hear you say that."

She was so happy, she was about to burst. "That I was wrong?"

"No, you loved me."

"I never said I loved you," Viola argued. Marcus put a finger to her lips to shush her.

"Just admit it, Viola. You, Viola Anne Haversham, are desperately in love with me despite the fact you always claimed no man could ever measure up to your impossibly high standards."

"What makes you so sure of yourself?" Viola nudged her forehead against his. She wanted to tell him he'd been the one she set all her standards by, but it could wait.

Marcus pinned her with a serious expression. "I know how I feel about you. I can only hope you feel the same for me."

"And what, exactly, do you feel for me?"

"Damn it, Viola! You are going to make me say it first, aren't you?" His dark eyes locked with hers as he cradled her face between his hands. "I am desperately in love with you. Please put me out of my misery and say you love me in return."

"It is true I adore you, Marcus," Viola answered with a tilt of her lips. She did not plan on making it too easy for him to discern her true feelings.

"But do you *love* me?" Marcus was not one to leave anything to chance. He would make her say it.

"Of course I do." Viola laughed wobbly as she gave in to his pleading expression. "I've loved you since I was fifteen. I was just too stubborn to admit it."

Marcus's smile could rival the sun as he bent down to kiss her and Viola was not surprised her passion mounted just as quickly as it had in the carriage. Somewhere in the back of her innocent mind, she'd known it would be like this between them.

A knock sounded at the door and the pair separated reluctantly. Viola's butler stuck his head in the door and informed them Robert was waiting for them in the morning room. Harris had been with the Havershams since he was eighteen and he was considered family. Therefore he was allowed liberties not many servants could claim. When he noticed the two of them standing so close together, he allowed a small smile to appear on his wrinkled face. "About time." He winked at Viola slyly before shutting the door to allow them a moment of privacy.

"God bless that dear, considerate man." Marcus took advantage of the time to press another quick kiss on Viola. He threaded his hands through hers as they went to join her father.

"How do we act now?" Viola whispered as they walked into the hall. She felt like shouting it from the rooftops Marcus loved her, but she was going to let him decide when they would announce it.

"I would not like having to hide my feelings

for you. I've hidden them for far too long already, but it's entirely up to you how we proceed."

Viola's eyes twinkled at him. "I suggest we tell them immediately. Then they would not find it unusual if I kiss you anytime I desire."

"Not anytime you desire," Marcus said with a low laugh. "You'll have to show some restraint."

"Perhaps a little."

"It's settled then." Marcus squeezed her fingers gently. As they entered the room, her father's gaze immediately locked on their entwined hands. He looked up with a hopeful expression and Viola nodded. His wide smile clearly indicated he approved of the match.

*****

On the evening of a masked ball hosted by her father, Viola's spirits were high. Her father was planning on announcing her betrothal to Marcus that night and he'd been hinting to his friends for almost a month of the joyous occasion. Viola stood in her room and admired herself in the mirror. Her new blue silk was stunning and she knew Marcus would approve. Blue had always been his favorite color and it complimented her complexion favorably. Marcus had given her a demi-mask especially dyed to match her gown. Tiny diamonds were sewn into the upper edges of the mask to draw attention to her eyes. Viola ran an approving hand over the skirt of her gown before turning to leave her room. Her father waited for her at the bottom of the staircase and he beamed up at her.

"You are exquisite, my darling." Robert took her hand to lead her into the ballroom.

"Thank you, Papa. Has Marcus arrived yet?"

"He and Kingsley arrived a few minutes ago. I imagine he is inside doing the circuit."

As she walked toward the ballroom, Viola trembled with the need to see Marcus. He'd been in London this past week and she'd been unable to see him. The past few months had only reinforced her feelings for Marcus and she could not imagine living without him. Three weeks ago, he'd suddenly grabbed her and kissed her passionately. While she was still dazed from his kiss, he reached into his pocket and pulled out a ring. He asked her to marry him and Viola tearfully agreed. She had thrown herself headfirst into planning the grandest wedding England had ever seen. With the help of Margaret, she'd handwritten nearly five hundred invitations which were waiting in her room to be posted after her father's announcement that evening.

As they entered the glittering ballroom, Viola's gaze wandered around the room. She smiled brightly when she spotted a familiar pair of broad shoulders at the edge of the ballroom. She made a move to join Marcus, when a hand touched her elbow.

"Dearest Viola, you look beautiful." Greenley's smile did not quite reach his eyes.

"Thank you," Viola answered distractedly and stood on her toes to keep sight of Marcus.

"I wanted to be the first to congratulate you on your impending nuptials. I hope you and Kingsley are happy together."

"How did you…?" Viola began to ask.

"How did I know you two are betrothed?"

He grinned wickedly. "A lucky guess. Although I must say I am disappointed." His hand traveled to Viola's elbow and she fought an involuntary shudder. His attitude cooled considerably once she began appearing with Marcus in public. She felt uneasy whenever she happened into him and she wanted to escape at the first opportunity. Though she was not frightened of him, she sensed he wanted more from her than she was willing to give.

"Are you searching for Kingsley?" His look seemed calculating. "I believe he was speaking to Agnes Weatherington a few moments ago."

"Agnes?" Viola echoed as she turned her head to search out Marcus. She was dismayed she'd lost track of him. Agnes had been following Marcus around like a lost puppy for several months. Viola warned Marcus that he needed to dissuade her, but he'd been reluctant to hurt her feelings. Viola worried the girl would be more seriously hurt when she learned of their betrothal tonight.

"Could I tempt you with a breath of fresh air?" Greenley continued at her side. "Mayhap he stepped out for a moment."

Viola allowed him to lead her toward the glass doors at the edge of the ballroom. She didn't particularly want his escort, but she could not very well go outside without it. The fresh night air caressed her face and she looked for Marcus. She thought she detected a flash of blue in the gardens and leaned over the railings to get a better look.

"Do you think he went out in the gardens?" She barely waited for his response.

She dashed down the stairs leading to the

gardens, but he followed her at a leisurely pace. If Viola had stopped to ponder the moment, she might've realized the look of almost sadistic glee on his face. It was as if he knew a secret she did not. Instead, she rushed into the gardens to locate the person she'd seen. She heard low voices coming from the gazebo and she picked up her skirts to rush toward it.

Her father had built the small white structure for his wife on their tenth wedding anniversary. Her mother had been bedridden at the time, but there was a clear view of the gazebo from her mother's bedroom window. Viola wondered what Marcus could be doing out here when her father was minutes away from announcing their engagement. Who could he be talking to? She put one foot on the bottom step of the gazebo. She heard the rustle of clothing and froze in disbelief. It took a moment for her to realize what she was seeing and then she covered her mouth with one hand. She must've made some sound because the male on the bench glanced up in surprise.

Viola's face paled when she recognized Marcus as the lover sprawled between the spread thighs of a masked woman. His buttocks, smooth and tanned, slowed their movements as he noticed her. Viola's eyes darted to the woman lying beneath her fiancé. Viola was shocked to see it was Agnes. She would recognize Agnes's distinctive eyes anywhere. What was even more shocking was the fact Agnes had an exact duplicate of the mask Marcus had given Viola. Had Marcus given her a mask also? A surge of pain hit her. It was so strong, she nearly crumpled to her knees. Viola wanted to tear her eyes away from the half-dressed couple on the bench, but her eyes refused to look away.

Marcus glanced between the two women in dawning horror and he quickly removed himself from Agnes. He haphazardly buttoned up his breeches and straightened his coat. Viola's eyes roamed over his messed hair and wrinkled clothing with distaste.

He held out his hand to her. "Let me explain."

Her eyes narrowed. "No need. I assure you I understand exactly what went on here."

"I thought she was you, Vi."

Viola lifted her skirts to run, but Viscount Greenley appeared and held her back. He looked at the couple in the gazebo with great amusement. "For shame, Kingsley. Diddling another lady on the night your betrothal is to be announced."

"Betrothal!" Agnes screeched as she began to gather up her discarded clothing. Her outraged face clearly indicated she had no idea of Viola's and Marcus's involvement. She gave Viola an apologetic look. "I'm sorry. I didn't know." Showing a bit of backbone, Agnes slapped Marcus across the cheek. "You, sir, are a beast."

Marcus raked his hand through his hair with frustration. "I thought you were Viola!" He tried to explain, but it fell upon deaf ears. Half dressed, Agnes ran from the gazebo. Marcus turned back to Viola and pleaded with his eyes.

"Vi, I swear to you I thought she was you. She was wearing your mask, so I assumed it was you."

Viola's eyes brimmed with tears and they

spilled across her cheeks unchecked. Though they had shared many passionate moments together, she and Marcus had never done what he'd just done with Agnes. She'd dreamed of making love with him on their wedding night and now all her dreams were ruined. She shook with anger and hurt and wanted nothing more to do than leave. She would've run, but Greenley still held her arm.

Marcus walked toward her. "Viola?"

Viola stared at his outstretched hand. Tearing her arm from Greenley's grasp, she stepped closer to Marcus. "I never want to see you again." She turned on her heel and walked away with her head held high. Though her magical night had turned into her worst nightmare, she refused to let even an ounce of pain become visible.

Chapter Eight

Viola, safely locked in Catherine's room, found the memories from three years ago still had the power to affect her. After Marcus's defection, she returned to the ball, pretending as if nothing had happened. She shivered with shock, a delayed reaction, until Robert called for attention. Her father attempted to toast the happy couple, only to be interrupted by Marcus's father. Robert's face mirrored his concern before he smoothly made a toast to Taylor and Margaret, who were expecting their first child.

Later that night, Viola confided in Margaret and spent almost an hour crying in her cousin's arms. The next morning she refused Marcus's numerous attempts to see her. Within a couple of months, Agnes was found to be *enceinte* and Marcus was forced to marry her.

He'd made one last effort to see her on the day he wed Agnes. Viola locked herself in her room and ignored Marcus's furious pounding on the door. He knocked for what seemed like hours, pleading for her to open the door. If her door hadn't been made of solid wood, he probably would've torn it from his hinges. Finally, he'd gone away and married Agnes as planned. Within the year, he was in India. With Marcus a continent away, she'd expected to have peace. Her hopes had been dashed and she feared her heart would never be whole again. Instead, she constantly looked over crowded ballrooms expecting to see him. While she went through the motions of the marriage mart season after season, her heart never became involved. Viola never intended to give anyone the power to hurt her as Marcus had. She kept her suitors at a distance until they finally all lost interest and turned their attentions to younger, more gullible females. The kind of female she'd once been, before her heart had been ripped out and stamped on by the so-called joys of love.

A knock at the door alerted Viola that her hiding place had been found out. She swiped at the tell tale wetness on her cheeks and cursed her weakness. Standing on wobbly knees, she unlocked the door and cracked it open to reveal her cousin.

"How are you?" Worry was etched in Margaret's face.

Viola opened the door wider. "As well as can be expected." Margaret reached out to hug her and Viola sighed against her shoulder.

"I didn't expect to see him again. I don't know which is worse, knowing that he is back in London or fear he would never return." Viola grimaced as she remembered the countless nights she had lain awake in her bed and dreamed of Marcus's return. Hidden under her bed was a trunk which contained every single handwritten invitation she and Margaret had happily created. Whenever she was feeling especially heartsick, Viola spread them out on her bed and considered burning them. In the end, she was unable to throw them in the fire and she would restack them in the trunk. Though the paper was beginning to crumble and the ink fading, Viola hesitated at destroying the last visible evidence of her and Marcus's failed courtship. It appeared she would never completely get over losing him.

Margaret patted her back comfortingly. "It is quite understandable for you to feel torn. It's difficult to forget your first love. But you don't have to see him again if you don't want to."

Viola laughed and wiped her drying eyes with the hem of her skirt. Like they'd been able to stop him from seeing her earlier. "Marcus is very capable. If he wants to see me, I'm sure he will find a way. Besides, it has been three years and I cannot continue avoiding him."

"Do you really want to avoid him?"

Viola narrowed her eyes. "I don't care to ever see him again. He's a brute, forcing his attention where it is not wanted."

" I know you do not think highly of him, but kindly remember his father is dying. He's not expected to be on his best behavior at such a time."

"I suppose you are right." Though it pained her to do so, Viola put aside the animosity eating away at her. "If I chance to see him again, I will try my best not to antagonize him."

Margaret's expression grew pensive. "He looked good, did he not?"

"I really didn't have the chance to get a good look at him before he began manhandling me," Viola petulantly answered. She refused to admit she still found him just as handsome, if not more so, as he'd been all those years ago.

*****

Marcus slammed the front door to his townhouse. He strode angrily to his study, poured a glass of brandy and threw himself in his chair to drink it broodingly. The alcohol burned as it made its way down his throat. He'd never liked the stuff, but he was in such a foul mood that the oblivion offered would be much more tolerable. For three years, he'd rehearsed what he would say to Viola when he saw her again. When he finally got the chance, he mucked it beyond repair. He'd known she would still be upset with him, but he needed the chance to explain to her what he believed happened the night of the masked ball.

After leaving Haversham the night of the ball, the look of heartbreak on Viola's face haunted him. He directly set out for the home of the London seamstress he'd commissioned to create Viola's mask. The poor woman had been interrogated mercilessly. He'd learned an unnamed gentleman offered a small fortune to have a replica of the mask he had presented to Viola. Marcus had been unable to determine the identity of the man, but he had his definite suspicions. During his short marriage to Agnes, he'd also found out the mask had been delivered to her home earlier in the week along with a request to wear it to the ball. The note had not been signed, but Marcus suspected Greenley was involved in the entire mess. He'd vowed to confront the man, even visiting his estate, only to find he had fled the country when it became apparent he'd lost his entire inheritance.

When Viola had fled from the gazebo, Greenley stayed behind to taunt Marcus. Marcus had fought him, but he still felt the need for revenge. Because of the viscount's villainy, Marcus had lost his one true love. He'd made the worst mistake of his life which would eventually culminate in Agnes's death.

His marriage to Agnes had not been a love match, but they suited each other tolerably well. When he'd lost Agnes and the baby, he was surprised by the amount of pain he felt. He'd expected to mourn the babe, but he'd not realized he would mourn the loss of his wife so greatly. Agnes had filled a tiny part of his life which was empty without Viola. He'd had someone to come home to at night, and while she was not the person he would have chosen to spend his life with, she made a more than adequate companion. Now he lived with the painful knowledge he was responsible for the loss of two innocent lives.

One night when Agnes was about five months pregnant, she came into his study and stood there watching him. The glow from the fire gave reddish tones to her hair and for a moment, she reminded him of Viola. "You still miss her, don't you?"

Marcus didn't look up from his ledgers. "Yes," he said simply while his fingers tightened around the pen in his hand. He'd never hidden the fact that he was in love with Viola from his wife. Just as Agnes never hid the fact she fancied herself in love with him.

"I know I'm not the person you would've chosen for a wife had the circumstances been different, but I believe we rub along well."

Marcus looked up at her and smiled fondly. "Indeed we do."

Agnes's face brightened and her hands flew to her stomach.

"Oh, she is kicking! Feel!" She grabbed his hand and placed it on the slight bulge of her belly.

Marcus felt the tiny kick and grinned proudly.

"Our son is quite active."

"Our daughter," Agnes corrected with a mockingly stern look. Marcus pressed an affectionate kiss on her cheek as she embraced him. "It's a miraculous feeling to have your baby inside me."

Marcus had looked forward to his impending fatherhood with pride. Though the baby was the reason he would never be able to marry Viola, he was not resentful of the innocent life he had created. The child was his and he would love it regardless. Agnes and the baby could hardly be held at fault for his own mistake.

During the months of her confinement, Agnes glowed with good health. They spent many hours fantasizing about their unborn child. She encouraged Marcus to talk freely of his feelings for Viola and he felt it helped him get over the mind numbing pain from the loss of his best friend. Though he never felt an all-consuming love for Agnes, he grew vastly fond of her during their short marriage.

In the end, Agnes's prediction of the baby's sex had come true. She'd given birth to his daughter, but Agnes slipped away before she could even see the baby. Marcus supposed it was for the best since their daughter had been weak and died in his arms minutes after his wife. He'd cried when the tiny body was taken from him and wrapped in clean, white cloths.

The next day, Agnes and the baby were buried together in the Kingsley cemetery. Marcus left the private ceremony, only attended by his father, Lady Weatherington and Taylor, and immediately set about packing for India. He decided to oversee his trading business there until the pain of losing his wife and child left him. He'd only expected to be gone for a couple of months. He was surprised when three years passed. Nothing had changed. He still missed Viola with a pain that gnawed at him every day of his life. Not a morning passed by when he didn't wish Agnes and the baby were alive. He'd run from the demons chasing him, but was unable to shake the memory of what he left behind. Now he was back to face the imminent loss of his beloved father. Marcus tossed back the remainder of his brandy and cursed the cards fate had dealt him.

*****

Viola returned to her father's townhouse on St. James Street and was surprised to see the candle still burning in his study. She rapped softly on the walnut door before pushing it open.

"Why are you still awake?" She came into the room, softly shutting the door behind her.

Her father looked up from his book and pulled off his spectacles. "I was waiting for your return."

Viola perched herself on the arm of his chair and ruffled his white hair fondly. "What have I done now?"

"Marcus has returned." He spoke bluntly, his eyes searching for her reaction.

"I know. He visited Taylor and Margaret today."

"Then you've seen him?" Her father's face clouded with concern.

"Just for a moment," Viola rushed to soothe

him. His heart was not strong and she didn't want to excite him. "It was of no importance."

"Poor Marcus." Robert gave a regretful shake of his head. "He lost his wife and baby and now his father is on his deathbed." Robert gave Viola a sad look. "And the one person who can give him comfort refuses to see him."

"Don't tell me you are on his side?" First Margaret, now her father. Why was everyone making her out to be the villain? "Do you not remember what he did?"

Robert struggled to his feet. "Marcus made a mistake. We all do. But sometimes circumstances are beyond our control. Give him a chance to explain. He's hurting right now and I hope you can show a little compassion. Why don't you just forgive him?"

Viola sank down into the chair her father just vacated. Why was every one of her acquaintances siding against her? Did they not understand she'd lost everything when she lost Marcus? The last three years had been the worst of her life and she was hurting just as much as she had the first day. If she were charitable, she supposed Marcus was not entirely responsible for what had happened. It was apparently a case of mistaken identity. But she could, and would, fault him for not realizing it was another he was embracing. Her pride refused to let her believe he would not realize the difference when he held her and when he held another. Viola reluctantly agreed if she were masked, she would bear a striking resemblance to Agnes. They'd been of the same height and coloring. Both wore the same mask.

She closed her mind to the thoughts of *what*

ifs. Even if she'd forgiven him all those years ago, it would've made no difference.   Marcus would've married Agnes anyway when he realized she was expecting his child.   She knew he would never overlook such a responsibility.

Her father was still waiting for an answer. Forgive Marcus? Not bloody likely. But to her father, she gave a dismissive wave of her hand. "It is of no importance now. The past is in the past."

"Is it?" Worry was still evident in her father's clear blue eyes. "If you are over him, why do you remain unattached? Why do you push away every gentleman who tries to court you?"

"Perhaps I like my freedom?"

"Or perhaps an old flame has yet to be extinguished? I know you, Viola. You were not meant to live your life alone."

"I'm not alone. I have you."

"But what will you do when I'm gone?"

"Don't talk like that, Papa." Viola didn't like to be reminded of her father's advancing age.

Robert shook his head sadly. "The years are catching up with me. It's best to prepare yourself that I won't be around forever." He patted her head as she gave him a misty-eyed look. "I'm leaving early in the morning to travel to Kingsley Hall so I'd better be off to bed. I fear my old friend does not have much time and I would like to be with him."

Viola mumbled goodnight to her father and watched as he shuffled out of the room. She kicked off her slippers and stretched her feet toward the fire to warm her chilled toes. Why did everyone insist they knew what was best for her? Viola had never intended to marry and the one time she'd relented, everything ended in disaster. Marriage wasn't meant for everyone and it was a trap she fully planned to avoid. She thought of what her father said about being alone. Her whole life, it had just been her and Robert. What would she do when he was gone? She wasn't as naïve to believe he would always be there, but she hoped to have him a while longer.

What her father didn't know and she wasn't prepared to tell him was that she wouldn't be alone. She'd given it much thought and decided she wanted a child of her own. She didn't think it necessary to have a husband. A lover could get her with child just as easily as a husband. The stigma of illegitimacy to her unborn child was a drawback, but she could move to a place where no one knew her. Pretending to be a widow would explain why the father was absent.

Where could she go, she thought to herself as she tapped a fingertip against her pursed lips. America sounded like an excellent place to start a life for her and her child. She rested her head against the back of the chair and forced both her mind and body to relax. It had been a long, exhausting day. She could think about her future at a later date. Her eyelids began to feel heavy and she allowed them to drift closed. Her last coherent thought before she fell asleep was why Marcus had to come back now.

Chapter Nine

One week later, Viola sat beside her father in the second row of the crowded church and clenched her hands together in her lap. She hated funerals, especially when it was the funeral of someone she'd known closely. Marcus's father had always been extremely kind to her and she had regarded him fondly. When the letter arrived from her father to inform her of the duke's passing, she'd debated on whether or not to attend the services. In the end, her need to respect the memory of the duke had forced her to travel south to Kingsley Hall.

The high collar of her black bombazine dress scratched unmercifully and the air inside the tiny church was stifling, but she'd made the right decision by coming. Her father held himself stiffly at her side as she patted his arm comfortingly. Her eyes involuntarily strayed to Marcus, who sat alone in the front row. Only the observant would notice the tense way he held himself, his back barely touching the back of the seat. Marcus bowed his head as the cleric gave a moving eulogy.

Viola's heart went out to him and she knew the pain he must be feeling. Marcus idolized his father and they'd been extremely close. Viola looked at the emptiness of the front pew and felt another lurch in the region of her heart. Marcus, as her father feared for her, was now truly alone. He'd been an only child and possessed only a handful of distant relatives, much of whom would be too old to travel.

When the services ended, Marcus stood to

walk out of the church and Viola briefly allowed her gaze to meet his. His dark eyes were shadowed with the grief he struggled to hide. She gave a small nod, which he returned after a moment's hesitation. At the front of the church, Marcus was forced to stand and accept condolences. Dressed all in black, he held himself stiffly as a few words of comfort were murmured to him by those who were exiting. Viola wished there was a way she could avoiding confronting Marcus, but Viola's father was taking the death of his friend hard and she had to lend him support as he walked toward Marcus.

As they came closer to him, Viola saw the blank look in Marcus's eyes and her heart clenched in sympathy. She remembered the death of her mother and how wretched she'd felt at the funeral. Marcus had sat beside her throughout the entire service and held her trembling hands between his. If not for him, Viola doubted she would've been able to make it through the service. Circumstances had changed so drastically since her mother's death ten years ago she was unable to provide the same comfort to Marcus now. Without such hesitation on his part, Robert took hold of Marcus's hand and patted it gently.

"Your father was a great man." The catch in Robert's voice was clearly audible. "And I'm proud to call him my friend." He choked up and moved away to gain control of his feelings. Viola was left standing with Marcus. She shifted from one foot to another as she thought of something appropriate to say.

"I'm sorry for your loss." She hoped the pity she was felt wasn't apparent in her eyes. Tears pricked the back of her throat and she swallowed convulsively. She would not cry in front of him, even if it were for his father.

"Thank you for coming." His smile didn't quite touch his eyes. "My father always looked upon you as a daughter."

It was left unsaid, but Viola knew how much the duke yearned for a marriage between her and Marcus. She also knew he never gave hoping they would reach a reconcilement. She'd often visited the duke throughout the years and he'd pressed her to write Marcus. She promised him she would think about it, but she never allowed herself to do what she considered a weakness. Thinking about Marcus filled her with regret and unbearable heartache and she was reluctant to allow those feelings to surface.

"Your Grace."

Marcus turned his head as an elderly lady came forward to offer her condolences. Viola abruptly realized that Marcus was now the Duke of Kingsley. He held himself with the natural bearing of an aristocrat, but Viola never imagined him in the role of duke although she'd been aware the title would pass to him eventually. Marcus's responsibilities had greatly increased with his father's death and she wondered how anyone could possibly hold up under all the pressure. Not that she was worried about him, but Marcus already owned a trading business that took up most of his time. With the dukedom on his shoulders, it appeared he would have to work twice as hard.

Not wanting to linger, she spared one last glance at Marcus before hurrying to her father's side.

"How are you holding up?" she asked her father as she approached the tree he was leaning against.

"It's not easy to bury your loved ones, but I'm holding up as well as can be expected for an old man." Her father motioned toward the front of the church, where Marcus was still talking to the elderly lady. "I worry about Marcus. He never knew his mother since she died at his birth, but his father was the world to him. The loss of his family in such quick succession must surely be taking a toll on him."

Viola could think of no response, so she avoided the subject. "You are tired. I'll see you home."

Viola ordered the carriage be brought around and she assisted her father up the stairs. He was not as strong as he used to be and she had to steady him as he climbed in. Her father's health had taken a turn for the worse in the past year and she worried about him constantly. His heart had caused slight troubles for him since he was a young man, but it just lately begun taking a toil on his overall health. She followed him up the stairs and sat down in the opposite seat. Her father fidgeted uneasily. He shifted again and Viola finally asked him what was the matter.

Her father hesitated slightly. "I invited him to dinner tomorrow night."

"Who?" Viola had the beginnings of a headache. Surely he did not mean what she thought he meant?

"Marcus."

"You invited him to our house for supper!

Why would you without consulting me first?"

Her father's body may be weak, but his tone was firm. "I expect you to conduct yourself as befitting your station. You will put aside your animosity and be courteous to our guest tomorrow night."

While part of Viola pitied Marcus, she was quite sure she couldn't be in the same room with him for any great length of time. "I will do my best."

"That is all I can ask of you, I suppose."

*****

As Marcus readied himself for supper with the Havershams, his mind replayed the events of the past week. He'd concluded his business in London and headed to Kent as soon as he was able. After arriving at the Hall, Marcus had immediately gone up to his father's room and prepared himself for what he would find. His normally robust father was a shell of his former self. He was pale and frighteningly emaciated where he'd once been tanned and in fit shape. Marcus had never been one for sickbeds and it had taken every ounce of his self-control to walk into the room. His father had been weak, but he'd ordered Marcus to sit and listen to the most surprising tale.

As a young man, his father had fallen in love with his estate manager's daughter. Elise was young and totally enamored of the young duke. Their affair had lasted but a few months before the girl had been forced to marry another. A second nobleman desired her and she was married hastily. Later his father learned Elise was pregnant and gave birth to Marcus's half brother, a brother Marcus never knew existed.

"My brother. Who is he?" He was shocked

and disappointed when the duke said the name of his older brother. "Greenley? You cannot be serious."

"I am very serious." The duke made a great effort to raise himself up in bed. Marcus rushed to assist his father and was dismayed at how fragile his father felt in his arms. "He is my son and I want you to find him for me. Promise you will try to help him."

Marcus hesitated to agree. "You want me to help the man who ruined my life?"

"How can you be so sure he is at fault?" Although his father was very much an invalid physically, his tone of voice was as strong as ever and Marcus felt like he was a young lad who had once again made some minor infraction. "Find him and learn the truth."

Marcus clenched his hands together, but he promised his father he would do his best. Marcus would find Greenley because his father wished it so, but God help him if he turned out to be the one responsible for making his life a living hell.

"Your half-brother has not had an easy life." The duke seemed intent on making Marcus pity Greenley. "The elder Greenley suspected Rafael was not his natural son, but he didn't want to cast shame on his beloved wife publicly. Privately though, he made his life a living hell. He suffered much abuse from his stepfather."

"Why did you not do something sooner?" Marcus was still reeling from his father's revelation, but he knew his father would never tolerate the abuse of anyone, much less one of his sons.

"Elise made me promise not to tell anyone. She was afraid of the scandal it would cause." The duke straightened in bed and his sorrowful gaze locked with his son's. "As he grew older, he began to resent his mother for denying him a different life."

"So he knows you are his father?"

"Yes. Elise told him shortly after the elder Greenley died. He stormed out in anger and barely spoke a word to her before her death. She made me promise I would take care of him and now I pass that duty to you."

"What if he is the one responsible for me losing Viola?" Brother or not, Marcus wouldn't be able to forgive such a transgression.

"Then he is not the man I imagine him to be and you can consider yourself to be released from your promise."

Marcus left his father's room that night with a great weight on his shoulders. The few days he had left to spend with his father passed much too quickly until the afternoon his father passed away. Marcus had seldom left his side, but they refrained from mentioning Greenley again. Even though it was unspoken, Marcus was aware of how much his father desired for him to locate him. He'd given it much thought, but Marcus was still unsure of how to approach the problem of locating his half brother.

Alone in the room he'd grown up in, he'd refused to take over his father's suite, Marcus lathered his face and slowly scraped a razor across his cheek. He should let his valet do it, but Marcus wanted to be alone. He'd had enough of everyone coddling him since his father's death. The blade slid along his skin with a slight tug. He wiped the blade on a towel swung across his shoulder and took another swipe.

Inevitably, his thoughts turned to Viola and the upcoming supper. He cursed when the blade slipped and nicked his chin.

"Damn," he muttered as he glanced in the mirror. He tilted his chin to see the cut. It was not too noticeable, just a slight nick that had drawn a few drops of blood. He wiped the lather from his face and tossed the towel aside in irritation. He'd not cut himself shaving since he was fifteen. This whole mess with Greenley was interrupting his concentration. The sooner he was done with it, the better.

Calling out for his valet, he ordered pen and paper be brought to him. He knew a man in London who excelled at ferreting out people who preferred to stay hidden. He would find Greenley and fulfill the promise he had made to his father.

After doing that, he planned to put all his efforts in wooing Viola back to his side.

*****

Viola listened to her father's excuses and shook her head violently. "You cannot expect me to dine with him alone!"

Robert, propped in his bed, coughed before pinning her with a fierce glare. "Viola, I cannot help that I have taken ill. I invited Marcus to supper and you must entertain him. Besides your aunt will be there."

Viola huffed. "You know as well as I do that Aunt Gertie will be nodding off at the table before the second course is served. Don't ask me to do this, Papa."

She may pity Marcus for his loss, but she didn't trust herself to be alone with him. The old hurt threatened to choke her.

"It's too late to back out now. Now hurry before you are late." Robert shooed her out of the room. "Make my excuses to Marcus. He is a duke now, and if you cannot respect him as an old friend, then I expect him to be treated with the respect of his title."

"The high rank of his title does not necessarily indicate a similar elevation in character," Viola muttered under her breath.

"Viola, this is no time for your thoughts on society. Just try to be civil. That is all I am asking."

"Yes, Papa."

She arrived downstairs just as a footman opened the door to admit her unwanted guest. She watched him take off his greatcoat and hand it to the servant. The black wool slipped across his broad shoulders and his arms moved fluidly to hand over the garment, revealing unusual grace for someone of his size. His gaze swung to hers and he strolled forward at a leisurely pace. She paused on the third step to await his approach. The advantage in height put her at his eye level.

"Good evening, Viola." His voice was deep and tinged with a hint of sadness. She could see the strain in his eyes and she hardened her heart against him. Though she sympathized with him for the death of his father, she wouldn't let him past her defenses again.

"Good evening. My father regrets to inform you he has taken ill, but he asks that you remain to dine with me."

Marcus's face mirrored his concern. "I hope it

is not serious?"

"No, it is a mere cold. Unfortunately Father's health has been ailing so his body cannot fight illness easily."

"I'm sorry to hear he will not be joining us."

"I will be sure to convey your concern." Viola descended the last few stairs and brushed past him quickly. Marcus offered his arm to her, but she pointedly ignored it and hurried ahead of him.

She led the way to the dining room where Aunt Gertie already napped. Viola sighed. She'd been right. Gertie would be no help tonight. She sat at one end of the large oak table. Marcus took the seat opposite her as she signaled for the servants to bring in the first course. Viola leaned back as a server placed tray in front of her. Though the dish was one of her favorites, she found she had no appetite. She poked at the food aimlessly with her fork. With Marcus in the same room, she would never be able to eat. Her insides were a bundle of nerves and she feared even one bite would make her ill.

"Are you not hungry?" Marcus set down the knife he held in his left hand. Viola was startled she'd forgotten he was left-handed. It was odd how time dulled so many memories yet left others permanently burned in the brain. She wished all her memories could be forgotten as easily.

"Not particularly."

"Good. Me neither." Marcus waved away the footman who came forward to replenish his wine during the second course. He folded his hands on top of the table and looked at Viola. "Thank you for having me over. The Hall seems extremely barren with only one inhabitant."

Viola once again suppressed her compassion. She would not let it weaken her resistance to Marcus's damnably strong appeal. "Do you plan to stay on at the Hall or take up another residence?" She prayed he would choose to move. She didn't relish the thought of living so near to him. She reached for a wineglass to hide just how interested she was in his answer.

Marcus smiled as if he knew the direction her thoughts were taking. "I'd imagined I would stay on at the Hall. It is what my father wanted."

"Is it what you want?"

Marcus nodded and leaned back in his seat. "I've always considered Kent as home. I cannot imagine myself living elsewhere. Perhaps I will do some renovations on the estate. The stables would benefit from expansion, don't you think?"

Viola hid her surprise at being asked her opinion. Surely he knew she would try to dissuade him from any endeavor which would tie him to the estate and thus leave him closer to her? She looked at his encouraging face and could not discern any ulterior motives, so she answered honestly. "The stables are a bit small for such a large estate."

"My father was never very interested in having horses at the Hall. When the stables were designed, I'm afraid he didn't pay much attention to the plans before he agreed to them. Most of his horse breeding was done at another estate."

Though she wanted to remain unattached, Viola's interest was caught. She loved horses, as he well knew. "Do you plan to breed the horses here?"

"Possibly." Suddenly Marcus pushed back his chair and stood up. He held out a hand to Viola. "The air is stifling. Come, let us take a walk."

Viola looked at his outstretched hand in dismay. It fell to his side as she came to her feet unassisted. "It looks like rain."

"It is England. It always looks like rain." He led the way to the glass doors at the edge of the dining room. He held open the door as she passed through. "While I was in India, I found that I missed the rain most of all. It's funny how you miss some things you never imagined you would."

Viola shot him a look and had to bite her tongue to keep from asking him if he missed her. The look that flashed in his eyes indicated he knew what she was thinking and she abruptly turned her head to look at the rose bushes. Biting her lip, she hurried forward but he merely lengthened his strides to catch up with her.

Marcus stayed by her side as they walked further into the gardens. The flowers were just beginning to bloom and the pleasant aroma drifted on the breeze between them. It was too romantic a setting, so she decided to pursue a safe topic of conversation.

"Did you enjoy India?"

Marcus put his hands on his hips as he regarded her. "It was a shock at first to be in such a different culture. It was vastly interesting, but I soon grew tired of the country."

"Why did you stay?"

Marcus turned away from her to pretend interest in a flowering rose bush. Viola realized he must have stayed away because England reminded him of the wife and child he'd lost. She wanted to kick herself for asking such an obtuse question. They'd been walking in a straight path along the rose garden, but Marcus suddenly angled to the left and Viola knew he was deliberately avoiding the gazebo. She glanced at the structure, not surprised that the sight of it could still bring back the horrible memory of him and Agnes entwined. If she closed her eyes, she could recall the look of shock on Marcus's face when he realized he'd been caught. Marcus noticed the look she gave the gazebo and his eyes grew shuttered.

"Viola, about that night," Marcus began to speak, but she held up a hand.

"Let us not ruin what little peace we have." She turned on her heel and headed back to the house. Marcus called out to her, but she pretended not to hear his plea. She'd almost made it back to the house before he tried again.

"Viola, you cannot keep running from this."

She turned her head to see him still standing in the same spot. She could tell he was glaring at her even though a great distance separated them.

"You really want to discuss this now?" Viola planted her hands on her hips. Marcus merely lifted an eyebrow and she angrily strode back to him. "Have it your way then," she said as she drew closer. "Go ahead. I'm listening." She crossed her arms and regarded him, silently daring him to explain.

Marcus rubbed the back of his neck with one hand as he thought of how to begin. "I was set up all those years ago."

Viola snorted. "Likely story."

Marcus held up his other hand for her to let him finish. She closed her mouth with a snap and glared at him. He started to speak slowly, as if what he would tell her was very difficult to say.

"I went to London and discovered someone had commissioned an exact replica of your mask. That person then sent it to Agnes and requested she wear it to the ball. Someone had planned for me to get your identity confused with Agnes."

"Who would do something like that?" Viola was unconvinced. Who could be that deceitful? "How could they expect it to work?"

"Greenley was the one to urge you to visit the gardens, was he not? He obviously wanted you to discover Agnes and me."

Viola's immediate response was to disagree, but she thought back to the events of that night. Greenley *had* seemed extremely eager for her to venture into the gardens. In fact, it was his suggestion for her to search the gardens. "Supposing you are correct, how could he have known his plan would work?"

"He obviously knew of Agnes's infatuation with me. When I mistakenly identified her as you, he knew she wouldn't protest if I made advances toward her. It was all a horrible mistake."

"That doesn't explain everything. When you had her in your arms," Viola's voice trailed off, but she regained her composure quickly. "How could you not tell it was someone else?"

Marcus's eyes darkened with regret as he looked away. "I was celebrating our betrothal and I fear I imbibed more than was necessary."

Viola was aware of Marcus's intolerance for alcohol, so the story seemed plausible. "If this is true, then it seems horribly unjust."

"It most definitely is." Marcus lifted his eyes back to hers. "I know I disappointed you terribly, but I would like a chance to make it up to you."

Viola moved away from him with short jerky steps. "You can't erase what happened. I will always have the memory of you and Agnes." She waved her hand violently in the general direction of the gazebo. "I believe it is permanently branded in my mind."

"Then let us unbrand it." Marcus came forward to take her hand and lead her down the path to the gazebo.

"What are you doing?" She dug her fingernails into his wrist until she was sure she drew blood, but still he didn't release her. "Have you lost your senses?"

Marcus hauled her to the edge of the gazebo and lifted her up the stairs. He turned her so they were face to face. "This is the scene, is it not? We will have to give you a new memory to replace your old one."

Viola's outraged gasp was silenced as his lips came down hungrily on hers. She raised her fists to pummel his chest, but her fingers curled and her hands returned limply to her side. His kiss still had the amazing power to curl her toes, a feat only Marcus had accomplished though she had been kissed by several men since he'd left England. She'd naively believed the heart did not have to be involved for her to enjoy another man's embrace. After several useless attempts, she'd stopped allowing her suitors take such liberties. Still caught up in the kiss, Marcus slanted his mouth across hers and forced her lips apart. Viola was shocked when his tongue swept past her defenses to delve into her mouth. The velvety sweep of his tongue teased her senses and she heard herself moan. She'd never let anyone but Marcus kiss her in a manner like this.

Marcus's hands traveled down her back to cup her bottom and lift her against him. The hardness of his desire rode low on her belly and she had an overwhelming desire to rub against him. Marcus's tongue dueled with hers as Viola lifted her hands to grip his hair. He tore his lips from hers and slid his mouth toward her ear. He nipped lightly at the lobe and Viola's knees weakened. His warm breath whispered across the sensitive skin of her throat and she shivered. She arched her head to give him greater freedom of movement. When he'd teased her unmercifully and she was about to cave in, he lifted his head and gave her a wolfish grin.

"Is that a better memory?" His eyes held satisfaction at her reaction.

His attitude was like a splash of cold water in the face of her desire. She had to fight the urge to slap his arrogant face. "I'm sure you had much opportunity to practice with Agnes. Did she like it when you did that to her?"

Marcus's face visibly tensed and he recoiled from her in disgust. "This is not about Agnes. This is about us." He jabbed a finger at his chest before pointing to her. "You and me."

"It can never be about us." Viola moved

down the stairs. "There is no more us."

She turned on her heel and marched away from the gazebo. Away from Marcus. Away from certain heartbreak.

Chapter Ten

Early the next morning, Viola packed a basket of food and headed toward the stables. She needed a distraction so she wouldn't think about Marcus and the sudden upheaval his return caused. Memories of his kiss the night before still had her reeling. As her horse was saddled, she let her eyes roam over the rolling hills surrounding Haversham and decided she would ride over to visit Hannah Creech.

Hannah, the daughter of Viola's childhood nanny, was married to the local blacksmith and was expecting her fifth child. The Creechs owned a sizable plot just east of Haversham. Kingsley Hall was located due west, but Viola refused to admit she chose to go east solely because it was the path that was unlikely to force an encounter with Marcus. Viola adored the children and looked forward to afternoons spent with the large family. The closeness of the family filled the empty space inside of her that longed for a family of her own. As her horse rounded the bend, the children came out of the house and ran forward to greet her. The oldest girl, Anne, reached her first and held up a hand to assist Viola off her horse.

"How was London?" the twelve year old asked in an excited voice. "Was it all very exciting?"

Viola nodded as she reached into her basket and pulled out several copies of the *London Times*. "You can read all about it and get caught up on all the latest *on dits*." She handed the newspapers to the wide-eyed girl.

"Thank you so much!" Anne clutched the papers to her chest. Viola was aware of the girl's infatuation with London and she made a mental note to ask Hannah if Anne might accompany her to London someday. The bubbly girl would provide endless entertainment and she would dearly love the company. Anne moved away as her younger siblings crowded Viola and waited for their gifts. Viola handed the twins, Elizabeth and Diana, a doll each and a tiny sailboat to Paul, the only boy. The children thanked her before running to show their new toys to their mother.

Hannah stood in the doorway and dutifully exclaimed over each of her children's toys. She gave Viola an amused look as she walked toward her. "You really shouldn't spoil them so."

Viola grinned at the motherly scolding. "I like buying gifts for them."

"It's your money." Hannah waved her hands and tried to shoo the children away. "Go and play, children. I want to speak with Lady Viola for a few moments."

The children scattered and Viola was able to see Hannah clearly for the first time in months. Viola looked at her friend's obviously pregnant stomach and motioned toward it. "You look like you are about to give birth any day now."

Hannah rubbed her belly and smiled. "Three more weeks. Then the midwife expects a normal, healthy baby." She bent to pick up the basket of laundry at her feet and Viola cried out in dismay.

"Do not dare pick that up," Viola ordered as she bent to take it from her. "I will hang up the laundry and you can come keep me company."

Hannah shook her head at Viola's concern. "I'm not an invalid. I can do my own housework."

"Not while I am here." Viola carried the basket to a line strung between the house and a tree. She pinned a sheet to the line and looked over at Hannah worriedly. "I really wish you would agree to let me send over a maid for a few weeks. You should not be exerting yourself at such a time."

Hannah laughed and her blue eyes twinkled with merriment. "Me? With a maid? Do not be silly. I have Anne to help me."

Viola looked at the young girl, who was bent over the newspapers and reading them avidly. A lock of blonde hair was twisted around her forefinger and seemed oblivious to anything going on around her. Anne would be some help to her mother, but she was too young to handle any real emergency that may occur.

"I suppose you are right," she finally conceded. It was not her place to force Hannah to do something. "But if you ever need anything, promise you will send for me."

"I will, but you worry too much for someone so young." Hannah handed a peg to Viola, which she used to pin a shirt.

"I can't help it." Viola reached for another shirt. "It's my nature to worry about things." She finished the first basket and starting on the second when the children's cries alerted her to the fact they were no longer alone.

"Papa!" Paul cried out and raced on chubby legs to greet his father.

Viola and Hannah both turned to see Patrick Creech walking toward them. The large brawny man picked the boy up effortlessly and swung him onto his shoulders. Paul squealed with laughter and clutched handfuls of his father's hair. Viola eyed the scene enviously. How she'd always wanted children of her own!

Hannah moved forward to greet her husband and he kissed her cheek. "How is my lovely wife?" He patted her stomach tenderly. They shared a private look before he looked up and saw Viola. His smile widened. "Lady Viola, how nice to see you!"

She picked up a pair of trousers and pinned them to the line before waving. "Hello, Patrick. It's good to see you again."

"I've just run into a friend of yours in town." Patrick informed her. "He's offered to help me patch my roof and should be along shortly."

Surely he could not be referring to Marcus! "And who would that friend be?" Viola waited with baited breath.

"The duke himself," Patrick answered with a chuckle. "Can you imagine? A duke patching my roof." He noticed the laundry at Viola's feet and he shook his head in amusement. "And the daughter of an earl hanging out my laundry."

Viola had to admit the image of lords and ladies involved in such menial tasks was faintly ludicrous. She laughed at Patrick's obvious amusement. "I am useful for something after all."

Viola turned back to the laundry and hurried to finish her task. If she were lucky, she could be finished and long gone before Marcus appeared. The sound of a horse just as she hung the last sheet made her groan. So much for luck. She ducked behind the sheets on the line and peeked at the newest arrival. Marcus sat astride a stallion and was dressed casually in a white shirt and fawn colored breeches. Though he was dressed no differently than Patrick, Marcus's breeding was apparent in the way he held his head and his air of sophistication. He looked every inch the duke and no one would ever mistake him for a commoner.

Marcus climbed down from his horse and the children ran up to him. He handed each a piece of candy and Viola watched as he swung one of the younger girls up in the air. He caught her as she fell and placed her back on her feet. He repeated the process with the other two children before greeting Anne. The oldest girl gazed up at him in awe as he lifted her hand and kissed her knuckles. Viola's hand tingled with remembered feeling of the many times he had done the same to her. As she looked at Anne's starry-eyed gaze, she realized he must have the same effect on women of any age. One look from Marcus was enough to turn any woman's mind to mush. Viola was probably the only woman on earth who'd ever been able to deny Marcus anything.

"Hannah, you look radiant!"

Hannah blushed and lowered her head as she quietly thanked Marcus. Her eyes darted to the clothes line and Viola ducked once again behind the sheet. The wet fabric tangled about her legs and she barely prevented herself from landing in a heap. She strained to hear the conversation across the yard.

"We were just about to have tea."

Viola slapped her forehead in consternation. Why did Hannah have to go and mention that?

"We?" Marcus glanced around the apparently deserted yard. "Who else is here?"

Drat! Now she supposed she would have to make an appearance. She stepped out from behind the sheet just as Marcus looked her way. His eyes focused on hers and she could almost feel the tension radiating from him. She resisted the urge to straighten her messed hair and instead pinned him with a casual regard. Her knees felt stiff as she walked toward him and she focused on putting one foot in front of the other.

"Good morning, Marcus," Viola said politely as she reached Hannah's side.

"Viola, what a surprise." Marcus smoothly came forward to take her hand. He bent over it and his eyes locked with hers in warning. "I didn't expect to see you again so soon."

Viola gritted her teeth and snatched her hand from his as if burned. In a way, she supposed she had been. Whenever he touched her, it was as if fire had been set to her skin. "I can assure you I did not plan it this way."

"I didn't suspect you had." Marcus smiled at her before moving to rejoin Patrick. Viola bit her tongue on a violent rejoinder.

"How about tea now?" Hannah gave Viola a curious look.

"That would be wonderful," Viola answered with relief. Anything to get her out of Marcus's presence would be welcome. Hannah led Viola into the house and set about making tea. Viola accepted a cup gratefully and looked at Hannah over the rim.

"I did not know Patrick was such good friends with Marcus."

"Oh, they have been friends since they were little children. Patrick said they used to get into the most trouble. Once Kingsley entered school, they saw less of each other."

That would probably explain why Viola had been unaware Marcus and Patrick were such good friends. She would've been too young to remember, barely three at the time.

"I remember you and Marcus were also inseparable as children," Hannah continued cautiously. She paused to take a sip from her teacup. "Whatever happened between you two?"

Viola lifted her shoulder in a shrug. "You know how children are. I supposed we grew apart much the same as Patrick and Marcus."

Hannah set down her cup and leaned forward in expectation. Her blue eyes held a hint of disappointment. "My mother used to tell me all about the trouble you two got into as children. Then as you got older and I witnessed you together myself, I must confess I thought you would make the best couple."

"Marcus and me?" Viola forced a laugh. "Nothing could be further from the truth."

Obviously the tale of her and Marcus's abrupt courtship had never reached the ears of Hannah and she preferred it stay that way. The fewer people who knew, the better.

"I was so disappointed when he married. I met his wife once you know?" Hannah mentioned as she refilled Viola's cup.

"You did?" Viola was surprised. "When was that?"

"Shortly after they were married. I ran into her in town. She was very polite, but I sensed a sadness in her."

"What would she be saddened about?" Viola's thoughts were spoken aloud. "She married the man she was in love with and was about to have his baby."

"Maybe she knew the man she married was already in love with another?" Hannah's pointed comment grabbed Viola's immediate attention. Hannah must know about her brief courtship with Marcus. A glance at her face confirmed it.

"How did you know?" She wondered if there was anyone in the country who hadn't guessed.

"You didn't have to tell me. It was written all over his face every time your name was mentioned. And you positively glowed when you talked about him. Only a fool would not realize you two had fallen in love. That was why I was so surprised to learn of his marriage."

"It is true we courted, but things have changed. I do not feel the same way any more." She was loath to inform Hannah of the sordid details in its entirety. Viola set down her cup and stood. "It is getting late and I must head home."

"I didn't mean to pry. Please do not leave on my account." Hannah held out her hand. "I can see I have offended you."

"You did not offend me. It is late and I really must check on my father. He's been ill and I should not leave him alone."

"Are you sure I have not upset you?"

"Quite positive," Viola said with a forced grin. "Why should I be upset?"

Hannah opened the door and Viola stepped outside. She noticed Anne staring up at the roof and Viola turned her head to see what had the girl so entranced. It became clearly evident and Viola's eyes widened at the sight. She soaked up the vision of a shirtless Marcus perched on the roof. The midday sun caused sweat to bead on his muscled chest. Viola stared at the sight of his taut abdomen and the way his muscles bunched as he hammered a slate tile in place. His shoulders were broad and smooth lines of muscle delineated his long arms. He turned to reach for another shingle and his back was displayed for their viewing. His smooth skin was darkened by the sun and the muscles clearly evident. His breeches hung low on his hips and revealed almost an indecent amount of skin. Viola's palms itched with the need to run her hands across his naked skin. She tried to ignore the fluttering in her stomach caused by the sight of his gorgeously displayed body.

"Oh my, would you look at him!" Hannah exclaimed as she approached Viola and Anne. She held a hand to her chest and took a deep breath. "Now that is a tempting morsel if I ever saw one."

Viola's shocked eyes flew to Hannah's face.

"What? Can I not look?" Hannah turned her face back up to the roof.

"He is wonderfully handsome." Anne sighed dramatically. "He looks just like one of those marble statues Viola showed me at Haversham."

"I adore a man who is good with his hands," Hannah continued as if her daughter had not spoken. "Look how easily he holds that hammer. Oh, and he is left handed. You know what they say about left handed people?" Hannah shot a knowing glance to Viola, who looked at her blankly.

"No, what do they say?"

Hannah cast a glance at Anne before whispering in Viola's ear. "They make the best lovers."

Viola absorbed the thought. "Where did you hear that?"

Anne grinned. "It's an old family legend."

So if she were ever to take a lover, she could choose someone who favored his left hand. Though Viola suspected it was just a myth, there was no sense in not putting it to the test.

"I wish I were six years older," Anne continued to rhapsodize.

"I wish I were the sort of person to engage in an affair," Hannah muttered half-teasingly. It was common knowledge that Hannah adored her husband and they were completely faithful to one another.

Viola looked at the other two women in amazement. Clearly something was wrong with this situation. Anne was too young to be eyeing a grown man so eagerly and Hannah was married. And pregnant to boot. If anyone should be looking, it should be herself. Viola looked back up at the roof.

Why did he have to be so damnably attractive? Her palms itched to touch his skin. Desire, long suppressed, quickly filled her thoughts.

She imagined the two of them alone. The freedom to touch him, the opportunity to taste his skin, the chance to see him completely nude. Her nipples hardened into peaks. With a quick glance at Hannah, she felt ashamed. Here she was, fantasizing over Marcus in the company of her dearest friend's family.

Marcus stood up to stretch his arms above his head. All three women collectively sighed and he must have heard because he suddenly glanced down at them.

"Hello ladies." He shot them a cocky grin. The muscles of his arms and chest rippled fluidly as he placed his hands on his hips. Was it Viola's overactive imagination or did he purposely flex his muscles just for their benefit?

"Hello yourself," Anne called out and her mother groaned.

"What am I going to do with this one?" Hannah laughed as she led her daughter away. Anne glanced over her shoulder and waved coyly at Marcus before her mother forced her to turn back around. Viola was left standing in the yard alone and she looked back up at Marcus when he said her name.

"Are you leaving?" His voice was as deep as she remembered and gooseflesh broke out on her skin at the husky sound.

"Yes." Viola's voice came out hoarse and she coughed to clear it. "Yes, I am."

"Can you hold the ladder while I come down?"

She hesitated, which led him to add. "Please."

Viola nodded and went to steady the ladder

propped against the side of the house as he began to climb down. She glanced up once to sneak a glance at his attractive derriere before moving her eyes away. When he reached the ground, Marcus bent to pick up the shirt he'd discarded on a tree stump. He pulled it on, but left it unbuttoned. Viola ran her eyes over his gleaming chest. She wanted to run her hand across his skin and see if it was possibly as firm as it looked. She had her suspicions it would be.

"Did you ride over?"

"I did," she answered distractedly. Marcus's hair was damp with sweat and it clung to his forehead. Viola could detect the scent of sweat, soap, and a vague hint of a smell that belonged exclusively to Marcus. She inhaled deeply of the intriguing scent.

"I will escort you back." Marcus turned to look at the roof. He cupped his hands around his mouth and called out to Patrick. "I will return tomorrow to help. I'm off to see Viola home."

Patrick's mouth was full of nails and he waved to indicate he'd heard. Viola tried to dissuade Marcus from his purpose. "Not necessary. I can see myself home."

"I insist." Marcus went to retrieve their horses. Viola followed him reluctantly and took the reins of her horse when he offered them to her. As he helped her into the saddle, his fingers lingered on her calf a moment longer than was necessary. She straightened and gave him a sharp look. He removed his hand, amusement in his gaze. He mounted his horse and they set off.

"I didn't know you and Hannah were acquainted," he mumbled around the reins he held in his teeth while his hands were free to button up his shirt.

"She is the daughter of my nanny. We were friendly as children and I enjoy visiting her family." She watched as the tempting view of his chest was quickly covered by the white lawn of his shirt.

"The children are a handful."

"You're good with them. They seem to adore you."

"They only like the gifts I bring them." Marcus's dark eyes gleamed as he laughed.

"No." Viola shook her head. "You played with them. I think they enjoy that more than the presents."

They fell into companionable silence and Viola concentrated on her riding. It had been many months since she'd been home and able to ride horseback. Her father's London townhouse did not support a stable, so she feared she was a little rusty. She glanced over at Marcus and was not surprised to see he still looked as if he were born to a saddle. She ran an appreciative eye over his mount.

"Where did you get the stallion?"

"I bought him a year ago from an Arabian prince and brought him home with me."

"You visited Arabia also?"

"For a couple of months."

"Were you able to ride while you were there?" She only asked to make conversation. She told herself she wasn't interested in what he'd been doing in the years he had been gone. Politeness was her only motive.

"If you can call it riding." Marcus grinned.

"Mostly I rode camels until I bought Pyrenees."

"Really?" Viola was envious. Oh all right, so she was just a little interested in what he'd been doing. "What was that like?"

He laughed. "Bumpy. Really bumpy, but it got us where we were going."

"Did one ever spit on you?"

Marcus tossed her a suspicious look. "Why? Are you planning to give the camel a medal for daring to disrespect me so?"

"A commendation would definitely be in order."

"It's good to see you have not lost your deranged sense of humor. Thankfully I was never spit on." His brown eyes twinkled as he turned to look at the path they traveled. "A camel is not the best conversationalist, so I'm afraid I spent much of my time in solitude when I traveled the country."

Viola continued to question him of his travels. The conversation turned to India, which was where he'd spent the majority of his time. She'd never been outside of England, but she would dearly love to travel. Her eyes showed her excitement as he described the many palaces of India, including the Taj Mahal. It was unbelievable the magnificent structure had been built solely to show a man's love for his wife. Viola idly wished someone felt strongly enough for her to make a similar grand gesture. Soon Haversham was before them and Viola rode her horse up to the gate. She pulled back on the reins and turned to glance at Marcus.

"Thank you for seeing me home."

"It was my pleasure." Marcus inclined his

head to nod in response. His horse pranced with restlessness and Marcus motioned toward the magnificent stallion. "I believe Pyrenees is trying to hurry me along. I will see you later then."

Viola watched as Marcus rode away. She'd spent a great length of time in his presence and not had one bad thought the entire ride home. Maybe she had finally gotten over her heartbreak. Viola smiled as she walked her horse to the stable. For once, it had been just like old times.

Chapter Eleven

"Good morning."

Viola bent down to kiss her father's whiskered cheek before sitting down for breakfast. She poured herself a cup of chocolate and stirred in a little sugar. "You are looking better. How do you feel?"

"Like a new man." Her father bit into a scone, which he ordered for every meal, ravenously. He licked his lips with a great smack and patted his slightly rounded stomach. "I've had nothing but broth for an entire week and I am famished."

Viola watched as he finished his scone and reached for another. "Your appetite certainly seems to have returned with a vengeance." She picked up a slice of toast and buttered it. "What do you have planned for today?"

"I am riding over to the Hall in a couple of hours. Marcus invited me over to see the improvements he is making on the stables."

Viola dropped her toast and leaned forward with interest. "He's enlarging the stables? Is he planning to breed horses then?"

Robert overlooked the fact that Viola was supposed to be ignorant of the process of raising horses. He always treated her like an equal and Viola could not have loved him more for it. "I believe he might. Would you like to ride over with me? I'm sure Marcus would not mind an extra guest."

"I'd better not," Viola said reluctantly. Though she would love to see the improvements, she didn't want to tempt fate with the strange truce she and Marcus had found a few days before. "I have a lot of things to do before I return to London in a couple of days."

"Suit yourself." Robert pushed back his plate and stood up from the table. "I need to meet the estate manager soon. If you change your mind, meet me at the carriage at ten o'clock."

Viola nodded to signal she would before her father walked out of the room. She lingered over her breakfast while she debated on whether to visit Hannah or join her father in his ride to the Hall. In the end, she decided on visiting Hannah. Within a few days, Viola would be leaving for London and she wanted to convince Hannah once again to accept the loan of her maid.

She finished breakfast and asked the cook to pack a picnic lunch before going to her room to finish writing a letter to Margaret. She regaled her with all the sights and sounds of Haversham in the springtime, but discreetly left out any mention of Marcus. A few hours later, she gathered her basket and set off for the Creech's.

As she left the house, Viola was glad to see there was not a cloud in the sky. It would be a perfect day for a picnic. A pleasant breeze carried the faint scent of roses and she inhaled deeply. It was quickly becoming spring, which had always been Viola's favorite season. She turned her face up to the sun and reveled in the warmth of the sun across her face. She'd left her bonnet at home and would probably have a pink nose by the end of the day, but she loved letting the sun warm her skin.

When she appeared at the Creech's, she learned Hannah was still in bed. Viola visited her friend who assured her it was quite normal and her exhaustion did not indicate a more serious problem. Viola insisted on taking the children off her hands for a few hours and Hannah gratefully agreed. Within a few minutes, Viola and the children set off to spend the afternoon at the lake on her father's estate. She held the youngest girls' hands while Paul and Anne lagged behind carrying a picnic basket between them.

"Here is a good spot." Viola helped Anne spread a blanket out beneath a tree. The branches shaded them as they sat down and dug into the basket. Viola laughed as the children ignored the roasted chicken and reached for slices of cake. "I agree. The cake is my favorite too."

The children finished their dessert quickly and left to explore the shores of the lake. Viola warned them to be careful and kept a watchful eye on them as they kicked off their shoes and waded in the water. She knew the water must be freezing, but the children seemed to enjoy themselves. Anne stayed behind to help her repack the basket before joining her siblings in the water. Viola watched as they splashed each other and laughed with delight.

"You seem to be enjoying yourself. Is that a smile I see?"

Viola's looked up at Marcus. He was developing a disturbing tendency of sneaking up on her. "Maybe. It's not difficult to enjoy yourself on such a lovely afternoon. Where is my father?"

Marcus dropped down to sit beside her on the blanket and he stretched his long legs out beside hers.

"Your father returned home several hours ago."

"Why are you out this way?"

Marcus turned his face to the sky, the warm breeze ruffling his hair. "I felt like a walk."

She watched the play of sunlight across his face, entranced by the utterly peaceful look on his face. "How are your plans for the stables progressing?"

"Quite well. The carpenters will begin building later this week. Within a few weeks, I am going to London to purchase some brood mares." He looked over at her questioningly. "Would you like to accompany me? You've always had an excellent eye for horseflesh."

Viola would love to go to the sale, but she refused. "I do not believe a lady would be welcome at the sale. It would be quite forward of me, would it not?" Viola would normally never let such a reason deter her, but she was loath to spend more time than was necessary with Marcus.

"I suppose you are right. Women are expected to go through childbirth, yet cannot participate in horse breeding. It seems a little peculiar."

"You'd better lower your voice. Someone might hear and proclaim you a radical."

"What is the use of being a duke if one cannot affect change?" He lifted his eyebrow in a perfect arch. "I am allowed to be a tad bit lenient in my view."

"Do not let your rank go to your head. It might explode and I would hate for my lovely picnic to be ruined." Viola motioned toward the basket.

"Would you like something to eat? There is some cheese and chicken. I am afraid the children finished off the cake."

Marcus shook his head. "I am not hungry." He rested his back against the tree and ran his eyes across the lake. "I can recall when you and I used to frolic in the water much as they do now."

Viola smiled to herself. "It seems like a lifetime ago." When he made no answer, she tilted her head to look at him. He looked unsure of what he was about to say.

"Viola, I want to apologize about the other night. I should not have been so forceful."

She gave him a pointed look. "Forceful? I could think of several adjectives to better describe your behavior."

"I'm sure you can." Marcus's dark eyes mirrored his apologetic look. "I did not mean to hurt you."

"You didn't hurt me." Viola waved away his concern. "I accept your apology."

"So?" Marcus's face widened in a smile. "Do we have a truce?"

He looked so much like the old Marcus that Viola could not refuse. She was close enough to see the tiny laughter lines at the corner of his eyes. Her gaze traveled across his strong features and she felt a familiar tug in her heart. He was getting too close, so she jerked her gaze away and motioned toward the children.

"I should probably take the children home. It is getting late."

Marcus climbed gracefully to his feet and

reached down to help her up. As he walked toward the shoreline, Viola admired his efficiency of movement. He reminded her of a panther, all sleek muscles and pure lines. Her gaze moved down his back and fastened on his thighs. The form fitting breeches molded to his muscles like a second skin. Her gaze lingered and she tried to imagine his limbs unclothed. She imagined running her hands over his thighs and moving up to caress his firm buttocks. Her own knees tingled at her wicked thoughts and her face heated. She should be ashamed at the sinful direction her thoughts had taken, but she could no more look away than she could have stopped the sun from shining. Though she'd desired him years ago, her reaction to him now was startling in its fierceness. Before it had been the youthful desire of a girl, now it was something unlike she'd ever experienced with another man. Her thoughts were interrupted when the children finally noticed Marcus and began shouting out greetings.

"Marcus!" Anne ran forward to greet him. "I didn't know you were going to join us." Viola managed not to smile as the young girl batted her eyelashes up at the much older Marcus.

"I did not know myself until just a few minutes ago." Marcus ruffled her hair as Anne smiled rapturously at his attention. Anne was joined by her siblings, who also clamored for his attention. Marcus fought to keep his balance as the children crowded around him and begged to be tossed in the air. He shot an amused look over at Viola before giving in.

He took turns throwing each child over his

head and Viola smiled at their obvious enjoyment. Their shouts of joy echoed across the lake as Viola moved to stand next to Anne. Marcus would make the best father someday. Viola wondered if they would've been blessed with children had she and Marcus been able to marry. The regret that she would never have his children caused her chest to ache.

"Who would like to ride piggyback?" Three hands shot up in the air in answer to Marcus's question. He tapped his finger against his lips and pretended to think. "How about Miss Elizabeth?"
The girl smiled shyly as he bent down to one knee, yet she wrapped her chubby legs around him without hesitation.

"I wish I were not so old."

Viola turned her head at Anne's sigh. The girl was eying Marcus with unabashed curiosity.

"Why is that?" Viola bit her lip to keep from smiling. Once she herself had looked upon Marcus in such a manner.

"Then I could ride piggyback." Anne's second sigh was just as heavy and regretful.

She fully understood Anne's feelings because she envied Elizabeth a little herself. Viola linked arms with the girl. "Come along. It's time to get you home."

"Is he not the most handsome duke ever? He is just like one of the heroes in my novels."

" Not quite so heroic," Viola disagreed. "But he is moderately attractive."

Anne rolled her eyes and her young face showed her disbelief. "How can you say that? I think he is perfect."

"You are young and do not understand all there is to know about gentlemen."

The smitten girl was not to be deterred. "If you are talking about sex, don't worry. I heard all about it from my friend."

Viola sputtered and her mouth opened and closed several times as she tried to think of an answer. "Well. I expect you know all there is to know then."

Their conversation brought to mind the conversation she and Marcus had the night he came back from Eton. It was funny how history repeated itself, she thought with a glimmer of a smile.

"Are you going to marry Marcus?" I really wish you would, but if you do not, do you think he will wait for me to grow up before he marries someone else?"

"What makes you think I should marry him?"

Anne rolled her eyes and sighed dramatically. "Because he is a duke and you have known him forever, of course."

"But if I marry him," Viola couldn't help teasing. "Who will you marry?"

*****

Marcus's arms ached from carrying the children all afternoon. Elizabeth clung to his neck tightly and he was finding it hard to breathe. Diane and Paul each rode a hip and their knees were digging into his sides. His knee was beginning to ache and it was getting harder to walk on it by the minute. He did not know how their father, Patrick, did it. One afternoon with the brood and Marcus was worn totally out. It was a relief when they finally reached their home and he could put them down.

They rushed off to inform their parents of their afternoon and he took a moment to stretch his aching back.

He noticed the smile Viola was unsuccessfully trying to hide. "May I ask what is so entertaining?"

Viola's eyes twinkled at him as she shook her head. He rolled his shoulders, grimacing when the muscles screamed in protest. "I am too old for this."

"You are barely five and twenty. Don't tell me three little children are too much for you."

"I do say that. They nearly killed me. And I swear Anne looks at me as if she were trying to imagine me unclothed. It's damned disturbing."

"You enjoyed every minute of it." Viola moved past him to untether her horse. "Enjoy your walk back to the Hall."

Marcus groaned and his head dropped toward his chest. "Don't remind me. It is nearly a mile."

"You said you felt like a walk," Viola reminded him as she swung up into the saddle.

"That was before I hauled three children across the countryside."

The new leather of her sidesaddle creaked as she settled on the top of the horse. He noticed with some surprise that she was actually riding side saddle. She'd always ridden astride when they were alone and abhorred the position ladies were forced to ride in public. "New saddle?"

"It was a gift from my great-aunt. It would be rude of me to not use it at least once." She grinned and took hold of her reins. "I'd best be off. Have a nice walk."

He grabbed her horse's bridle before she could gallop off. "You can't just leave me here."

"Did you or did you not say you wanted to walk? I distinctly recall you saying that."

"That was before those little monsters wore me out. Have pity on me."

"I suppose I could offer you a ride, but I'm riding side saddle." She clicked her tongue with mock pity. "We won't both fit."

Marcus looked up at her with a dark frown. "We can ride bareback like we used to. Besides, my knee is beginning to ache. You should take pity on me considering you were the one to cause the injury."

Viola flushed with guilt, as he knew she would. "Are you sure we both will fit? We haven't ridden like that since we were children."

It would require them to be put in an extremely intimate position. Marcus felt his cock jerk at the thought. It didn't take much imagination to know her bottom would jostle against his groin the entire way home. It would be pure torture, but one he was willing to suffer.

"We'll fit." *Almost as well as they would fit in bed.* Marcus felt another spurt of desire at the thought. He remembered how curious she'd been at eighteen and wondered if any part of her still longed to be his lover. Not a day had passed where he didn't dream of her. He wanted to spread her pale thighs and bury his head between her legs. He wanted to know her taste, her smell. God help him, he wanted all of her.

Marcus helped her from the saddle. Before he

sat her on her feet, he allowed himself the pleasure of sliding her down his body. He quickly removed the saddle from the horse and rested it against the side of the house. "I will come back for it tomorrow," he reassured her when she gave him a questioning look.

Marcus mounted first and reached for her hand. He tugged and she landed in a heap in front of him. Her horse skittered nervously at the added weight, but Marcus calmed it with a few murmured words. He wrapped a steadying arm around Viola's waist as they began to move.

The motion of the horse caused Viola to lean against his chest. His thighs bracketed hers, their legs brushing with every sway. It was an improper embrace and he felt it when she stiffened her spine. He wrapped his arm tighter around her, his hand brushing the underside of her breast as he did so. She pivoted to glare at him.

"It was an accident." He grinned devilishly. She faced forward and he wasn't surprised she leaned forward to put as much distance between them as possible. "We are on a horse, Viola. I'm afraid I'm quite limited in what I could do to you now."

His breath ruffled the hair at her nape and he was pleased to see her shiver. She was not as immune to his touch as she would like to pretend. She turned again, her green eyes sparkling with challenge, as she deliberately relaxed against his chest. He frowned when she moved her hips further between the cradle of his thighs. He clenched his teeth together and forced his body to not respond. He didn't imagine it would be comfortable to ride a horse while in an aroused state. Viola wriggled again and he clamped his hands on her waist.

"For the love of God, stay still!"

Viola looked back at him with a gleam of triumph and Marcus realized he'd been had.

"You little minx! What are you trying to do to me?"

"I'm only demonstrating two can play that game."

"You plot your revenge by attempting to injure me?"

Viola laughed at the look of offense on his face. "I planned no such thing. I merely wanted to demonstrate you should not torment me so."

"I torment you?" Marcus gave a silent cry of joy. "What an interesting statement."

"I assure you it's not as interesting as you imagine." Viola tossed her head. "I'm not tempted by you in any way."

"Care to make a wager?" A glint of mischief appeared in his eyes. This could be the chance he'd been waiting for. The opportunity to prove to Viola that while her mind may not want him, her body still desired him.

"What sort of wager?" Viola was clearly suspicious of the look in his eye.

"I bet you could not last more than two minutes of me touching you before you begged me to kiss you."

"You cannot be serious! What sort of touching?"

"Nothing too inappropriate. I will not do anything that would shock you."

"What do I get when I win?"

"Anything you want." Marcus shrugged dismissively. She wouldn't win so the point was moot. "When I win, my forfeit will be a kiss whenever I choose. The only requirement is you give me my full two minutes. Is it a deal?"

Viola puzzled over the details of the wager. "I can have anything I want?"

He could tell her thoughts were turning to his stallion, Pyrenees. He would make an excellent addition to her father's stables. His stud fees alone would make a small fortune. "Anything," he agreed.

"In that case, I agree. You have two minutes." She began to count the seconds aloud.

When she reached fifteen, he leaned forward and nuzzled his cheek against her neck. Viola held herself stiffly as his hand crept up her arm and touched her collarbone. He traced the delicate line of her neck with his fingertips and he felt her tremble beneath his hands. He reached the front of her gown and slid his hand forward to cup her breast through the fabric. The heavy weight fit in his palm perfectly. She made a strangled sound as his hand moved back and forth across her nipple. He was rewarded when it hardened and pressed against his palm. He could feel her heart pounding in her chest and her skin flushed.

"Forty-one," she counted out and he heard the tremor in her voice. It was only a matter of time before she broke down. He still remembered how sensitive Viola had been to his touch and he used that knowledge ruthlessly. One hand continued to trace the curve of her breast while the other slid to her stomach. She held her breath as his fingers moved lower. At the last moment, he slid his hand to the side and caressed her thigh.

Reaching for the hem of her skirt, his hand moved under the material. He tossed aside the layers of clothing to finally touch her legs. Though their courtship had been passionate, he'd never touched her bare legs. The feel of her under his hands was extremely satisfying. His fingers danced over the bare skin of her thighs, which she tried to clamp them together. It was useless endeavor since she was astride a horse. Marcus moved his fingers closer to the juncture between her thighs and his breath came in quick pants. Finally, he would touch the part of her that had haunted him for years. He forced himself to calm as he inched his hand closer.

"Seventy eight," she breathed as he cupped her mound fully. She immediately grabbed his wrist. "You said nothing too indecent."

There was a slight hitch in her voice, revealing she was affected, but he obliged her by moving his hand back to the warm skin of her thighs. "Are you ready for me to stop? Two minutes are not up and I'm afraid that would concede defeat."

Viola removed her hand and she clutched at the horse's mane as he ran his hands across her bare thigh. "Ninety nine," she continued counting.

She pressed against his hand and he knew it was only a matter of time before she turned to him. He lightly stroked the crease of her thigh, his fingers ruffling the damp hair guarding her slit. She was wet. His cock was ready to explode at the thought.

"You can end this by kissing me," Marcus whispered into her ear. "Unless you want me to continue?" He used his knuckle to press against the nubbin of flesh between her legs. "Your choice, Viola. Do I stop or…" His knuckle was joined by a second. "Do I continue?"

Viola twisted in the saddle. "Damn you!"

She roughly pulled his head down for a kiss. Her open mouth met his and they fused together hungrily. His tongue tangled with hers as they both fought to be the one in control. He'd forgotten how fiercely dominant she really was. Viola's teeth nipped at his lips and he turned her to face him. She moved restlessly against his hand, which was still under her skirts.

Her thigh brushed his arousal and he groaned. He shoved her skirts to her waist, baring the lower half of her body to his gaze. Other than skirts and petticoats, she was nude. The fact she wore nothing underneath her skirts sent a jolt of pure lust through his body. His hand returned to her thighs and his control slipped away. He spread the lips of her slit with his thumb and forefinger as his middle finger touched the damp opening to her body. Her breath came faster as his finger slid inside her. She was tight, her muscles surrounded his finger like a glove. She made a slight whimper which Marcus took for a sound of pain. He withdrew his hand immediately as eyes flew open and she looked at him accusingly.

"Why did you stop?"

Marcus nearly laughed at the look of outrage on her face, but he managed to hold in his amusement. "I didn't want to hurt you." God, what a lie. He wanted to spread her legs and thrust his cock deep inside her. He wanted to brand her as his. He wanted her to scream his name. None of which would be pleasant for her the first time.

"You didn't hurt me." Her eyes gleamed with curiosity. Her lips moved wordlessly as she thought of how to exactly phrase the sensation of having him touch her so privately. "It was just slightly uncomfortable at first."

"Shall I continue then?"

"Oh my God!" She threw her head back with a moan as he touched her again. Using her own wetness, he spread it around so his finger slipped easily inside her. One finger was joined by two. He came in contact with the barrier of her virginity, which he avoided carefully. No need to cause her excessive pain.

His gaze remained locked on his hand moving between her legs. Wanting her to see for herself the reaction she was unable to hide, he used his other hand to turn her face down. "Open your eyes, Viola."

She did as he asked, the pupils of her eyes dilated with desire. There was no way she could miss seeing the wetness of her body or the way her thighs clenched against his hand.

"Do you like the way I touch you?" When she didn't answer, he stopped moving his hand. "Tell me, Vi."

She gripped his wrist, her grip surprisingly strong. "Damn you, Marcus. You know I do."

He smiled to himself. Content he'd re-awakened her passion for him. His hand curved, his palm expertly kneading the center of her desire.

Her inner muscles tightened. He felt her convulsing around him as she let out a strangled cry. He fought to control his lust as she came apart in his arms. Never had he experienced such a violent reaction to another woman. His body screamed at him to throw her to the ground and complete her initiation into lovemaking. Battling his urges, he pulled her skirts down and turned her to face forward once again. Viola was still limp and leaned back against his chest weakly. Marcus supported her with one arm as he urged the horse on. He was still painfully aroused, but he had no intention of taking Viola in the woods. She deserved a slow wooing, not a quick tumble in the bushes.

"I do believe you won the wager," Viola murmured after several minutes of silence. She glanced over her shoulder at him. "When are you planning on claiming your forfeit?"

"If I told you it would spoil the fun." He was unsure if he would be able to touch her again without exploding. How he would ever survive the rest of the ride home with her body pressed against his? And he'd been right, it was damned uncomfortable to ride a horse with a raging arousal.

Viola was quick to come out of her daze. He was aware of her cleared head when she straightened in the saddle. He was oddly relieved and regretful at the loss of her closeness as she leaned forward to put distance between them once again. He topped the hill leading to the Hall. The sight of his family's ancestral home didn't give him the pleasure it normally did since it signaled the end of his time with Viola.

He rode to the front of the house, the only

sound to be heard was the clopping of the horse's hooves on gravel. He pulled back on the reins and prepared to dismount.

"What we did today cannot happen again," Viola warned as he swung off the horse to the ground.

As he gained his footing, he studied her face. She chewed at her lip in nervousness and he found the habit quite arousing. She pointedly ignored his hand, which was still resting against her leg.

"Are you saying you did not find it pleasurable?" His eyes dared her to deny she had just not scaled the heights of passion in his arms.

Her face turned crimson and she closed her eyes. "You know I cannot deny my body's response to you, Marcus. It is highly unfortunate, but I am not looking for a reconcilement."

Marcus's jaw clenched with frustration. "I don't recall making such a proposition."

Viola's gaze was far too knowing for his comfort. "Then we will not let this happen again?" Her long eyelashes swept forward to hide her eyes from him.

"I promise not to do anything you don't want me to do," he answered evasively. It would be up to him to convince her she did want him. In more ways than sexual, but he would utilize whatever methods were available to him.

"In that case, we are understood. Good day, Marcus." She turned her horse headed away. Marcus waited until she was almost beyond earshot. "You still owe me a kiss. Consider this your warning."

*****

Marcus stared at the man in front of him with irritation. "What do you mean, you cannot find him? Is your career not based on being able to locate even the most difficult to find people?"

Owen Rivers clutched his hat between two brawny hands nervously. "Aye, Your Grace. We tracked his whereabouts to Paris, but there the trail ends. Our inquiries yielded no results. No one has seen hide nor hair of him for weeks. We have reason to believe he may not even be in Paris any longer."

The large man seemed ill at ease in Marcus's elegantly appointed study. He was better suited to prowling the streets of London's most seedy areas. He seldom had the need to venture out of his element, but Marcus was an exception. An extremely influential, high paying exception.

Marcus slammed his hand down on his desk and cursed. He'd hired the most competent man he knew to find his half brother only to meet with failure. "Are you absolutely sure no one knows his whereabouts? Possibly a landlord or a mistress?"

Owen shook his head. "We offered very ample reward, but no one was able to provide any useful information in our search." Owen reached into his pocket and pulled out a crumpled playbill. "He was last seen attending this opera. At intermission, he went to get refreshments and the young lady he was with claimed he never returned."

"Something is terribly odd about this." Marcus studied the playbill with a fierce frown. "Do you think he realized he was being followed and gave us the slip?"

The look of offense on the investigator's face

put Marcus's doubt to rest. "None of my men have ever failed at their task, I assure you. If he realized he was being followed, it would appear my men were not his only pursuers."

"He couldn't have just disappeared into thin air." Marcus walked to the liquor cabinet and poured himself a brandy. The liquor slid easily down his throat as he sipped. It seemed his tolerance for alcohol grew stronger every day. "Would you care for a drink?" He held up the bottle for inspection.

"Not while I am on a case," Owen declined with a polite nod. "Alcohol dulls the brain."

"That it does, my friend." Marcus saluted the investigator with his glass. "Must explain my recent fondness for the stuff." Marcus pinned the investigator with a serious expression. "What do you propose to do now?"

"I have men still in Paris trying to locate the viscount. I started a casual inquiry about London in case he turns up."

" Do you have any reason to suspect he is back in England?"

Owen cleared his throat nervously. Marcus crossed his arms across his chest while he waited for him to speak. "Well? Speak up, man."

"I have it from reliable sources that the viscount often spoke of a particular lady while he was abroad. My sources indicate he seemed to be obsessed with her."

Marcus's blood ran ice cold as a suspicion began in his mind. "And you believe he may have come back to England with the sole purpose of confronting her?"

Owen nodded and watched Marcus closely for his reaction. "The viscount has not appeared to be stable for many years now. I would not disregard any apparent motive he may have."

"Do you think him capable of harming this lady?"

Owen's stone face expressed his opinion. "Let me put it to you this way, Your Grace. If I cared about the lady in question, I would take every precaution to see she is safe guarded at all times."

"I see," Marcus murmured. His mind raced with the knowledge that Viola may be in danger. "Thank you for your efforts, Rivers. Please report back to me the moment you learn anything else."

Owen stood at Marcus's dismissal. "Me and my men will redouble our efforts to find him. Meanwhile, I suggest you see to Lady Viola's safety."

"That will be all, Rivers."

Marcus waited until the investigator was seen out before showing a reaction. He cursed violently and slammed his fist into the wall. He barely felt the throbbing of his hand as his mind raced. If Greenley so much as harmed a hair on Viola's head, Marcus would personally see him in hell.

Chapter Twelve

Viola stood in the hall and directed the footmen as they carried her trunks down the stairs and loaded them into her carriage. She was leaving for London within the hour and her packing had already taken up much of her morning. After seeing the last box put in the carriage, she went to search out her father. She found him in his study and was surprised to see he was not alone.

Her face flamed when Marcus turned his head to look at her and the memories of one afternoon nearly a week ago weakened her knees. As she had ridden away from him that day, her body tingled with remembered sensations. It had taken all of her resolve not to turn around and beg him to make love to her. In one moment, he'd forced her to realize she would never be able to let a complete stranger make love to her. The only man she would ever want was Marcus and she doubted anyone could make her feel the way he did with just a look. The thought of his touch made her belly tingle with excitement. It was truly disheartening to know that the only man she could ever want was the one person she could not allow herself to love again. Deliberately she hardened her resolve and ignored the effect he had on her senses.

"Marcus, I did not know you had arrived." She smoothly moved into the room to stand by her father. Her father looked a little peaked and she frowned. "Are you unwell Papa?" She placed a hand against his forehead. "You are not getting feverish again, are you?"

Robert reached up to grasp her wrist. "Don't worry about me. It is you we have to worry about now."

Viola's face mirrored her confusion. "What do you mean? I'm perfectly well." She turned to Marcus and was surprised to see he also looked tense. "What is going on?"

Robert opened his mouth to speak, but Marcus held up a hand for silence. "I'm not sure we should tell her. There is no reason to cause excessive panic."

"Perhaps you are right. We're not completely sure he means to harm her anyway."

Viola lifted an eyebrow questioningly. "Harm who? Would anyone care to tell me what is going on?"

Marcus stepped around her father's desk and led her to a chair. "Perhaps it is best if you sit."

He gently forced her to take a seat. She sprawled into the chair and cast worried glances at her father and Marcus. She gripped the arms of the chair to pull herself to a more ladylike position. "I am leaving for London in a few minutes, so could we hurry this along?"

"I do not think you should go to London." Her father's expression remained tense.

"Why ever not? You have known I was leaving for days now. If you'd objected you would've said something earlier."

" That was before all this began."

"Before all what began? What is going on?"

Marcus bent down to her eye level and

pinned her against the chair. She drew back and held his gaze as he spoke. "You may be in danger."

His calm words took a great length of time for her to decipher. She remained mute for a few moments before her lips twitched. "Is this some sort of joke?"

"I assure you we are quite serious." Marcus paced the room. He thrust his hands into his closely cropped hair and brushed the ends back from his forehead. His hair stuck up at odd angles, but didn't detract from his appeal.

"Who would want to hurt me? I have no enemies."

"Did Greenley ever do anything in the past that may lead you to believe he was mentally unstable?"

Viola's mouth dropped open in astonishment. "Greenley? Of course not. He was perfectly sane."

"So he never indicated an undue obsession with you?" Marcus continued to pace the floor, but he glanced at her quickly. "Did he ever do anything to suggest you may be in danger?"

Viola shook her head and looked at her father helplessly. "No. At least not until…"

Marcus pounced at her words. "Not until what?"

"Not until you began showing interest in me." She arched her eyebrow. Marcus's dark eyes roamed over her face, looking for any sign she mislead him. He seemed to accept her explanation. "I don't understand. Are you suggesting that Greenley will try to harm me? He is not even in the country."

"I've had men trailing him.   He left Paris suddenly and we have reason to suspect he may be in London."

"You hired someone to track him!" Viola was shocked. "Whatever for?"

Marcus was irritatingly closed lipped about the entire affair.   "Suffice it to say I have long suspected him of villainy."

"This is about the mask, is it not?"   Her disapproval was evident in her tone. "You did this because of an old grudge?"

Marcus's jaw clenched. "You cannot possibly begin to understand my need to find Greenley."

Viola waved a hand expansively. "Then tell me. Why be so secretive about it?"

"It is of no importance. My involvement with him bears no significance to his obsession with you."

"I think you should let me be the judge of that." Viola crossed her arms and leaned back in the chair. "After all, if you are not completely honest how am I to know you're not doing this out of spite?"

In two great strides, Marcus reached her side and grasped her upper arms tightly.   "Because I bloody well tell you so."

Viola's eyes locked with his and they regarded each other fiercely. The touch of his hand against her skin sent sparks down her spine and she could tell from Marcus's look he felt the same thing. Her father coughed to remind them of his presence. Marcus released Viola and put his hands on his hips. "You should not go to London."

Viola focused her attention on her father. "Do you seriously think I will be in danger if I go?"

Her father nodded, his thumb and forefinger pinching the bridge of his nose as if he had the beginnings of a headache. "Marcus has it from reliable sources. We cannot ignore such a warning."

There was no help for it. She was going to have to delay her trip. "How long until I can travel again?"

"Not until Greenley is located."

"But that could be months! You cannot expect me to hide out indefinitely just because you suspect he would do me harm?"

"Until he is located, you must take extra precautions," her father broke in. "You will be escorted at all times when you leave the grounds. I will have the servants increase security precautions about the estate."

"This is unbelievable. I suspect next you will have armed guards outside my door." She said the last sarcastically. Marcus exchanged a look with her father and Viola raised an eyebrow in expectation. "What else are you not telling me?"

Her father cleared his throat and fixed his gaze on a point on the wall beyond Viola's head. "Um, there is one more thing." He halted and Viola nodded her head encouragingly for him to continue. "Until the viscount is located, Marcus will be staying here at Haversham."

Viola laughed out loud. "As what? My personal bodyguard?"

Marcus leaned against the mantle and regarded her calmly. "You can refer to me as anything you like, but I will be here to oversee your safety. Your father's recent health may prevent him from being able to protect you himself and he asked for my assistance in that regard."

"Well, isn't that just wonderful?" Viola asked in a falsely bright voice. "Not only am I to be imprisoned, but I have my own warden. Lucky me."

Marcus folded his long frame into the chair beside her. "While I am here, you must defer to me before leaving the house. I am to be appraised of your whereabouts at all times."

Viola stood with dignity and straightened her skirts. "I still believe this is entirely ridiculous." She was not looking forward to being under Marcus's control. She certainly did not look forward to having him live in the same house with her.

"Nevertheless," her father ordered. "You will do as we say. Until this threat has passed, we must exercise extreme caution."

*****

"I'm off for the chamber pot in case anyone would like to accompany me." Viola gestured expansively as she stood up from the dinner table. Marcus and her father glanced up at her with identical expressions of amusement.

"That is not necessary," Marcus said with a twist of his lips. "I am sure you know the way." He took a sip from his wineglass and eyed her over the rim. He could almost feel the tension radiating from her in waves.

Viola tossed her head defiantly. A curl fell from its pin, but she ruthlessly shoved it back. "How shocking! You have hounded me so all afternoon that I'd begun to worry if you would ever desist."

"There is no need to be rude, Viola." Robert

paused with his fork halfway to his mouth to reprimand his daughter.

Her eyes moved to Marcus and her expression clearly said that she believed him the cause of all her problems. He set down his wineglass and pretended to be engrossed in his dinner. Viola huffed loudly and departed with an angry swish of her skirts. Marcus watched the intriguing sway of her hips and fought the urge to go after her and pull her into his arms. It was a double-edged sword to be so close to her, but unable to touch her. If their enforced closeness did not bring them closer to a reconcilement, he had no doubt he would go insane. He'd obviously been crazy to offer his help to Robert in keeping Viola safe.

"I don't believe she is too happy with the arrangement," Robert said conversationally.

"No, she's not." Marcus gave a grim shake of his head.

"Do you truly believe all this is necessary? Or are we being overcautious?"

"Would you like to take a gamble with your daughter's life?" Marcus faced Robert with a serious expression.

"Of course not," was the older man's quick answer.

"Good. Neither would I." Marcus's face hardened with resolve. "I'm not going to let anyone hurt Viola."

"Including yourself?" Robert asked pointedly. At Marcus's surprised look, he continued. "I know you still have feelings for Viola. Though she tries to deny it, I suspect my daughter returns those feelings. I would not like her heart to be broken a second time."

"I can assure you I intend no such thing. If it takes the rest of my life to make it up to Viola, I will do it. My feelings for her remain unchanged."

"I still have faith in you, Marcus. You are a good man and I could ask for no better husband for my daughter."

Marcus held up his hands in hesitation. "Do not put the cart ahead of the mule. I can barely get Viola to stay in the same room with me much less propose marriage to her."

"Give it time, son." Robert's face held a hint of a smile. "She's always been stubborn, but she'll come around someday. Takes after her mother that way."

"Sometimes I wish things had never changed between us. If I'd never fallen in love, perhaps things would have been different." Marcus sighed heavily. "I would not have killed Agnes. I would not have broken your daughter's heart. I'm the reason she is so distant and refuses to accept she is capable of loving again."

Robert shook his head sadly. "It is an unfortunate situation. Until you came back, I'd despaired on Viola ever showing emotion again. I know it does not seem like it now, but Viola will realize she needs you." He patted Marcus's shoulder comfortingly and looked away when it became apparent there was nothing he could say to change Marcus's mind. Robert worried about his daughter constantly. He wanted to know when he was gone, she would not be left alone like Marcus had been. If only the two of them could realize, as he himself could plainly see, that they belonged together. Robert was concerned for Viola's safety, but he was still capable of protecting his daughter. The main reason he had asked for Marcus's help was in the hope they could move past their differences. He was betting their forced closeness would bring them together. If they did not kill each other first.

Robert inclined his head and pointed upstairs. "I hope she is not fashioning a rope out of bed sheets."

"Where Viola is concerned, I've learned it's better to not doubt she is capable of anything. I'd better go and check on her."

Marcus excused himself and headed upstairs to make sure Viola was in her room and not planning an escape. It would be just like her to run away to London than be forced to face him on a daily basis.

As he climbed the stairs, he mentally envisioned the layout of the floor that housed Viola's suite. Her rooms on the third floor were conveniently next to his and he would be able to hear if she needed help. Viola had argued most vehemently over him being given the neighboring suite, but Robert had ignored her protests. Shaking his head in silent amusement of the fuss she'd put up, Marcus knocked on her door. She called out it was unlocked. He pushed open the door and stepped inside.

Viola was seated across the room brushing her hair. She saw his reflection in the mirror and tossed a glance over her shoulder. "What is it now?"

"I came to make sure your windows were safely locked," he lied as he walked toward her.

He'd never been in her bedroom and he found himself intrigued by her choice of décor. Instead of being overly feminine, her room was done in varying shades of blue and quite simple. Her bed was large and dominated most of the room. Marcus's imagination ran away as he envisioned himself and Viola entwined under the silk sheets. He imagined her pale limbs open to him, her dark hair spread out on the white pillows. He tore his gaze away from the bed and reached out to test the window. It was made of heavy glass and didn't budge as he pushed on it. He nodded with satisfaction.

"Does everything meet with your approval?" Viola set aside her brush and stood to face him. His cock jerked at the sight of her in her nightclothes. Though she was covered from throat to ankle, it required little imagination to see what she looked like underneath the frilly lace. She was tall and slender but pleasingly curved in all the right places. He detected the tiniest hint of a shadow between her legs. A shadow just a few days ago he'd seen under bright sunlight. His eyes roamed over her body leisurely. Moonlight streamed through the window behind her, just enough light to outline her breasts and indentation of her hips.

"It is all quite satisfactory." His lips twisted into a smile.

Her eyes narrowed suspiciously at his double meaning as she reached for the robe lying across the back of her chair. She pulled it on and tied the belt around her waist. Though the sheer robe did not offer much in the way of concealment, she probably felt safer with it on. He watched her actions with an amused expression. "You do not have to fear I will ravish you." He walked past her to test the window on the opposite side of the room. "I've never been in the habit of attacking innocent young women who have been put into my safekeeping."

"The possibility did not even enter my mind." She sat down on the edge of the bed and watched him warily. "Besides, when have you ever been in the habit of protecting young women?"

"That is true." Marcus flashed the grin he knew from personal experience most women found irresistible.

Unfortunately, Viola was not most women and she continued to glare at him.

After testing the second window, he came to stand beside her. He was close enough for their knees to touch. He moved closer, her legs involuntarily parted to give him room to stand. It put them in an interesting position, one he planned taking full advantage of.

"Is there anything else you require tonight?" She probably did not mean it as a double entendre, but he could tell from the look in her eyes she believed he was taking it as such.

"You still owe me a kiss," he softly reminded her.

Viola's gaze flew to his. He widened his eyes innocently while hers narrowed to slits of green. After several moments of silence, she sighed heavily and tilted her head with an exaggerated pursing of her lips. "Go ahead then," she said with a resigned sigh. When he did not immediately move closer, she cracked open one eye and glared at him.

Marcus grinned at her martyred expression. "Not exactly what I had in mind."

"It is the best you are going to get." Viola shrugged her shoulders. "So either you take it or leave it."

With purpose in his actions, he put a hand on both of her knees and determinedly pushed them farther apart. She tried to clamp them closed, but he stepped between her legs before she could.

"What are you doing?" Even though she spoke in anger, her eyes darkened with desire.

"I'm giving you a kiss." He grasped the hem of her night rail and pulled it to her waist. As he'd suspected, she was nude underneath.

Her breath hitched, the muscles in her thighs slowly relaxing as she realized his intent. "This is not a kiss."

"No?" He trailed a finger across her thigh and dipped forward to tease the edge of her slit. She was already wet for him.

"No." Viola was unsuccessful at biting back a moan.

He bent and pressed an open-mouthed kiss against her right thigh. "What about now? Is this a kiss?"

Her fingers tangled in his hair, but she didn't push him away. "No."

He got to his knees in front of her. His gaze locked between her legs. The hair shielding her femininity was dark and glistened with the wetness of her arousal. The urge to taste her gripped him.

He swiped his tongue across her swollen nether lips, the taste of her nearly making him come undone. He used his lips and teeth to tease the bud of her desire. She jerked against his mouth and moaned with pleasure. The fingers in his hair tightened almost painfully.

Abruptly, he stopped. "Was that a kiss?"

Viola tilted her head to meet his gaze. She was shaking with unfulfilled desire, but her expression was full of stubborn determination. He knew she would not allow him to win this battle. "No."

He sat back on his heels and made a great show of wiping his mouth. Her legs remained open, tempting him to come back for a second taste. He ignored his painful erection and got to his feet. He made it halfway across the room before she spoke.

"Marcus!"

He turned and swept his gaze over her impassively. "Yes?"

She made a vague gesture toward herself. "You're forgetting your kiss."

It took every ounce of his self-control to turn away. "Perhaps another time."

He could be patient and claim his kiss at a more appropriate moment. As the door shut behind him, the sound of something crashing against the wood made him chuckle.

*****

Over the next several days, Viola grudgingly accepted Marcus's constant presence at Haversham. She still doubted the need for him to constantly watch her, but she could tolerate him if need be. She reluctantly admitted she was appreciative of the attention he showed her father. Her father's spirits had increased greatly with Marcus's company. Since the duke's death, she'd worried about her father and Marcus was relieving some of her concern.

On the third day of her forced confinement, she was kept indoors because of a violent thunderstorm. She paced the length of the library and gazed regretfully out the window at the downpour. She had longed for an afternoon ride and a visit with the Creech's. The sudden storm had prevented her plans completely.

"You remind me of a caged lion." Marcus suddenly spoke from the open door of the library.

Viola whirled to face him. "I cannot stand to be trapped indoors." She sat down at her father's desk, tapping the fingers of her left hand and propping her chin on her right. "I am bored." Briefly, she thought back to a few nights before. She'd definitely not been bored when Marcus had touched her with his mouth. The memory of his tongue against her heated skin made her clamp her thighs together with renewed arousal.

"Could I tempt you in a game of cards? It might help to pass the time."

Viola leaned back in the chair and studied him as he walked toward her. His shirtsleeves were rolled up to his elbows and his casual attire indicated he also had nothing pressing to attend to. Usually he spent the afternoons at the Hall attending to concerns with his estate. He'd been doing double duty by guarding her and overseeing the renovations at the Hall. The storm must have ruined his plans too. "A game would be nice. Anything to take my mind off this damnable weather."

"You better not let your father hear you speak in such a way." Marcus grabbed a pack of cards from a table across the room and brought them to her.

"Why? He is the one who taught me how to curse." She reached for the cards and shuffled. She dealt the cards efficiently and sat back to wait for him to make his first discard.

He studied his cards carefully before looking over them at her suspiciously. "Did you cheat when you dealt these cards?"

She shook her head. "No. Why?" Marcus taught her how to cheat at cards when she had been fourteen and she was surprised she still retained the skill.

"This is why." He tossed his cards face up on the table. He had the worst hand imaginable.

She hid a smile. "That was rotten luck!" There was a glimmer of amusement in her eyes as she looked at him.

"That was not luck," he argued. "You purposefully dealt me a poor hand. Do not try to fool me. I taught you how to cheat in the first place. Do you think I would not realize it?"

"One could hope."

Marcus gathered the cards and reshuffled. He dealt a second hand. Viola picked up her cards and stared at them for a few moments before pinning him with a stern look. "What is this?"

"I don't know what you mean." Marcus carefully arranged the cards in his hand. His lips twitched as he looked up at her with glimmering eyes.

"You wretch!" she exclaimed as she tossed

her cards on the table and crossed her arms. "Maybe card playing is not the best occupation for us. You cheat too much."

"Me?" Marcus raised an eyebrow. "You started it."

"Well, you taught me how," she argued back as she gathered up the cards to put away.

"True. If cards are out of the question, what do you suggest we do?"

Viola looked up at him and his eyes regarded her hotly. Her body flushed in response and it did not take her imagination long to envision a highly indecent way to spend the afternoon, one which would require him getting rid of all his clothes and showing her more of his tempting body. She wanted to know the feel of his mouth again, the touch of his hands. Ruthlessly pushing those thoughts out of her head, she leaned back in her chair and laced her fingers over her stomach in a passive manner.

"What do you suggest we do then?"

His eyes roamed over her leisurely and her skin reacted as if he had physically touched her. Suddenly she felt hot and cold all at once. "What had you planned on doing this afternoon?"

"I wanted to visit Hannah. She should be having the baby any day now." Viola's sharp eyes detected Marcus's response to Hannah's condition. He would probably have an aversion to childbirth, especially since he'd lost his wife and child in such a situation. Viola was jolted into realizing how hard that must've been on Marcus. Up until now, she'd been so focused on her pain she'd never spared a moment to consider Marcus's own suffering.

"I never told you how sorry I was about Agnes and the baby."

Marcus turned his head away and his shoulders stiffened. "Thank you."

Viola lapsed into silence as she tried to think of a way to liven the sudden gloom. Her mouth opened and closed several times before Marcus spoke.

"Did you know it was a girl?" He turned back to her.

Viola was hypnotized by the flare of pain in his eyes and her heart ached for him. "No, I was not aware." She stood to circle the table and put her hand on his shoulder.

"She barely lived an hour." Marcus's eyes were unfocused as if he were staring at the past. "She was so small."

He cupped his hands together to illustrate the size of his dead daughter. Viola gently patted his shoulder and he covered her hand with his much larger one. He pressed a kiss to the back of her knuckles and Viola held her breath as he looked up at her.

"For the longest time, I blamed myself for their deaths."

Viola sucked in a surprised gasp. "Marcus! How could it be your fault?"

"It was my fault Agnes was pregnant. If not for me, she might still be living."

Viola cupped her hands around Marcus's face and turned it up to face hers. She pinned him with a serious expression. "Agnes wanted nothing more than to be your bride. The fact she died cannot be helped. Women die in childbirth all the time. It was not your fault."

"But it was my fault I hurt you," he whispered. "And for that I can never forgive myself."

Viola's eyes slid closed and she nodded. "I cannot deny I was hurt dreadfully. I have thought much about that night and I realize it was not entirely your fault. You must move forward and stop blaming yourself."

"Do you think you could ever forgive me for what I did?"

Viola opened her eyes to see that Marcus had risen from his chair, standing right in front of her. Her gaze was level with his neck and she stared at the buttons on his coat for the longest time. "Perhaps I already have."

Marcus gathered her to him and they clung to each other. Her head rested on his shoulder and he rubbed her back comfortingly. Viola was aware of every inch of his body that was pressed against hers. Being in his arms again was comforting. They stood there for several moments until a knock at the door separated them. Viola reluctantly stepped away from him as Harris entered and handed her a note on heavy paper. Viola thanked the elderly butler as he shuffled back out of the room.

"Who is it from?" Marcus looked over her shoulder at the note.

"I'm not sure. It has no address." Viola frowned as she turned the paper over in her hands. The note was sealed with wax, but no emblem had been imprinted. She broke the wax seal and scanned the contents once to herself. Her face drained of color as she passed the paper to him wordlessly.

"What is it?" He took the note and lowered his eyes to the bold writing. He read it to himself as she looked over his shoulder at the threatening words. He scanned it a second time angrily. "Hell!" he exclaimed as he looked at the heavy writing. "Do you recognize the handwriting?"

Viola shook her head. "No, I don't think so. Who do you think wrote it?"

"It has to be Greenley." Marcus looked at the paper again. "The writing appears to be masculine. Who else would want to warn you away from me?"

Viola reached for the note as she reread the cryptic words aloud. "Do not trust Kingsley. Death will follow." She looked up at Marcus disbelievingly. "Is this a threat to me?"

"I am not sure." Marcus shook his head. "We must assume it is. Whoever wrote that note knows I am here. He must be watching the house."

Viola sank into the chair as she realized someone might possibly wish for her demise. Her father and Marcus's overprotection suddenly seemed warranted. She did not realize she was shaking until Marcus grasped her shoulders and asked if she was all right. She nodded numbly and forced her head up. "I am fine," she assured him.

"Viola, I promise nothing will happen to you." His dark eyes grew hard with determination. "You must trust me."

"I do." Viola was surprised to realize it was true. "I trust you."

Chapter Thirteen

That night, Viola found it hard to sleep. She lay awake in her bed and stared at the ceiling for what seemed like hours. Someone was actually planning to kill her or at least frighten her into thinking it. It was inconceivable to her. Marcus and her father assumed Greenley was the author of the letter, but Viola had her doubts. Though she knew he had a darker side, she didn't think him capable of harming her. He'd shown a marked interest in her, but it had never been to an obsessive degree. He knew she preferred Marcus and he accepted it however grudgingly. Surely he would not be the person who wrote the note?

Viola turned over on her side and pressed her head into the pillow. She willed herself to go to sleep and she was finally able to doze off. When she awoke, sunlight was streaming in the window and she grimaced. She turned on her back with a groan and rubbed her eyes tiredly. It was morning already? Viola tossed aside her covers and heaved herself off the bed. Half an hour after summoning her maid, she was dressed and headed downstairs to find her father and Marcus. She was informed they had left early in the morning to meet with a gentleman at Kingsley Hall.

"They left me here alone?"

It was unlike Marcus to leave her unprotected at such a time. Since receiving the note, he'd barely let her out of his sight. In truth, she was frightened and it helped to have him near.

The butler allowed a small smile to show. "No, Lady Viola. I can assure you that you are well protected."

"Oh," Viola answered meekly as she sat down for breakfast. Marcus had probably armed all the servants. She smiled at the thought of Harris, her elderly butler, with a weapon. She doubted he could hurt a fly, much less protect her if it became necessary. She took a cautious sip of her chocolate and reached for a scone when the door suddenly flew open. Viola's eyes flew to the doorway and widened in alarm at the sight of the distressed girl being ushered in by a harassed footman.

"Anne? What is wrong?" Viola rose to meet her halfway as Anne rushed toward her. "Is it your mother?"

Anne looked up at her with red-rimmed eyes and she sniffed loudly. She ran a thin arm across her nose and appeared visibly shaken. "Mama is having the baby. Papa went to get the midwife, but it is taking too long. I think something is wrong."

"What do you mean?" Viola asked frightfully. "Is someone with your mother?"

"No!" Anne shook her head. "She sent me to come and get you. She doesn't want to be alone."

"We must hurry then." Viola took Anne's hand and rushed to the door. "Do you know how to ride?"

"A little."

"Good. It will be much faster on horseback."

Viola ordered two horses to be saddled and she paced impatiently as the task was done. Normally, she preferred to saddle her own horse, but her fingers were shaking so badly she doubted she would be able to do it quick enough. She helped Anne into the saddle before mounting her own horse.

"Hang on tightly," she warned Anne right before they took off at a gallop. Anne clung to her horse in terror, but she managed to keep her seat. As they came within sight of the Creech home, Viola dug her heels into the side of her horse and pushed him to hurry. She dismounted quickly and helped Anne down before hurrying into the house.

"Hannah?" Viola called out as she scanned the house. Moans were coming from the back bedroom and Viola entered at once. Hannah was curled up into a ball, soaking with sweat. Viola froze in the doorway as she looked at her obviously suffering friend and she wondered what she had gotten herself in to. She had never assisted with a birth, but she had a vague idea of what needed to be done.

"Where are the younger children?" Viola paused to roll up her sleeves as Anne came up behind her.

"I took them to Mrs. Oliver. I didn't think they should be here."

"Good decision, Anne. Can you get some cloths and hot water?"

As Anne rushed to do her bidding, Viola walked to the bed Hannah lay crumpled on. She touched her friend's forehead and found it was burning with fever. "Hannah? You're going to have to help me. I have no idea what to do."

"Viola?" Hannah's eyes were closed, her breathing rapid and uneven.

"Is something wrong with the baby?"

Hannah moaned and her eyes flew open to gaze unfocusedly at Viola. "It hurts so much. None of the others have hurt this much." Her hands hugged her large belly and Viola could visibly see the contractions taking place under the distended skin.

Anne returned to the room and she staggered to the bed with a pot brimming with water. She placed it on the floor and looked at her mother worriedly. "Do you suppose the baby is turned the wrong way?"

"What do you mean?" Viola looked over her shoulder at Anne.

"Papa once had a mare that was breech. He said the baby horse tried to come out the wrong way."

Viola nodded as she thought about it. She knew such things had happened. One of her father's mares had died from such a situation.

"You may be right." Viola placed a cloth on Hannah's forehead. "I don't know what to do though. How long has your father been gone for the midwife?"

"About two hours."

"That long? They should be here by now." Viola looked at her laboring friend with concern. She wondered if Hannah would be able to hold out until the midwife got there. She did not want to deliver a baby herself. Hannah moaned again and Viola stroked her arm gently. "The doctor will be here soon."

"There is not enough time," Hannah croaked out. "The baby is coming."

"Oh dear," Viola whispered. She looked at

Anne with wide eyes. "What do we do now?"

*****

Marcus returned to Haversham and inquired immediately after Viola. No one seemed to know where she had gone and terror entered his mind. He'd just returned from a meeting with Rivers, the investigator, and was informed that Greenley's whereabouts were still unknown. Suppose the viscount had taken her? He'd hired several men to patrol the grounds, yet none seemed to recall seeing her leave. A frantic search was conducted and an hour later, a stable boy finally informed him Viola and a young girl had taken two horses and fled east. He was able to tell Marcus that Viola appeared worried and he quickly deduced something must be wrong with Hannah. She'd probably gone into labor and it was just like Viola to dash off to help her friend. Marcus quickly mounted his own horse and took off for the Creech's.

Two horses were indeed grazing in the meadow beside the house as Marcus reached the yard. He recognized the horses from the Haversham stock. He dismounted and headed into the house. A loud scream came from the back of the house and Marcus paled. He put a hand against the wall and tried to steady himself as memories of Agnes's labor flooded his mind. Willing himself to focus, he walked down the hall and entered the bedroom. As he opened the door, he was greeted by the shocked faces of two women. Viola and Anne wore identical looks of amazement as he strode into the room and rolled up his sleeves. He supposed it was unusual for a man to be attending the birth of a child that was not his own. In fact, most men did not even attend the birth of their own children. Marcus had always believed if he were to have children, he would like to be at his wife's side the entire time. The only thing that had kept him from Agnes' side was the complications she'd suffered. Since Patrick was not present, he would stand in his stead.

"What are you doing here?" Viola asked when he reached her side. Her hair lay in damp strands against her cheeks and her eyes were filled with concern for her friend.

"I could ask you the same question, but it will wait." He turned his gaze to Hannah Creech. The poor woman was pale and lay limply against the pillows. Shaking off the memory of Agnes, Marcus bent down and placed a hand on Hannah's belly.

"How far apart are the pains?" He glanced at Viola, who chewed her bottom lip and nervously twisted her hands.

"They are almost constant now, but we believe the baby needs to be turned."

Hannah screamed again. He winced. There was not much to be done for a breeched baby. If she were a horse, he could possibly reach in and turn the baby himself but he doubted it would work on a human. "Are you sure the baby is breeched?"

"No, I'm not sure. I've never attended a birth. Can you help her?"

Marcus cut a glance toward Anne as he motioned for Viola to come to him. "When horses are breech, you can sometimes force the foal to turn." He kept his voice low and shot a warning glance at Anne.

"Can you do that to Hannah?" She turned to

look at her writhing friend. "She can't take the pain much longer."

"I don't know, but it is worth a try. If we leave her like this, she and the baby will die." He looked at Viola's slender hands and gripped them in his own much larger ones. "You will have to do it. My forearms are too large."

Viola's face paled and she swayed. Marcus hauled her up. "Viola, you have to be strong if you want to help Hannah."

She snapped back to her senses in an instant. "What do I need to do?"

"Wash your hands. They'll need to be clean."

Viola stuck her hands in a pot of hot water and began washing her arms carefully. "Anne, why don't you go check on your brothers and sisters?"

The girl glanced at her mother one last time before rushing out of the room. Marcus moved to stand with Viola and handed her a cloth to dry her hands on.

"How do I turn him?"

"Reach up until you feel the baby. Position him so his head will come out first." Marcus grasped her by the shoulders and pressed a comforting kiss on her forehead. "Do you think you can do this?"

Viola straightened her shoulders and nodded. "If it will help Hannah, I'll try anything."

He moved to the head of the bed to distract Hannah with softly murmured words of comfort. Viola closed her eyes and said a quick prayer before pushing up Hannah's nightgown and positioning her arms.

"You can do it, Viola."

She jerked her gaze to his and Marcus smiled encouragingly at her.

Viola's mouth firmed into a straight line as she carefully eased her hand into the birth canal. She seemed surprised she was actually able to reach inside. She moved forward a few more inches and Hannah groaned loudly. Viola paused and shot him a worried look. He motioned for her to continue.

"Can you feel the baby?"

Viola bit her bottom lip in concentration. "I feel something. Maybe a leg." She looked to him for direction.

"Okay, now ease him around." Marcus held his breath as Viola followed his instructions. "Did he move?"

"A little I think." She tried again. "I feel his head!"

"Thank God!" Marcus breathed as Viola went to wash off the blood on her hands. She hurried back to his side.

"How long should it take now?"

Hannah appeared to be not in as much pain as before. He felt the tension leave his body in slow waves.

"Not long." He reached for her hand and laced his fingers with hers. Hannah's contractions seemed to have slowed. Neither one of them spoke as they waited. It seemed like hours, but was probably only minutes, until the door opened and Patrick rushed inside.

"How is she?" He spared a quick glance at Marcus, but didn't comment on the oddity of the situation. The midwife followed at a harried pace and immediately began her ministrations.

"The baby was breech," Marcus explained. "Viola turned him around."

The midwife made a cursory examination of Hannah and nodded in agreement. "You did exactly the right thing. It should be an easy delivery now, but we will have to be cautious of the blood loss."

No longer needed, Marcus moved toward the door. Viola was right on his heels. He held the door open for her as he spoke to Patrick. "We'll be right outside if you need us."

They stepped out of the room, both of them visibly shaken. Viola sat on the sofa. He sat beside her and draped an arm over her shoulder.

Her voice trembled as she spoke. "I do not know how Hannah does it. The pain must be unbearable."

"Do you not want children?" The small couch forced them to sit closely together and their knees touched.

"Once I did. Now, after seeing Hannah suffer, I do not know if I have the courage to do the same."

She left the words unspoken, but he knew she had once dreamed of having his children. They'd spoken of it often during their brief courtship. In his own dreams, he envisioned a lovely baby girl who was the spitting image of Viola.

"I don't know if I could ever want children again. I wouldn't want anyone to face death just to have my baby."

"Not everyone dies, Marcus."

"No, but just about everyone I care for seems

to."

"I'm not going anywhere." Viola gave him a small smile. "So you will always have at least one friend."

It was true he cared for her, loved her even, but he was surprised she would admit that she knew it. Even more surprising was her offer of friendship. It was less than what he wished, but more than he'd hoped for. Marcus pulled her close for a moment. The sound of a baby crying came from the next room and they glanced up simultaneously as Patrick came out of the bedroom.

"It's a boy!" Patrick exclaimed with a robust laugh as he cradled his new son to his chest proudly. "A healthy baby boy."

Viola jumped to her feet and hurried over. The baby blinked up at her owlishly as she touched his cheek. "He's so soft!"

Marcus came to stand beside her and gazed at the baby with a relieved smile. "How is Hannah?"

Patrick adjusted his new son's blanket. "She is fine. The midwife says she will have to take it easy for a few weeks, but will be back to normal in no time. She'll be up for visitors in a couple of days."

Viola sighed in relief. "Thank goodness! Tell Hannah I will come back as soon as she's ready."

"Aye, I will. And thank you both for everything you did for my wife."

Patrick went to check on Hannah, leaving Marcus and Viola alone once more. Weary beyond belief, Marcus gestured toward the door.

"Are you ready to go home?"

"Home sounds wonderful," Viola answered

with a heartfelt sigh.

Chapter Fourteen

By the time they reached the edges of Haversham, Marcus's anger had returned in full force. It had been pushed aside during Hannah's plight, but Marcus remembered the panic he felt at Viola's disappearance and he was once again flooded with ire. Viola rode quietly on the horse beside him, unaware of his growing irritation. Her shoulders sagged wearily and she was barely able to keep her seat. When he'd imagined someone had taken her, he'd been filled with impotent rage. His relief at finding her safe barely managed to lessen his anger. In his present mood, he feared he would say something he would regret. Cursing low, he stopped his horse and dismounted quickly. Viola looked at him in confusion.

"What is it? Why are you stopping?" she asked as she pulled back on the reins.

"Viola," Marcus said between clenched teeth. "Just keep riding."

His warning went unheeded as she slid off her horse and walked toward him. "What is wrong, Marcus?"

"Damn it, Viola! Do you not listen to one damned word I say?" Marcus strode away from her. "I told you to keep riding."

Her chin lifted with determination. "I am not yours to order about. My father may have convinced you to protect me, but no one tells me what to do."

"Obviously," Marcus muttered as he swung back to face her. The tall grass barely hampered him as he stalked toward her. His nostrils flared with anger as he glared down at her. "Do you not even comprehend that your life may be in danger? I told you not to leave the house."

"What was I supposed to do?" Viola shouted. "Let Hannah die?"

Marcus ran his hands through his hair in frustration. "No, but you should have asked one of the men to escort you."

"There was not enough time. Anne came to me and I did the first thing that came to mind."

"You must be more careful," Marcus began to admonish. He was distracted from his tirade when he noticed the glint of metal from the nearby woods. A shot rang out just as he shouted for Viola to move. He threw himself at her and knocked her to the ground just as a bullet whizzed by them. He felt a sear of pain above his left shoulder and grunted at the sharp sensation. He fell in the soft grass beside Viola and was relieved to see she appeared unharmed. Her green eyes were wide as she struggled to her feet. Marcus reached out a hand to stop her.

"Stay down!"

Viola sank back into the grass. Her eyes widened until the green was almost swallowed by the black of her pupils. "Someone shot at us!" Her expression mirrored her dawning comprehension. "Thank goodness they missed."

"That is not entirely true." Marcus pointed to his wounded shoulder. It hurt like hell, but he doubted the bullet did anything more than scratch his skin.

"Dear Lord! You were shot?" She stared at

blood seeping from his coat. "Does it hurt?"

"It doesn't feel comfortable." Marcus smiled at her to show it was not a serious injury. "It is little more than a scratch."

Viola lifted a disbelieving eyebrow. "Let me see."

She assisted him out of his coat and tugged at his shirt until she was able to view his wound. He was right, the bullet had grazed him leaving only a deep groove across his shoulder. He was bleeding, but not excessively. It would probably heal within a few days and leave little more than a small scar. She averted her eyes from the wound and he saw her take several rapid breaths. For someone who despised the sight of blood, as he knew Viola did, she was being faced with it quite often today.

"Am I going to live?" he teased. She was close enough he could see the gold flecks in her eyes and the small sprinkling of freckles across the bridge of her nose. Her eyes mirrored his humor.

"I'm not sure. We'll have to wait and see."

"Then how about fulfilling the wish of a dying man?" He leaned back and watched her with lowered eyelids.

"And what would that wish be?"

"A kiss." Marcus spread his arms wide. "A last kiss from a beautiful girl."

"Woman," Viola automatically corrected him as she slowly moved closer to him and placed her hands against his chest. His muscles leapt under her fingers. He wondered if there would ever come a time when her touch didn't send tingles down his spine. If he had it his way, she would always be able to incite such a reaction from him.

"Pardon me.   A kiss from a beautiful woman." He reached out with his uninjured arm to place his fingers behind her head and urge her to him. Viola put her hands on his chest for balance as she dipped her head to place a chaste kiss on his lips.

"That was not a proper kiss," Marcus argued.

"Nevertheless, it is all you are going to get."

Marcus lifted an eyebrow. "You forget, you still owe me a kiss."

"I think you got much more than a kiss the other night. My debt has been paid."

The reminder of the night in her bedroom had his cock throbbing with remembered desire.   "I thought you said that wasn't a kiss. You can't back out on our agreement now."

"I just kissed you."

He'd been shot and they might still be in danger. It was ridiculous to try to seduce her at a time like this, but he had to know the feel of her lips again. He lay back on the grass with indolent ease.

"You gave it freely." Marcus placed his hand behind his head and regarded her calmly. "I can still claim my forfeit anytime I want."

"Now is not the time." Viola climbed to her knees. "You are shot and clearly delirious."

"Now is definitely the time and if I'm delirious it is because of you."

Marcus surged up to wrap his good arm around her waist and tumbled her into his lap. Viola's small squeak of outrage was silenced by his lips as he claimed his kiss. Her kiss had the power to make his brain feel like mush. She relaxed against him in surrender. His lips teased the seam of her lips and she opened her mouth to kiss him deeply. He turned her so she was pinned to the ground by his body.

The damp grass soaked her back, but he could think of nothing besides kissing her and the wonderful feelings it evoked. His hands restlessly moved against her waist, his fingers longing to contact her naked skin. His mouth moved lower and kissed the tender skin of her neck. Viola's hands moved to the waistband of his breeches and tugged his shirt loose. Her hands roamed under the fabric and greedily touched the smooth muscles of his back. She spread her fingers wide and clasped him to her as his mouth roamed to the low neckline of her gown and he pressed his lips against the rise of her breast. Viola let out a breathy moan as he undid the top buttons of her gown. Slowly, he slipped it to the side and bared her breast to his gaze. She was only covered by a thin chemise and her body was clearly visible under the transparent fabric. He kept his eyes on hers as he bent down and placed his lips against her breast. He drew her nipple into his mouth and lightly sucked. He moved to the other breast and repeated the action.

His body was alive with sensation. He would stay in the tall grass forever if she kept allowing him to pleasure her. He brought his lips back to hers. She kissed him hungrily and tried to unbutton his shirt, but her awkward fingers refused to complete the task.

"I want to touch you," she argued when his hand closed around hers. Her eyes locked with his in silent battle until he finally released her hand. She forced her fingers to cooperate and she managed to undo the first few laces of his shirt. It was enough so she could slip her hands inside to caress the hardened muscles of his chest. A light dusting of hair sprinkled his chest and narrowed across his abdomen to the waist of his breeches. Viola seemed captivated by the feeling of the springy hair against her questing fingertips. Marcus sucked in a breath as her hand moved lower to caress the muscles of his abdomen. He grasped both of her wrists in his hand and pinned them above her head.

"No more." He leaned down to kiss her and silence her arguments.

Instead, she averted her head and pressed her lips against his neck. Marcus groaned in defeat and dropped his head to the side as she lightly nipped his skin. Her tongue flicked out to taste the salty skin of his neck. She moved her lips against his jaw and finally reached his mouth. Her eyes dared him to kiss her again.

"You are a hellion," he remarked as she moved her mouth closer to his. Her hands were still captured by his, the sensation of being in control thrilled him. He finally obliged her and pressed a kiss against her smiling lips. Viola's legs moved restlessly under his and she experimentally wrapped one against his hip. Their bodies came into immediate contact. His cock pressed into the vee between her thighs. She moved her hips under him and rubbed against him shamefully. Through the thin silk of her skirts, he could feel the heat of her slit. She was ready for him, even if she refused to admit it. He flexed his hips to simulate fucking. He groaned as she arched her hips under his to bring him closer.

He wanted to tear off her clothes and fuck her until they both couldn't move. If he couldn't bind her to him with love, he would make her a slave to passion. Suddenly he had to know she desired him. "You want me. Say it."

She ignored his command and kissed him. Her hands drifted to the waistband of his breeches and delved underneath. Her fingertips brushed perilously close to his cock. He rubbed against her again. He bent his head and lightly bit her nipple. "I want to hear you say it, Viola."

"Just kiss me, Marcus."

He lifted his head and pinned a dark gaze on her. "I won't do it unless you say you want me."

The desire clouding her eyes slowly receded. He cursed low under his breath. He'd pushed too hard, but damn it he wanted to know she ached for him as much as he did for her. She tugged her wrists from his grasp. He released her instantly and Viola shoved against his chest. He obliged her by rolling to the side and she scrambled from underneath him. She got to her feet shakily and caught her breath.

"We'd better get back. Your shoulder needs to be seen to." She looked around the clearing carefully. "I think it is safe now."

Marcus stood and scanned the nearby woods. If the shooter was still there, he would've had a plain target. Hell after their romp in the grass, they would both be dead by now. He grabbed her hand and led her to the horses, berating himself for putting her in danger. The sooner he had Viola safely inside her home, the better he would feel. His shoulder was steadily bleeding and their interlude seemed to have made it worse.

*****

Once at Haversham, Viola grew concerned for Marcus. His wound had yet to stop bleeding and she wondered if perhaps she had been too hasty in judging the seriousness of his injury. She was in no way knowledgeable of gunshots after all. What if their antics in the grass had harmed him further? Doubts assailed her and she held herself responsible for hurting him. If she'd listened to him in the first place, none of it would have ever happened. As they entered the hall, her father came out to join them and he paused at the doorway of the library.

"What happened?" Robert's face paled as he looked at the smear of blood on Marcus's shirt. "Are you injured?"

"Marcus was shot."

Marcus's face was ashen. He'd held himself up stoically, but the loss of blood was taking its toil. He was beginning to weaken and she put a hand around his waist to steady him when it looked as if he would fall. Her father hurried to assist her and together they forced Marcus toward the stairs.

"Did you see who did this?" Robert asked as he and Viola staggered under Marcus's weight.

"No. I only heard a shot and then Marcus knocked me to the ground."

"The bullet was meant for you?" Robert's face clouded with worry and Viola felt a sudden stab of fear. Who could want her dead? And what lengths would he go to?

"We cannot know for sure," Viola tried to

reassure her father. "Perhaps it was a hunter who mistook us for a deer."

"What were you doing away from the house?" Robert asked as they finally reached Marcus's room and lowered him to the bed. Marcus sprawled across it and grunted when his injured shoulder protested the movement.

"Hannah was about to have the baby and it was breech. I went to help." She bent to help Marcus to a comfortable position. "Marcus arrived and we were able to save the baby."

"You assisted with a birth? An actual birth?" Her father's tone was disbelieving.

"Why do you doubt me?" Viola straightened and placed her hands on her hips.

"You almost faint at the sight of blood. I'm amazed you were able to help."

"You do what you have to. And, in case you have not noticed, Marcus is bleeding and I have yet to submit to a fit of vapors." She turned her attention back to Marcus. A stain of red spread across his otherwise pristine shirt. "Do you suppose we should call the doctor?"

"I suppose we should. I will send one of the footmen to fetch him."

Viola was left alone with Marcus and she twisted her hands as she wondered what to do.

"I am not going to die." Marcus spoke suddenly and she whirled about in surprise. He'd been silent the past few minutes, so she'd assumed he was unconscious.

"I hope not." Viola rushed to his side. "How do you feel?"

"Terrible." He propped up on the pillows. "I don't suppose you could fetch me a glass of brandy?"

Viola raised an eyebrow. "Brandy? You plan to knock yourself out then?"

"I have developed a certain tolerance for brandy. It has little effect on me now, other than a slight dulling of the senses. If you would kindly fetch me a glass, I would be happy to prove it to you."

Viola shrugged her shoulder. "If you insist."

She went into the hall and asked one of the maids to fetch a bottle of brandy and a glass. She muttered under her breath the entire way about the stubbornness of men in general. She came back to the room to see Marcus trying to pull off his bloodied shirt. With only one capable arm, he did little more than get tangled in the material.

"Let me help." She came forward and gently tugged his shirt away from his wound. It stuck to his skin because of the dried blood. It had to be painful. She bit her lip and firmly tugged. "There!" She removed the shirt and tossed it aside. Marcus's wound was swollen. She gave the inflamed area a worried look. What if it got infected? She put a hand to her stomach to quell a nauseous feeling. Marcus tilted his head and examined his shoulder with a slight grimace. "It is not too bad. It hurts much worse than it looks though." He gave her a reassuring grin.

"Then it must hurt dreadfully because it looks awful."

A maid returned with the brandy and Viola thanked her as she returned to Marcus's side. She poured him a glass and handed it over. He sipped it thoughtfully as she pulled a chair close to the bed. She had some unanswered questions. Mostly why Marcus believed Greenley was behind the note. Now would be as good a time as any to get answers.

"Do you really think Greenley is responsible?"

"I'm not sure. He certainly has reason to feel threatened by me."

"Why do you want to find him so badly?" Viola wanted to plead with him to tell her the truth. Surely he knew he could trust her? "What is he to you?"

Marcus turned away from her. "He is my half brother."

She stared at him in disbelief. "You are serious?"

"Completely," Marcus assured her solemnly. "Before he died, my father told me how he'd fallen in love with his estate manager's daughter. She was forced to marry another while pregnant with my father's baby. Greenley is my father's son."

"Then that would mean he…" Viola's voice trailed away and left it unsaid.

"If my father had married her, Greenley would be the heir." Marcus completed her unspoken thought. "Instead he was raised by a man who caused him nothing but grief."

"Does he know?"

"Indeed he does. My father did not learn of it himself until Greenley was nearly sixteen. It was too late for my father to claim him. Besides, Greenley's mother begged my father not to reveal the truth. When he learned of his true father, Greenley blamed his unhappy childhood on my father. He refused all my father's attempts to talk with him."

Viola's face lit with sudden understanding. "Your father made you promise to help him, did he not?"

"You are correct, but so far my attempts to find him have come to naught."

"But if it is you he resents, why do you think he would harm me?"

"I hired an investigator to track Greenley to Paris. My man discovered the viscount seemed obsessed with you. Or maybe it is all an elaborate scheme to prevent us from being together. Perhaps he thinks the way to hurt me would be to take you away from me."

"That is ridiculous." Viola stood and moved across the room. "How could he know you and I would even be on speaking terms again? Something is just not adding up." Viola tapped her chin thoughtfully. "I suggest we not assume Greenley is the villain."

"You sound like my father. Do not worry. I have not discounted the possibility of his innocence."

She turned back to him and caught the dark look in his eyes. "But you want it to be him. You still blame him for that night."

He didn't ask which night she referred to. He shifted higher in the bed, his skin bronze against the stark whiteness of the sheets. "Viola, I…"

His words trailed off when the door creaked open and her father and the doctor walked in. Though Viola was relieved the doctor was there, she was disappointed their conversation had to be cut short.

The doctor asked Viola to leave the room so he could begin his examination. She shut the door behind her and leaned against it. There was much to think about. Foremost, who would have reason to want either her or Marcus dead? Secondly, how would she be able to live in the same house with Marcus and not feel such an overwhelming desire to be with him?

Chapter Fifteen

After Marcus was shot, Viola began receiving warning letters at an alarming frequency. The fifth note arrived while she was alone in the library nearly a week after Marcus was injured. She took the folded paper from the footman and thanked him softly. She waited until the door closed behind him before breaking the wax seal and reading the contents of the letter. Her lips moved as she read the threatening words softly to herself.

The first shot was just a warning. You will not be so lucky the next time.

It sounded as if the writer was threatening Marcus instead of herself. The previous letters had seemed more directed to her, as if warning her away from Marcus. This time though, her name had not been carefully printed on the paper with dark slashes. She wondered if she should show the letter to Marcus and her father. Marcus was still recuperating and her father had still not regained his usual strength. Making a quick decision, she tossed the letter into the fireplace and watched as the flames destroyed the paper.

No sooner was the paper consumed by the fire than the door opened again and Marcus strolled in. His left arm was bandaged and anchored by a sling across his broad chest. He glanced up at her and she could see the faint shadows under his eyes that hinted at sleepless, worry filled nights.

He approached her and she forced a calm expression on her face. "Should you be out of bed?

The physician said you should rest for a couple of days."

"I am perfectly well." Marcus reached her, but the stiff way he held his arm told her it was still paining him. "I need to go to the Hall and see how the renovations are progressing."

"Are you mad? You are injured and are in no condition to travel! Does my father know you are out of bed?"

"It is only a few miles to the Hall. I can manage."

"But what if someone is waiting for you?"

She briefly considered telling him about the latest note, but decided to keep it a secret. If she told him about it, it would doubtless make him worry even more than he already did. A few days before he'd confessed to her his fears something would befall her or her father.

"Viola, you sound as if you are worried about me." He laughed lightly. "I thought I was the one who was supposed to be protecting *you*? Of course, a fat lot of good it does me when I am holed up in a sick bed all week."

"Of course I am worried about you, you fool." Viola plopped into a chair. "You saved my life after all." She worried her bottom lip between her teeth. "If you go, do you promise to be careful?"

"Of course," Marcus promised as he started toward the door. "You will stay indoors while I am gone, won't you?"

"Of course." Viola echoed meekly as Marcus left the room. She gave him a few moments head start before rushing from the room. She sneaked out of the servant's door in the rear of the house. There was no way she was going to let Marcus roam about the countryside unprotected. She put her hand in the pocket of her skirt and was comforted by the presence of a small pistol her father had given her. It was not loaded, she had not gotten that far in her training but it would be a definite deterrent to someone who meant to harm her.

She peeked around the corner of the house and saw Marcus top the western hill. She ran toward the stables at full speed. She wasted no time in saddling her own horse and mounting. As she set off across the stable yard, the head groom called out a warning. Viola assured him Marcus was aware she would be joining him. The groom looked unconvinced, but he could not argue for fear of being disrespectful. Before he could change his mind and stop her anyway, she dug in her heels and tore across the yard.

Viola kept her distance from Marcus so he would not realize he was being followed. He glanced over his shoulders once, but Viola darted into the trees before he could notice her. When they reached the Hall, Marcus rode toward the construction site of the new stables. Viola chose instead to ride to the front of the house and tether her horse so she could proceed on foot. She inched her way to the back of the house and was relieved when her presence went undetected. She hid behind a large tree and observed Marcus from a safe distance. His back was to her as he talked to the large man who was obviously overseeing the repairs. The man gestured expansively toward the stables and Marcus nodded his head in agreement. As the men were absorbed in conversation and Marcus did not seem to be in any immediate danger, Viola took the time to study the work being done on the stables. From the look of the repairs, she imagined Marcus's stables would be very grand once the work was finished.

The men spoke for several moments before Marcus patted the overseer on the back and moved away to remount Pyrenees. He turned to ride away and Viola abandoned her hiding place. She took her time heading back to the front of the house. She wanted to give Marcus a chance to clear the hill before she rode after him.

In no hurry, she trailed her fingers along the ivy-covered wall of Marcus's ancestral home. She'd not been here in years. As a child, she and Marcus had spent hours at the Hall. Coming here now was almost like coming home. She was distracted by her thoughts as she reached the front of the house. It took her a moment to realize what she was seeing. She blinked to clear her vision and groaned when she realized she was not imagining it.

Marcus had dismounted and stood beside her horse. His eyes locked with hers fiercely. A dark frown covered his face and he looked very forbidding as he strode toward her. Viola held her ground even though she felt like running as fast as she could in the opposite direction. If his frown was an indication of his feelings, then she was in big trouble.

"Did I not tell you to stay at the house?" His voice nearly shook with the force of his anger. His eyes were narrowed and intently focused on hers. Though she had seen him angry often enough, she'd never been the target of such a silent rage.

Viola bit her lip nervously as her eyes darted to the right. Just a few feet and she could safely reach the front door to the house. "You did."

"Then would you care to explain what the hell you are doing all the way out here?" Marcus's breath heaved harshly and Viola could tell his restraint was rapidly disappearing. Her eyes darted to the side again and his followed the movement. He smiled harshly at her and shook his head warningly. "Do not think you will receive any help in that quarter. I gave most of the servants a couple of days off while repairs are being done to the house."

Viola silently rejoiced. If the house were truly empty as he said, it would be easier for her to hide in one of the many rooms of the Hall. Marcus would not be able to enlist servants to aid him in his search. By the time he had found her, he should've calmed down enough to listen to her explanation. Viola took off at a run and managed to slip through the door just as Marcus lunged for her. She slammed the door behind her and gained a few precious moments before he shoved open the door and entered the house. Viola raced for the stairs and wasted a few seconds debating on which way she should turn. She'd not been inside the Hall since she was a little girl and she had forgotten which wing was the least used. She headed to the left and dashed inside the first door she came to. She belatedly realized she had entered Marcus's rooms.

Of all the rotten luck, Viola berated herself as she turned in a circle looking for something to jam against the door. All of the furniture had been removed other than his bed and as she eyed the heavy wooden piece, she knew there was no way she could move it by herself. Its weight was probably the reason it had been left behind.

There was a lock on the door, but it would be useless since he had a key. Instead of hiding, Viola stood in the center of the room and eyed the door. Seconds later, it creaked open. She reached into her pocket to pull out the small pistol, aiming it at the doorway with nervous fingers.

Marcus stood in the doorway and glared at her. When he saw the pistol she had aimed at his heart, his eyes narrowed dangerously. "Don't be foolish. Do you even know how to shoot?"

"I refuse to talk to you until you have calmed down." She kept her attention on the gun in her hands.

"Pointing a gun at me is definitely not the best way to calm me." Marcus growled. He glanced at her trembling hands and she could tell he was trying to think of a way to disarm her. She cautiously backed up. The gun was unloaded after all. What would she do if he really meant to harm her?

"Marcus, I am warning you. Stay back."

He ignored her warning and turned to lock the door.

"What are you doing?"

"What does it look like?" Marcus faced her. "I am locking the door."

"Why?" Viola felt the beginnings of real unease.

"So I can thrash you without anyone disturbing us."

"You will do no such thing. I am not a child you can put over your knee."

She continued to back up until her knees bumped into something soft. She glanced at the bed which blocked her retreat and turned her gaze back to Marcus. His gaze followed hers to the bed and her cheeks flushed. She did not trust the look in his eyes one bit. Suddenly she was conscious of the fact they were alone in his bedroom, surely not the safest place to be when he was in a temper.

Marcus crooked a finger at her. "Then stop acting like a child and give me the gun."

He moved away from the door and approached her slowly with his hand outstretched. A little reasoning might serve to cool his temper.

"I know you are angry I disobeyed you, but I only did it to protect you."

"Care to explain how you were going to protect me with an unloaded gun?"

Viola lowered her arm and stared at him dejectedly. "How did you know?"

"Viola, if that gun was loaded, you would've shot me already with the way your hands have been shaking. Whether you meant to or not."

"Oh." Viola put the pistol in her pocket. He came close enough so her skirts brushed his legs. She tilted her head back and searched his face to see if he was still angry with her. "What do you plan to do now?"

Marcus's eyes darkened as he looked at her. "I'm still debating on whether I should thrash you or not."

She gave him an arch look. "You wouldn't

dare."

He moved quickly, grabbing her by the waist before she could even gasp and tossed her on the bed. She landed with a bounce and her skirts flew up in an undignified manner. She brushed them back down and pinned Marcus with a fierce glare.

"That was uncalled for, you brute!" She tried to climb off the bed, but Marcus pushed her back down. "Stop manhandling me!" She fought to keep her balance on the soft mattress.

Marcus put one knee on the bed beside her and lowered his face to hers. They glared at each other for several moments in a silent battle of wills. Marcus's harsh breathing indicated his anger had returned, but Viola refused to back down. "You are acting like a complete beast."

"And you are acting like an idiot!" Marcus's anger suddenly exploded and he grasped her shoulders as if to shake her. "You promised you would stay inside. Why did you follow me? Do you not comprehend the danger you are in?"

"Do you not comprehend the danger *you* are in? Those notes are meant for you, not me!" Viola shouted back at him. She clamped her mouth shut when she realized what she had just revealed. Marcus's face tightened in suspicion and Viola sighed as she realized there was no way to hide the truth. "Notes? What are you are not telling me?" Marcus released her shoulders with a grimace. His left arm must be paining him.

Viola's gaze fell to the white sling on his left arm. "Your injury was just a warning."

As Marcus sat on the edge of the mattress, she

tucked her legs underneath herself and stared at his back. She supposed there was no help for it except to tell him about the note she'd received that morning. He listened quietly, stiffening as he learned she'd destroyed the evidence by burning it. Suddenly she felt extremely guilty for her rash act.

"I'm sorry I didn't tell you about it earlier, but I didn't want you to get upset and injure yourself further on my behalf." She crept to his side and cautiously touched his injured arm. "It is my fault you were shot and I could not bear it if anything else happens to you."

Marcus kept his head away from her and Viola could tell he struggled with his anger. She wished there was a way she could make it up to him, but she did not know how. Her hand lightly touched his back. His muscles twitched under her hands and she was overcome with the need to touch more of him. Her eyes gleamed with a sudden insight. Perhaps she could make it up to him while doing something she had been dying to do for days now. If only she actually had the courage to go through with it.

Chapter Sixteen

Marcus could not believe what Viola was suggesting. Were the notes truly meant as a warning for him? It seemed plausible, especially if Greenley was the author of the notes. His half-brother was obsessed with Viola and if Marcus was dead, nothing could stop him from pursuing her. Now he'd got Viola and her father involved in his troubles. Marcus buried his face in his hands and let out a harsh groan. What did he do now?

It took Marcus several minutes before he realized Viola had practically draped herself across him. Her breasts flattened against his back as she reached around him to unbutton his shirt. Though it almost killed him to do it, he reached up a hand to cover her fingers.

"What are you doing?" There was a slight hitch in his voice.

"I am taking off your shirt," Viola whispered in his ear as she untied another lace. She propped her chin on his shoulder so she could get a better view and he tilted his head until their faces were mere inches apart.

"Why?" Marcus could imagine the answer and he was more than agreeable, but he wondered if Viola really knew what she was asking for. She'd responded to him physically on more than one occasion, but he didn't want to take advantage of her.

"Why do you think?" Her husky voice swept over his skin and he couldn't repress a shiver of delight. Her delightfully feminine smell surrounded him as she pressed even closer.

"I think you are trying to seduce me," Marcus answered bluntly and turned his head to look at her. "Is that what you really want?"

"Yes." She ran a hand across his cheek. He fought the urge to press a kiss on her palm and stared at her instead.

"Do you really?" His eyes searched hers for any sign her heart was not in what she was suggesting. She was noticeably nervous, but other than that, he did not sense any hesitation. In fact, she seemed almost eager. Viola slid off the edge of the bed and came to stand between his splayed legs.

"Do you not want me?" She bent forward to lightly kiss his chin.

How the hell was he supposed to be noble when she was doing her best to seduce him?

"Hell, Viola! If you don't know by now, you're a fool."

"Then do something about it. Make love to me, Marcus." She smiled at him with the eyes of a siren. He'd never seen them look so green. He knew with sudden, blinding clarity he was lost. Accepting defeat, he took her in his arms and kissed her with all the passion he'd been repressing for so long. Viola smiled against his lips and he felt like smiling himself as she arched against him, pressing her delectable body against his.

The seducer became the seduced as he reached for the buttons on the back of her gown and undid them easily. Her gown drifted to the floor and he moved back to appreciate the sight of Viola clad in only her chemise. He loved that the current fashion dictated no petticoats. He didn't have to waste time removing clothing, but could reveal the prize in a matter of seconds.

She stood in front of the window, the afternoon sun clearly outlining her body. Her breasts were round and full and his palms itched with the need to touch them. His eyes roamed down her flat belly and he admired the length of her legs before looking upon the shadowed triangle between her thighs. He practically salivated at the thought of tasting her again. He had to see if she was as sweet as he remembered.

He bent his head and took her nipple between his teeth. He rolled the tight nub between his lips, delighting in the shattered groan she made. He repeated the action with the other and kissed his way down her belly. Anticipating what was to come, Viola widened her stance and gripped his shoulders. He tongued her slit through her chemise and he caught her as her knees gave way.

He moved his eyes back to her face and instead of looking down nervously, Viola regarded his passionate look with one of her own. He should've known once Viola got something in her head, she would not show any reticence.

"My turn." She finished untying his laces. She tugged the shirt from his breeches and he obliged her by tossing it over his head. She eyed his chest greedily and he couldn't prevent a puff of pride. He reached out to her, but the sling hampered his movements.

"To hell with this bloody thing." He viciously tore off the sling and tossed it aside with his shirt.

"Careful, Marcus. You'll hurt your arm."

"It would be worth it." He was already painfully hard and nothing so minor as an injured arm would deter him from his purpose. Viola must've sensed his thoughts because she suddenly glanced down. He grew even harder as she examined him. His hands moved to the waistband of his breeches and he was able to undo the first button before Viola stopped him.

"Let me do it." She pushed aside his hands and set to work unbuttoning his breeches. Each brush of her small fingers against his cock nearly sent him over the edge. Finally, the torture was over and he lifted his hips so Viola could slide his breeches down over his thighs. He helped her remove his boots and then he was bare before her. Viola's eyes widened as she looked at him and he nearly laughed at her expression of disbelief.

"I take it I am the first naked man you have ever seen?" He couldn't resist teasing her. Viola's eyes flew to his.

"Besides statues, of course you are." Her eyes traveled back down his body.

Marcus had suspected it, but he was still relieved he was the only man she'd seen. If he had it his way, it would remain that way for the rest of their lives. "Come here."

She moved to the edge of the bed where he sat. He reached for the hem of her chemise and hauled it over her head in one smooth movement. Viola did not show the slightest discomfort at being naked with him. Her bare skin was warm against his as she sank into his arms and kissed him. He wrapped his arms around her bottom and hauled her astride him on the edge of the bed. Her breasts flattened against his chest and the damp curls of her slit rubbed against his cock temptingly. The silky skin of her thighs caressed his hips as she moved closer.

"This is just like the first time we kissed, except we have no clothes on." The hair on his legs tickled the sensitive skin of her bottom and she rose up on her knees to tower over him.

Marcus tilted his head back to keep his eyes on her face. "Is it better this way?"

She smiled, her full lips parting slowly and seductively. "Much better." She moved her hips again, shamelessly wanting more. The breath sucked out of his lungs as she reached down and touched his cock. Her fingernails lightly brushed his skin as she trailed a path to the head. Her eyes, which had been curiously studying his body, moved back to his questioningly.

"What are you going to do now?" His lips twitched as he saw the dilemma on her face.

She motioned toward the bed. "Should we not be lying down?"

Marcus grinned broadly. "We could, but where is the fun in that?"

She looked down at their bodies and he could tell her mind was furiously whirling. He had a hunch Viola would enjoy the position since she would be the one in charge of the movements.

Now if only she could figure out how it was accomplished.

"It is just like riding a horse," he offered

helpfully. She gave him an irritated look for enjoying himself at her discomfiture.

"You could help me out a little, you know? I've never done this before. Unlike you."

The primness of her voice made him laugh. She was sitting nude upon an aroused male. Not exactly the time to act properly. She glared at him as his chest rumbled with the sound of his amusement. He stopped laughing long enough to lean forward and lick her breast. She gasped and clutched at his hair as he took a nipple into his mouth and laved it with his tongue. She flexed her hips instinctively and he looked up at her in approval.

"That's it." He put his hands on her waist to guide her movements. He tilted his head to take her lips in another one of his mind numbing kisses as she slid her hands down his chest. He groaned as her hands encircled his straining cock and caressed the velvety hard tip. His own fingers slipped to her slit. He pressed his palm in small circular movements. She bit her lip to keep from moaning. He used his free hand to touch her mouth.

"I want to hear you."

Viola stopped biting her lip. Instead, she sucked one of his fingers into her moist mouth and laved it with her tongue. He felt it all the way to his toes. She kept her hands on his cock, her small hands caressing him to throbbing fullness. He returned the favor. His fingers teasing her before slipping inside her damp warmth. She arched her neck backwards while simultaneously jutting her lower body forward. He felt the loss of her hands as she braced her palms against his chest. She cried out, the sound of her voice echoing in the empty room.

The sounds of pleasure she made was his undoing. She was more than ready for him and he had to be inside her. Marcus positioned her legs to receive him. She balanced herself on her knees, tensing slightly as he pushed her thighs apart. He pinned a look on her. If she were having second thoughts, he needed to know now.

"Do you want this?"

Viola smiled and opened her legs wider to receive him. It was answer enough for him. He took his cock in one hand and placed it at her opening. He pressed experimentally, her tight muscles opening to receive him. She nodded belatedly as he guided himself further into her. Putting his hands on her hips, he urged her to complete the joining. She lowered herself on his cock inch by devastating inch. When he thought he could take it no longer, she brought herself completely over him, breaking through her maidenhead in one quick downward lunge. He gave her time to adjust to the feeling of him inside her. Her forehead wrinkled into a frown and she moved her hips gingerly. She quickly halted with a small sound of distress.

"Are you all right?" Marcus wrapped his arms around her and pressed a kiss on her forehead.

"Yes." She gave a wobbly laugh before swatting him on his arm. "You did not tell me it would hurt."

"I'm sorry." Marcus rubbed her back comfortingly. "I thought you knew. Would you like to stop?" He did not know how he could, but if she asked him to stop, he would force himself to pull out of her. He flexed his hips as if to pull out and she protested.

"Don't you dare!" The tension seemed to leave her body. "The pain is gone now. We can finish what we started."

"As you wish." Marcus chuckled as she kissed him and rocked her hips forward seductively. Marcus groaned aloud at the feeling of her inner muscles gloving his cock so tightly. He'd made love to a virgin before, but no one had ever been as responsive as Viola. She excelled at this as she did at every other aspect of her life. She moved in slow, languorous rolls and Marcus reached down to clutch at the bed sheets as she undulated above him. His head tilted back to stare at the rapturous expression on her face as she rocked back and forth. He let her set the pace, but soon his hands were gripping her waist and urging her to ride him harder. His hips came off the mattress, putting an arm around her waist he rolled her until she lay underneath him.

Viola opened her eyes and gazed at him. "I thought you said lying down was not as much fun."

Her breath hitched as his thrusts brought her closer and closer to the headboard. She wrapped her legs around his waist and her fingernails dug into the skin of his back. He was amazed at how good it felt to make love to Viola. He wanted to take her slowly, but once he'd touched her, he had lost all control. It had been several months since he'd been with a woman, but somehow he doubted that was the reason he reacted so strongly to her.

"I was wrong," he grunted between thrusts. Viola brought his head down to hers and her tongue slipped between his lips to duel with his. His hands cupped her breast and he teased the tips to pebble hard attention. God how he loved her breasts and how they fit perfectly in his hands. But most of all, he loved how it felt to be inside her. He had dreamed of this moment for years and in his wildest imagination, he could not have predicted this overwhelming desire or Viola's passionate response. She arched her hips under his, bringing him closer to his peak. Her soft moans escalated until she cried out in release and sank down into the soft mattress. Her hands dropped to her sides as she gazed up at him in wonder. At the sight of her eyes widened in disbelief, Marcus put his hands under her bottom and lifted her for one final thrust as he joined her in her release. Tremors still shook her body as he poured himself inside of her. He knew he should spend himself on the sheets, but his body rebelled and he gripped her hips as he came.

Exhausted, he dropped his head on the pillow beside Viola. He turned so he was no longer lying on top of her. His chest heaved with his heavy breathing and it took him a moment to gather enough strength to turn and face her. His put his hand on her hip and urged her to snuggle against his chest.

Her green eyes shone radiantly. "That was amazing. Thank you."

"I should be thanking you." He brushed a tendril of sweaty hair away from her cheek. Viola's cheeks were flushed with exertion and her lips swollen from his kisses. She looked thoroughly sated and he felt a surge of satisfaction at being the only man to have her. His arm tightened possessively around her. He vowed no man would ever have her except him.

Viola's breathing returned to normal much sooner than his. Her eyes dropped to his shoulder and she touched it with the tip of one finger. "How is your arm?"

"It hurts like hell," Marcus admitted with a rueful grin and tried to collect his senses. "But it was worth it."

"So I take it I am a good lover?" The beginnings of a smile tilted the corners of her generous mouth.

"The best I've ever had." Marcus spoke honestly. She smiled brightly and puffed with pride. All too soon, her smile faded to be replaced by a frown.

"What are you thinking?" He didn't like the look on her face. It reminded him of the one she wore whenever she did something she thought was wrong. He would be damned before he let her regret what had just happened between them.

Viola lifted one eyebrow as she propped herself up on an elbow to regard him seriously. She tugged on the sheet to cover her naked breasts and a slight flush stained her cheeks. "Should we be getting back? It is getting late."

Marcus never wanted the interlude to end, but he knew she was right. Her father would doubtlessly realize she was missing and grow worried. "We should."

Viola slid off the bed to gather up her clothing and he reluctantly climbed to his feet to do the same. It had not escaped his notice that Viola had the disturbing habit of getting back to business quickly after their passionate interludes. While he was still in a daze, her mind cleared and she distanced herself before he could stop her. One day he planned to make sure she spent the entire night in his arms. There was much they still needed to talk about. Viola would have to agree to a reconcilement after what they had just done. Then he could spend the rest of his life making her go out of her mind with desire.

*****

Viola pulled on her gown and struggled to fasten the buttons on the back. Her muscles ached with every movement, making the task extremely difficult. Marcus noticed her struggle and he came over to finish buttoning up the gown for her. She held herself stiffly at the touch of his hands. Now they were clothed, Viola suffered in growing embarrassment.

She was no longer a virgin.

The ache between her thighs reminded her of all they'd just done. How would she be able to face him? Part of her longed to climb back in the bed with him and the other part of her wanted to run away as fast as she could. The battle between her head and her heart warred with each other and made her feel off balance.

"Are you ready?" Marcus buttoned up his shirt as he faced her. Her embarrassment must have been obvious because he smiled at her comfortingly.

Viola nodded weakly. "Let's go."

He took her hand and led her down the stairs. She could smell herself on him. His scent also lingered on her body. Between her legs, she ached and felt embarrassingly damp. Was this what it felt like after sex? She wasn't sure whether to be horrified or intrigued. If she were honest, she would have to admit that intrigue was the winner.

He held open the door for her. As she passed him, he patted her bottom. She whirled around with surprise, but Marcus only gave her a cocky grin. Clearly his mind was not filled with concerns. She sniffed to herself. Just like a man.

Their horses were standing where they'd left them. As Marcus helped her into the saddle, she winced with pain. Her thighs were sore and the hard leather of the saddle was uncomfortable.

Marcus noticed her pained grimace. "I'm sorry. I should have been more restrained."

"Don't apologize. It isn't your fault." Though she spoke with a steady voice, her cheeks flamed crimson. Marcus's dark eyes regarded her as he mounted his horse. The ride home passed with very few words being spoken. When they reached Haversham, Viola fled to the house while Marcus was left to tend to the horses. She rushed upstairs and locked herself in her room while recriminations echoed inside her head. What was she thinking to seduce Marcus? What if she were pregnant? She didn't know much about sex, but she did know it usually led to babies.

Viola was startled out of her thoughts when her maid knocked lightly on the door and poked her head in to ask if she was ready to dress for dinner.

"I feel a little ill. I'll have dinner in my room tonight." She could not go down to supper and she hoped her maid would make some excuse for her. She was not ready to face Marcus so soon after what they'd done. And what if her father could tell just by looking at her that she'd become a fallen woman? Viola felt sick thinking about how disappointed her father would be if he knew.

She ordered a bath and scrubbed herself clean, hoping to erase the memory of what she'd done. Her eyes took in the visible proof of his possession. Her nipples were rosy and her breasts were covered with marks made by the scrape of his stubble against her tender skin. The hair between her legs was sticky, both from her body's fluids and Marcus's. Even though she scrubbed, she couldn't wash away the memory of how good it felt to be in his arms. He looked at her as if she were the only woman he could ever desire. The look on her face probably said much the same thing. There was no man on earth who could measure up to Marcus. Having sex with Marcus had been an eye opener in more ways than one. At some point in the afternoon, she'd come to the realization she was still in love with him. She couldn't face losing him a second time.

When they had made love, it had taken every ounce of her will to keep from saying she loved him. She'd bit her lip and refused to utter the words. Right now it would only make matters worse. The threat hanging over their heads would have to be solved before she could seriously give their relationship a chance. That was, if Marcus actually wanted to have a relationship. She'd not given him much of a choice in the matter. His previous actions indicated he desired a reconcilement, so she would have to have faith he still wanted her.

Taking matters into her own hands, she

decided on a plan. It would require huge amounts of daring on her part, but she had to accomplish it if she wanted to spend the rest of her life with Marcus.

*****

"What do you mean she is gone?"

"We've searched everywhere, but there is not a trace of her." Robert's face was lined with worry.

This was not the news Marcus wanted to hear. He'd slept fitfully the night before and rose just moments before to be informed Viola had disappeared.

"Do you think someone took her?" Marcus's heart raced frantically. He should've known she would do something desperate after what had happened the previous day. Viola was sure to be reeling from self-recriminations and doubt. Especially since he hadn't told her he was still in love with her. Maybe if he had, she would not have been forced to do something as desperate as run away. He pushed aside his own guilt and stopped pacing long enough to listen to Robert.

"There is no sign of a struggle. Her maid said a few items of clothing are missing, so she had time to pack a bag. Maybe she went to London?"

"If she did, I'm going to wring her foolhardy neck." Marcus wasted no time in ordering his bags to be packed and loaded in his carriage. His immediate reaction was to take off on his horse, but he needed something to carry Viola home in. Knowing her, he would probably have to tie her down kicking and screaming. He dashed off a quick note to his estate manager and handed it to a footman to be delivered. Robert hovered at his elbow as Marcus scribbled his hasty instructions.

"So you're going after her?"

"Did you doubt I would?"

Robert shook his head. "Honestly, no. I know how you feel about my daughter."

Marcus hoped that wasn't true. If Robert knew what he planned to do to Viola as soon as he caught her, the man would never let him out of his sight. Marcus's valet rushed by with his bags and he turned to follow him out the door. He had one final request of Robert.

"In case she appears, send word to me at my townhouse."

Robert followed Marcus out the door. He reached out a hand and halted Marcus before he could go down the steps. "Did something happen between you two that I should know about?"

Marcus's head swung around to look at Robert seriously. He chose not to answer since it was apparent Robert already knew what had occurred. "I'm going to marry her. I hope I have your blessing."

"If my daughter agrees to marry you, rest assured I will fully support her decision. And if she doesn't, I will fully support her still."

It was not much in the way of comfort. Marcus gave a slight nod. "Thank you, sir."

Robert clamped a hand on his shoulder. His lined face eased into a smile. "But it is my sincere hope she chooses to marry you."

"Mine also." Marcus said his farewells and descended the shallow steps to the drive. He climbed into his carriage and rapped quickly on the roof to let the coachman know he was ready. The coach began to move and Marcus said a silent prayer he would find Viola safe and sound. And then he was going to make damned sure she never left him again.

Chapter Seventeen

"Viola, what a wonderful surprise!"

Viola looked up as Margaret descended the staircase and smiled wearily. "Forgive me for barging in, but I had nowhere else to go."

"What are you doing in London? We didn't expect you back for several months."

"I had a sudden change of plans." She dropped her valise and rolled her aching shoulders with relief. The trip from Kent had taken its toll and she was exhausted. She'd ridden throughout the night so she could make it to London before anyone learned of her disappearance. Her back hurt from being in the saddle so long and her eyes could barely focus. She gave Margaret an overview of all that had happened, conveniently leaving out any mention of her and Marcus. Margaret's face revealed her shock as Viola told her about the threatening letters and Marcus getting shot.

"I hope you are not planning on doing anything dangerous." Margaret gave her a stern look.

"I don't believe so." Viola had thought about the entire night and concluded she would be safe. "If it is really me they are after, I figured they would try to attack me while I am in London."

"But what if you are the target? What then?" Margaret's pinched lips and puzzled frown clearly indicated she did not approve of Viola's plan.

"Then I hope your husband will be able to protect me."

Viola knew her plan sounded foolhardy, but

it was the only way to draw out the attacker. It had to be done if she wanted to have a life with Marcus. One where she did not have to constantly worry he would be taken from her.

"Surely you realize this will be the first place Marcus, and need I mention a possible attacker, will look for you?"

It was indeed something she'd realized. "Yes, which is why I am taking up lodging elsewhere. I do not want to put you and Catherine in danger."

"But where will you go?" A frown still lingered about Margaret's lips.

Viola smiled and shook her head. "I know you are my cousin, and I love you dearly, but I cannot trust you will not tell Marcus where I am going. You have always acted like a babbling fool around him and if he asked you would probably tell him regardless of whether you meant to or not."

"You cannot be serious! How can we be sure you are safe?"

"I will let Taylor know where I will be staying. I trust he can keep a secret from Marcus?"

"I would suppose he could." Margaret put her hands on Viola's shoulders and stared at her seriously. "Are you absolutely sure you can protect yourself?"

"I will send word to Taylor if it appears I am in any danger."

"What do I say if Marcus questions me? You know I was never very good at deception."

" You tell him you did see me, but you have no idea where I am. It is the truth, after all. Surely you can handle that?"

"I really wish you would reconsider," Margaret pleaded with huge eyes.

"I cannot live the rest of my life constantly looking over my shoulder," Viola said determinedly. "I refuse to let someone else have such control over my life. I am going upstairs to rest for a few hours and then I must be gone before Marcus catches up."

Margaret followed Viola as she wearily climbed the stairs to the guest bedroom she used while in London. She finally asked the question Viola had been dreading since she first saw her cousin. "How are you and Marcus getting along?"

"We are tolerating each other," Viola hedged as she opened the door to her suite and tossed her small valise inside the room. "As well as can be expected in the circumstances. Why do you ask?"

Margaret shrugged her shoulder as she moved into the room to pull back the covers on the bed. "I just wondered. It must have been odd seeing him so often after all these years."

Viola had to bite her lip to keep from spilling the events of the past few weeks to Margaret. She readied herself for a nap and allowed Margaret to help her undress before climbing between the cool sheets. She yawned widely and focused a stern eye on Margaret. "Do not let me sleep for more than a couple of hours. I have to be long gone before Marcus arrives."

Margaret glanced at the clock on the mantle and nodded. "I will make sure you awaken before eleven."

"Thank you." Viola snuggled deeper into the covers with a heartfelt sigh. She was so exhausted.

Margaret had barely closed the door behind her before Viola was deeply asleep.

*****

The coach had barely stopped moving before Marcus sprung from it and rushed up the stairs of Taylor's London townhouse. He was shown into the library and he paced nervously while he awaited Taylor. After what seemed like hours, his friend finally appeared.

"Have you seen her?" Marcus asked without preamble.

Taylor's smile froze on his face and he lifted an eyebrow questioningly. "It is nice to see you too, Marcus." He sat down behind his desk and offered Marcus a glass of brandy. "What happened to your arm?"

Marcus shook his head impatiently and ignored the glass in Taylor's hands. "It is just a flesh wound, nothing to concern yourself about. I know she had been here, so where is she?"

"If you mean Viola, then yes she has been here. Unfortunately, she came and left while I was away from the house. I did not have a chance to see her although Margaret spoke with her briefly. She did leave me a note though."

"And where is this note now?"

Taylor's gaze flicked to the fireplace and Marcus knew his answer. "She made me promise to burn it as soon as I had read it."

Marcus's gut clenched and he leaned forward in his seat. "Did she happen to mention where she was going?" He barely managed not to reach out and shake the information from Taylor.

"Yes I believe she did."

"Would you like to tell me where she went?" Marcus asked in carefully modulated tones. He was still forcibly restraining himself from beating the truth out of Taylor.

Taylor shook his head as he leaned back in his seat and laced his hands over his flat belly. "My wife made me swear not to tell you."

Marcus placed his hands on the desk and narrowed his eyes dangerously. "If you do not tell me, I will be forced to beat it out of you."

Taylor held up a hand in warning. "Viola may have a good idea, Marcus. Think about it for a moment."

"The only thing I am thinking about right now is planting my fist in your nose." Marcus's fist clenched and unclenched in frustration.

Taylor ignored his warning and continued speaking, "If someone really wants to harm Viola, now is the perfect time to capture him. She is using herself as prey to draw him out of hiding and force him to reveal himself."

Marcus's mind raced with all the possibilities that could occur. He would never forgive himself if Viola were harmed. True, he did not relish the thought of not knowing who was behind all the threatening letters, but he did not want Viola to put herself in danger. "Do you have men watching her at all times?"

Taylor gave him a bland look. "Do you think I'm an idiot? I sent three of my best men after her. She should not be in any danger."

"Does she know you did that?"

"No and I hope you won't tell her I've set watchdogs after her."

"I wish Margaret would've tried to talk her out of this." He still did not agree with Viola's scheme, but it seemed he would be forced to let it play out.

"She did try. Have you ever tried to convince Viola to do something once her mind was made up?"

Marcus nodded in agreement. "Yes, I have."

"And how did that turn out?"

"Seeing as we are still not married, I guess I failed." .

"Then you understand how hard it would be for my wife to change Viola's mind?"

"She is the most damnably stubborn female I know."

"Especially when she thinks she is doing something to protect the man she loves." Taylor winked knowingly.

"What gave you that idea?"

"Come on, man! It is written all over her face. Yours too, if you want to know the truth. The sooner this mystery is solved, the better off you two will be." Taylor leaned forward and all trace of amusement fled his face. "Do you still believe Greenley is behind all of this?"

"I am almost certain," Marcus answered grimly. "I have men scouring the country for him as we speak."

"Well I cannot say I liked the man, but I never would have imagined he would stoop to this level. If you need any help, I can make any number of men available to you."

"Thank you. Hopefully it will not come to that, but thanks for the offer."

Marcus headed for the door after a final goodbye to his friend. There was still a few hours of daylight left and he planned to use them scouring the city for Viola.

*****

The first thing Viola intended to do was make herself visible. She visited nearly every shop in London and made sure she stopped to talk to everyone she recognized. She had no doubt the news of her arrival would be bandied about the drawing rooms of the *ton* later that afternoon. As she went from shop to shop, she was painfully aware of the hired thugs Taylor obviously ordered to follow her. When she had first seen them, she would have believed them to be criminals themselves, but if Taylor hired them, she knew they would be trustworthy. The man following her now was easily half a foot over six feet and had a shiny, bald head. He reminded her of a pirate she had once seen illustrated in a children's book. A scar ran down the left side of his face and caused his eye to droop alarmingly. He was definitely intimidating. Viola only hoped he was as honorable as Taylor obviously believed.

Viola went into yet another shop and glanced around carefully. It was nearly deserted except for a single customer who was talking to the modiste.

"The gown must be done in orange. I adore orange."

Viola grimaced when she realized who the customer was and she turned to head back out of the door.   Regrettably, a bell had tinkled when she walked in and a pair of beady eyes turned to focus on her.   Viola pasted on a weak smile and reluctantly headed to the front of the shop.

"Viola, how fortunate to run into you!   I am just finishing up an order for a new ball gown."

"I am sure it will be lovely," Viola replied politely to the Dowager Duchess of Bradford.   "You have impeccable taste."

"Thank you.   I do, don't I?"   The old lady smiled smugly as she patted the concoction of bright purple feathers on top of her hair.   Viola thought the hat looked like a bird had taken up residence in her hair, but she refrained from pointing that out.   The dowager continued rambling and Viola forced her mind to stop drifting and pay attention.

"I am having a small dinner party tonight. Only a select group has been invited.   You must come and keep me from boredom."

"I do not know if that is such a good idea," Viola protested.   "I have just arrived in London and I do not feel up to a party."

"Nonsense!"   The dowager imperiously waved her hand.   "You are young.   Young people always love a party.   It is at eight.   I shall expect you at seven thirty sharp.   I had better get going if I want everything in order for the party tonight.   Remember, seven thirty on the dot."

The dowager breezed out of the small shop, leaving Viola with a protest arrested on her lips. Viola sighed in resignation and quickly left the shop. If she had to attend the party tonight, she would need to go home and prepare herself.

*****

Marcus prowled the streets of London and questioned several proprietors of London's most exclusive shops. He had heard rumors of Viola shopping in the company of a disreputable servant. For two days, Marcus had searched nearly every shop in London searching for a trace of Viola. A few of the shop owners confirmed she had indeed been inside their establishment, but it appeared she did not visit anywhere twice. Viola was doing an excellent job at keeping herself hidden, damn her. When he finally located her, he was going to tie her to his side until she never wanted to leave again. Marcus was so intent on his search he did not realize his name was being spoken until he was right upon the lady.

"Your Grace, I did not know you were in London."

Marcus looked down and gave the Dowager Duchess of Bradford a small smile. "I have just come up from Kent for a short visit."

The dowager smiled knowingly. "Ah! You have come to fetch your lady home."

"I am afraid I do not know what you mean," he hedged. Was it really that obvious he was in love with Viola?

"Do not play daft with me, young man." She swatted his arm. "It is obvious the only reason you are in London is because Viola is here. When are you two going to stop denying you would be a perfect match?"

Marcus lowered his shoulders in resignation. "I assure you the fault is not mine."

"Balderdash!" The old lady spoke

vehemently and jabbed a pointy finger in his chest. "Have you told Viola how you feel about her? I can see by your face you have not, so do not try to put the blame entirely on her shoulders. How can you expect her to confess her feelings once again when they have already been trampled upon by you before?"

"If you are referring to my marriage to Agnes, I must confess you do not know the entire story. I never intended to hurt Viola."

"Nevertheless she was hurt and if you want her back you are going to have to try very hard to win her love. She is a very special girl and she deserves the best, not some fickle rake."

Marcus lowered his head and nodded to hide his smile of amusement. He was very fond of the dowager although she was blunt to a point. "Have you seen Viola lately?"

"Of course I have. Just a few minutes ago actually."

Marcus's eyes lit with sudden desperation. "Where was she?"

The dowager pointed a finger down the street at a small shop. "She was in that shop, but she left several minutes ago. She had a very unusual footman with her. If you ask me, he looked more like a sailor than a servant." When Marcus made a move to rush off, she detained him with a hand on his elbow. "You will never catch her. She left in a carriage."

"Do you know where she is staying?"

"No, but I did invite her to a small party of mine tonight. If you promise to behave, you are invited also."

"Thank you, but no. If she sees me there she

will rush off before I could talk to her." He had a sudden thought. "But, if you have no objection, you could help arrange a private meeting. Viola must not be aware I will be there. Do you think you can help me?"

The dowager rubbed her hands together and smiled. "I do so love a challenge. What do I have to do?"

Marcus smiled at her enthusiasm and quickly outlined his plans to get Viola alone during the dowager's party. It was not foolproof, but maybe it would work. Right now he was so desperate that he would try anything.

*****

"Good evening, Viola. I am so glad you could come."

Viola smiled and accepted a kiss on the cheek from the dowager. "Thank you for inviting me."

Viola abruptly noticed the dowager looked worried. Her hands were trembling and her bottom lip quivered slightly.

"Is anything the matter?" Viola put a hand on the dowager's small shoulder. "Can I do anything to help you?"

"Normally I would never presume, but since you asked there is one small favor I might request of you."

"Anything," Viola promised quickly. She had never seen the dowager look so meek and it worried her. If she could help out in any way, she would be glad to.

"I have not had time to pick out a wine and my guests should be arriving at any moment. How would that look to not serve wine to my guests?"

"Would you like me to get a servant to fetch the wine?"

"No that would never do." The dowager shook her head fiercely. "I do not trust that they could pick out a good vintage. Might I presume upon you to go to the wine cellar and make a selection?"

It was an odd request, but Viola nodded in agreement. "Of course. I am no expert, but I will try my best."

"Thank you, my dear. You are such a darling girl. Go down that hallway and turn left. The door to the cellar is the last one on the right."

Viola set off down the hallway after handing her cloak to the dowager's servant. Viola noticed it seemed deserted. Odd, considering the servants should be busy preparing the table for dinner. Viola shrugged and continued down the hall. When she reached the door to the cellar, she cracked it open and poked her head inside. It was pitch dark and Viola hesitated before entering. Her eyes took several moments to adjust to the darkness and she moved cautiously down the stairs. The door slammed shut behind her and she whirled about in fright. Seeing no one, she decided the hinges must be set in such a way that the door would close on its own. She had seen such a door before. Viola reached the bottom of the stairs and looked up at the wine rack in front of her. Most of the bottles were dusty and she reached up to take a bottle from its rack. The label was hard to read so she brought it closer to her face and squinted.

"An excellent choice, my dear."

Viola jumped at the sound of a voice and the

bottle slipped from her fingers. She winced at the sound of breaking glass and the splash of wetness on the hem of her skirts.

"Who are you?" She gave a cross look at the person hiding in the shadows.

"I do not think the dowager would appreciate you being so careless with her wine."

Viola groaned when she recognized the voice coming from the shadows. "How did you find me?"

"It was simple really." Marcus's voice grew louder as he walked toward her. "I ran into the dowager on the street and she was kind enough to invite me to her party. Of course I accepted once I learned you would be in attendance." Glass crunched under his boots as Marcus came to a stop right in front of her. "If you had truly wanted to stay hidden, I would not have suggested making yourself so visible."

"I only wanted to remain hidden from you." Viola took a step away from him. Her back came into contact with a wall and halted her progress. "I knew you would not let me carry out my plan."

"And what plan would that be?" Marcus lifted a hand to touch her cheek. Viola recoiled from his touch and turned her head to the side. If he touched her, she would lose all her resolve and throw herself at him before she could stop herself.

"To catch the person responsible for threatening you." Viola caught a glint of his eyes as he moved his head closer to hers.

"Why would you risk your life to save mine?" Marcus's breath feathered across her cheek as he asked the question. Viola's knees trembled although she locked her eyes with his in a silent battle of wills. She tried to push him away and evade the question, but his hands encircled her wrists and held her captive against the wall. "You still have not answered my question."

"Perhaps I do not intend to." She wished his closeness did not have such an effect on her. The will of her mind was clearly no match for the will of her traitorous body. She tried once again to get him to release her. "Let go of me at once."

"Not until you promise me you will go back to Haversham and let me handle this."

"You know I cannot," Viola argued fiercely. "I cannot stand not knowing who is behind all this! How can you be content to sit and do nothing?"

Marcus allowed his body to lean against hers until he was pressed full length against her. Her soft curves melted against the hardness of his body and Viola forced herself to remain unaffected. Her harsh breathing made her breasts swell and push against the plunging neckline of her gown. Marcus's eyes swept down and Viola could feel her skin flush beneath the heat of his gaze. Memories of that afternoon flashed in her mind and it took all of her strength not to throw herself at him again. She'd already made a fool of herself once and she did not intend to do the same twice.

"Viola, what you are attempting to do is madness! I appreciate your concern about my well being, but I cannot allow you to put yourself in such danger."

"It is not your place to *allow* me to do anything, Marcus. I am fully grown and can make my own decisions. I will do this."

"There is no way I can talk you out of this?"

Viola shook her head and gave him a determined look. "No."

His smiled turned dangerous. "I have ways of convincing you."

Her knees went weak as she realized his meaning. She warded him off with one hand. "The dowager is waiting for me." She caught the flash of guilt in his eyes and she huffed. "The dowager is in on this! Why that sneaky old woman!"

"Unlike you, the dowager still retains a modicum of common sense."

Viola's eyes narrowed to slits of green. "My plan is well thought out, I will have you know."

"But foolhardy." He lowered his forehead to hers. "Come home, Viola."

She almost gave in to his softly whispered plea. "I can't. Not until this is solved."

He kissed her softly, his lips moving warmly against hers. "Come home. You don't have to do this for me."

She shook her head. "No, Marcus." He tried to move away, but she gripped the sides of his face and kissed him urgently. "I'm doing this for us."

"God, you're stubborn!"

Her lids lowered seductively. "Just be quiet and kiss me."

Her back knocked into the wall with the force of the kiss Marcus gave her. She clawed at his shoulders, wanting to get closer. Marcus didn't move fast enough for her. He seemed content to kiss her the entire evening, while she was dying to feel him inside her again. She undid his breeches and lifted her skirts hastily. "I need you, Marcus."

He shoved his breeches past his hips, but didn't immediately take her. She sighed impatiently and drew him closer. She lifted her leg and wrapped his around his hip. "Please, Marcus."

He finally gave in. "Turn around."

She did as she asked, pausing to give him a questioning look.

He planted her hands along the wall and held them there with his own. "Just trust me."

She relaxed her posture and waited for him to continue. His hands tightened on hers as he stepped closer. She felt the brush of his cock against her bottom.

He nuzzled her hair away from her neck and kissed her. "Spread your legs."

"Good." He praised her as she did as he asked. "Now arch your back."

Her belly tightened with unfulfilled hunger. She began to suspect what he was about to do. She gasped as he filled her in one fluid stroke. Her fingers clenched into the stone wall of the cellar. He pulled out partway and slid forward again. This went on and on, driving her crazy as he brought her closer to the heights of ecstasy.

Marcus lifted their joined hands from the wall and pressed them at the point of her joining. She felt the velvety smoothness of his cock as it slid inside her. Unerringly, Marcus placed her fingers against the spot that gave her the most pleasure. He used her hands to give her even more pleasure. When she came, she slumped forward. The stone wall was cool against her bare shoulders and breasts. Marcus continued to pump into her, his movements controlled and fierce. She felt a rush of warmth inside her as he finally came.

He leaned against her, his body trapping her against the wall. Her body began to cool and she shivered slightly. Marcus moved to the side and reached for their clothing. They dressed quickly, both of them knew the dowager could stumble upon them at any minute.

Marcus helped button her gown. When he was finished, he gripped her arms. "Please come home, Viola."

She closed her eyes against his pleading. It hurt to disappoint him, but she had to do this. "No."

Marcus speared his fingers through his hair and groaned. "At least tell me where you are staying so I know you will be safe."

It seemed a little enough concession. She knew Marcus well enough to know he would never force her to do anything she didn't want to do. "Do you promise you will not visit me there? If you do, it would ruin everything and we will never be sure who the true target is."

"I have to know you will be safe."

Viola quickly rattled off her address and ignored Marcus's protest when he learned she was staying in such a disreputable district. "I'd better go. The dowager is sure to wonder what is taking me so long." She brushed past him and grabbed the first bottle of wine she could reach.

"Be careful," Marcus warned just before she disappeared through the door.

"You too." Viola took a moment to memorize his beloved face before closing the door and hurrying to join the party. Seeing Marcus again had only strengthened her resolve. She would find out who was responsible for those letters and then she could tell Marcus all she was feeling. Until then she could not allow herself the weakness of telling him she was in love.

Chapter Eighteen

For the next week, Viola carried out her plan and was seen about town nearly every day. She traveled the deserted alleyways of some of the most dangerous streets in London, but she had yet to be faced with anything more suspicious than a mother cat with its kittens. The men Taylor had forced to accompany her always trailed at a discreet pace and Viola feared they might be dissuading her possible attacker. As long as her guards were present, Viola doubted her plan would be able to work. After being followed closely by Amos, the man who reminded her of a pirate, Viola had had enough of his over protectiveness. She darted inside a dressmaker's shop and quickly ensconced herself in a deserted dressing room. Viola paced the room as she frantically thought of a way she could elude her guards. It would have to be at night, she thought. They each took turns staying up to watch the house. One man was posted outside her door and one prowled the grounds while the third man rested. If she timed it just right, she would be able to escape the house undetected.

She left the dress shop with a casually affected air. Amos gave her a warning glance before she turned her head and walked back onto the street. She headed back to the house she had rented with a new determination. If she went out alone that night and came to no harm, then she would know she was not the target. She could then focus her talents on ferreting out the person trailing Marcus. At the thought of someone wanting to harm Marcus, Viola's stomach clenched in anger. It would make it much easier to discern the author of the notes and person responsible for shooting Marcus once she knew which of them was the real target. If her plan went accordingly, she would have her answer.

*****

Marcus was standing across the street looking up at Viola's room when he saw her extinguish her candle and come to stand beside the open window. He huddled under a voluminous cloak and pulled the folds closer to hide his face. Viola leaned out of the window and looked down at the nearly deserted street. She waved cheerfully at one of the guards, who continued his circuit of the house. Once he was out of sight, Viola looked left and right before tossing out a length of rope and throwing one leg over the windowsill.

"Bloody hell!" Marcus exclaimed as he watched her climb down the rope. She was dressed in men's clothing and the tight trousers clung to the curve of her hips and bottom enticingly. Her hair was hidden under a woolen cap and she wore a shirt three times too big for her, but she still managed to look desirable. Marcus was still recovering from his shock as Viola reached the bottom of the rope and quickly dashed off down the street. He did not waste any time by alerting the guards. Instead, he took after her alone and hurried to catch up with her.

"I am going to kill her," he said to himself as he caught a glimpse of her disappearing around the corner. He walked faster, but the heels of his boots clinked against the cobblestones so loudly he feared she would realize she was being followed. No sooner had the thought crossed his mind when Viola looked over her shoulder and her gaze locked with his. Marcus had no doubt of his dangerous appearance. He was completely cloaked in black and his face was hidden. Viola's eyes showed her fright, but she turned her head and continued to walk nonchalantly down the street. The little minx even began to hum a bawdy tune about a sailor and a prostitute!

Marcus forced himself to walk slower so it would not appear that he was following her. Viola stuck her hands in her pocket and sauntered down the street. She turned into a dark alleyway and Marcus ran forward to overtake her. He recognized his mistake as soon as he felt the cold press of metal against his belly.

"Why are you following me?" Viola's voice was wobbly with fright, but she kept a steady hand on the gun pressed against him.

Marcus looked down at the offending weapon with distaste. One hasty move and Viola would permanently put an end to any thought of them someday having children. Marcus raised his hands in mock surrender and forcibly changed his voice to the rough timbre of a common laborer.

"I didna mean no harm, Miss," Marcus said in his affected accent. "I was only taking a shortcut home."

Viola's eyes narrowed suspiciously, but she moved the gun away a few inches. Marcus was determined to give her a lesson on the foolishness of going out at night alone in London, but he could not do so as long as she kept such a tight grip on her pistol. He doubted she would have gone out without a loaded gun this time. He waited patiently for her to make her move.

"Sorry. I thought you were following me."

Viola lowered the gun and stepped aside for him to pass. As soon as she did, Marcus's hand whipped out and took the gun from her unresisting fingers. Viola's screech of outrage echoed off the stone walls surrounding them as he tossed the pistol aside. Her face was pale with fright and he was almost moved to end his lesson, but his resolve hardened. If Viola did not learn of the danger she put herself in, she would continue doing it until she truly was harmed. It was up to him to make sure she never did something so dangerous again.

"I don't have any money." Viola stuck her chin out at a haughty angle as she faced him.

"It is not money I want," Marcus sneered.

Viola's shock was clear in her face as she looked down at her masculine attire. She was obviously unaware some men preferred young men to ladies. She recoiled from him in revulsion. "Surely you do not mean...?"

"Oh, but I do. Such a pretty young thing like you?" Marcus lightly caressed her cheek. Viola grimaced and pushed his hand away with a shiver. Her eyes narrowed in calculation and Marcus realized her intent a second too late to dodge the knee she aimed at his manhood. Pain exploded behind his eyelids and he doubled over to catch his breath. Damn! He should never have taught her that particular method of self protection.

"That will teach you to go around accosting

young boys," Viola said fiercely as she lifted her leg to kick him again.

Marcus ignored the pain still throbbing between his legs as he rose up to haul her against him. His arms clamped around her body as she tried to squirm her way out of his hold. Her thrashing legs came close to hitting their mark again so he tossed her over one shoulder and ignored her howls of protest.

"Let go of me, you beast!" Viola wailed as she used her fists to pummel his shoulders and back. He would probably be bruised by the morning. Marcus winced at the feel of her sharp teeth biting into the sensitive skin of his neck. She was surely drawing blood. He placed a firm hand against her buttocks.

"I would ask that you restrain yourself until we get home. Then you can bite me all you want." Marcus finally spoke in his own voice and Viola fell silent. Her teeth stopped their vicious biting, but her mouth remained pressed against his shoulder.

"Marcus?" she mumbled against his cloak. He felt her try to turn her head to look at him. She gripped the back of his cloak and pulled the material away from his head. She gasped when she recognized him. "You almost scared the life out of me! You should be ashamed. I thought I was about to be raped by a depraved animal."

" You could have been too, if I had not followed you," Marcus threatened. "Do you know how dangerous London streets are at night? There are all manners of criminals lurking about just waiting for an easy target. What were you thinking sneaking off like that?"

Viola remained stubbornly silent as he continued his tirade.

"What if someone had realized you were a woman?"

As usual, Viola ignored his question in favor of her own. "How did you find me?"

"I have been watching the house. I knew you would do something stupid sooner or later."

Viola's spine stiffened at the insult and she tugged his hair viciously. "I thought you promised not to come here?"

"And I thought you promised to be careful? It seems we both broke our promises."

They reached her rented house and he set her down on her feet. Her woolen cap had become lost in their struggles and her hair fell against her shoulders in glorious disarray. Her face was flushed with anger and her nostrils flared delicately with each harsh breath she took. Marcus waved away the three guards who came running as they appeared and the large men ducked their heads respectfully before hurrying back the way they had come. Marcus's stern look indicated they would have a harsh talking to at a later time, but at the moment he had to make Viola see how foolish her actions seemed.

He took Viola's shoulders and fought the urge to shake her. "You cannot keep putting yourself in danger." He looked at the rundown house she was living in and grimaced. It was not fit for the rats. "We are packing your bags and you are going back to stay with your cousin."

"You cannot tell me what to do. I am not leaving." Viola turned her back on him and began to walk away. She opened the door of her house and slammed it shut behind her. Marcus opened it so hard it bounced against the wall before slamming it shut once again. Viola stood in the center of the room and looked at him in frustration. "Do you not understand I am doing all this to save your hide?"

Marcus had to fight the urge to roll his eyes. The thought of her protecting him was ridiculous, but he was touched she held him in such regard. Surely it indicated a greater affection on her part than she was currently claiming. "Though I appreciate your help, I can take care of myself. It is not necessary for you to take such a risk."

"I am not giving up," she warned as he advanced on her. His face was cold and forbidding and she shivered at the look in his eyes. "You cannot make me."

"Yes, I can and you will," he said just before his head bent and he took her lips in a punishing kiss. Viola struggled against his tight grip and wedged her hands between them.

"Let me go." She gave an ineffectual push against his chest. "You know I cannot think when you are kissing me."

Marcus was heartened by the admission that his kisses affected her as much as they affected him. He reached out to pull her closer, but she twisted in his grasp. "I am serious, Marcus. Let me go."

"I can't," Marcus whispered achingly as his hands came up to frame her face. "God help me, but I cannot let you go."

*****

Viola stared into his face and closed her eyes

against the rush of tenderness that filled her at his words. Marcus pulled her back to him and this time she did not resist. She met his lips eagerly with her own and wrapped her arms around his waist to clasp him to her. Marcus lifted her off her feet and carried her the few feet to the couch. Her back had barely contacted the cushions when he was upon her. Their fingers made hasty work of each other's clothing until they were both naked. The wound on his shoulder was almost healed and she leaned forward to press a light kiss against the puckered scar. Marcus drew back to look at her, his face pinched with desire.

"I cannot wait," he apologized.

"It is all right. I do not want you to wait."

He positioned himself between her thighs and thrust deeply inside her. He buried his face in her neck as his lower body began to move rhythmically. She experienced a slight twinge of discomfort, but soon she melted against him in a whirlpool of delight. He slid partway out of her before slowly sliding all the way back inside. All of her body focused on where they were joined and she nearly cried out at the sensations.

"Am I hurting you?" Marcus lifted his head from her neck and looked down at her. A curl fell onto his forehead and she reached up to brush it away.

"Only if you stop," Viola said on a breathy moan as he came up on his elbows and adjusted the angle of his movements. The new position forced him deeper and her legs opened wider to receive him as he thrust harder. Viola cried up with pleasure, arching up to kiss Marcus's neck. She licked the red marks on his shoulders where she had bitten him and he shivered with pleasure. Remembering his taunts earlier, she delicately nipped the skin with her teeth. Marcus groaned and she became carried away. She accidentally bit him much too hard and she drew back in alarm.

"I'm sorry. Did I hurt you?" She touched the raised welt on his shoulder.

He smiled seductively at her. "Only if you stop." He copied her phrase with a wink and bent down to kiss her. Viola's tongue danced upon his and her hips arched up to meet his thrusts. Their skin grew slick with sweat and they slipped against each other pleasurably. Marcus began to move faster and Viola's cries became shorter until finally her body exploded and she cried out one last time. Marcus groaned and he made a move to pull out of her. Viola put her hands on his hips and urged him to stay inside her.

"Do not leave," she said as she gripped his hips and tightened her legs around him. Marcus reached out a hand to push aside her legs.

"But if I do not pull out, you may become pregnant," Marcus explained as he continued his frantic movements inside her. He was so close. If he did not stop now, it would be too late.

"I don't care." They'd done this two times already. Both times his seed had been released in her, so she didn't see the point in withdrawing now. Viola arched upwards and forced them both to the floor. They fell with her on top of him. Viola quickly resumed her movements. Marcus gripped her hips and held her to him as she ground down upon him and forced him to the most explosive climax of his life. Viola fell limply against his chest and he poured himself inside her with a satisfied smile. Her sweaty hair clung to his chest as she lifted herself and tried to slide off him.

"You are not doing it this time." Marcus clamped an arm around her waist and held her to his side.

"What do you mean?" Viola's face flamed as she tried to move away.

"You always distance yourself after we make love. I will not let you do it again."

"That is not true!"

"Yes, it is." Marcus began to count off the examples. "After I got shot, the afternoon at the Hall, in the wine cellar. You are always the first to pull away. Can you not be content to just lie here beside me for a while?"

Viola was afraid she would never want to let him go if she stayed with him. "It is cold on the floor." She gave a forced shiver.

"Then we will go up to your room." Marcus got to his feet and reached out a hand to pull her up. "It would be more comfortable in a bed anyway."

Viola looked down at her nakedness and bent to reach for her clothes. Marcus looked at her with amusement as his gaze traveled the length of her body. "It is not as if I have not seen it before."

Viola lifted her chin at a haughty angle and let her clothes fall to the floor. "Better?"

"Infinitely more so." He took her in his arms again.

Soon Viola was much too engrossed in his

intoxicating kisses to be concerned with her lack of clothing.

*****

"Where are you going?"

Viola lifted herself on one elbow and watched as Marcus pulled on his breeches and fastened them. The early morning sun streamed in through the unshaded window and fell across the broad expanse of his naked chest in tempting swirls. She'd spent the entire night in bed with Marcus. They'd made love more times than she cared to count and her face flamed as she remembered how wanton she'd been. Even now her body stirred to life as she looked at him. He truly had ruined her for any other man. She doubted she would ever find someone who tempted her even half as much as Marcus.

His lips lifted into a satisfied smile as he reached for a shirt and pulled it on. "I can see by your expression you have not forgotten last night."

The ache between her thighs and her sore muscles clearly attested that she would not forget the past night for many days to come. She tossed aside the sheet and got to her feet. "No, I have not and if you were any sort of gentleman, you would refrain from speaking of such."

"When have I ever given you the impression I was a gentleman?" Marcus came forward and pressed a quick kiss on her forehead. He looked at her sleepy face with tenderness. "I promised Taylor I would meet him to go over some investments. How soon can you be packed and back at Margaret's?"

Viola pulled away from him with a look of confusion. "What do you mean?"

"You promised me you would move back to your cousin's."

Viola's forehead crinkled as she tried to remember making such a promise. "Did I?"

"Yes you did and do not think you are going to talk your way out of it this time. I don't intend you to stay here any longer than it takes you to pack."

"What makes you think you have the right to order me around?" Viola wrapped the sheet around her body and tried to look properly insulted.

"Besides the fact I just spent most of the night in your bed?" Marcus raised an eyebrow questioningly.

"Besides that." Viola's face flamed with memories of how she had moaned in his arms, begging him to ease the ache inside her.

"Do not fight me on this one." He put his hands either side of her face. "If you care for me at all and value my sanity, you'll go back to Margaret's. You've been on your own for long enough."

Viola debated silently for several moments before nodding her head in agreement. He was right. She'd been alone for several weeks now and had yet to be faced by an attacker. Marcus was obviously the true target. There was no need to remain on her own any longer.

She wrapped her arms around Marcus's shoulder, heedless of the fact it made her sheet slip to the floor, and brought his head down to hers for a final kiss. "Give me two hours."

Marcus firmly kissed her, his hands tracing her body and leaving trails of fire wherever they traveled.

"Be careful," she whispered as he pulled away. Her eyes dropped to his newly healed arm meaningfully.

"I will tell your guards to escort you, so don't leave without them." Marcus kissed her again. "If you're not there in two hours, I will come looking for you."

Viola bent to retrieve her sheet from the floor as he left. She was retying it around herself when the door opened again. She glanced up and gave him a questioning glance. "Did you forget something?"

"I was just wondering."

"About what?" Viola prodded when he appeared reluctant to continue.

"When is the wedding?"

"What wedding?" Viola suspected she knew whose he meant.

"Ours," Marcus emphasized with a stern look. "I fully intend on making you my duchess before the end of the summer."

"We shall see." Viola shrugged noncommittally and tried not to laugh at Marcus's bemused expression. He shut the door and she pressed her forehead against the wood with a sigh. "We shall see," she whispered to herself.

Chapter Nineteen

"Viola, I have been so worried about you!"

Margaret rushed forward and enveloped her in a hug so tight Viola could barely breathe. When Margaret finally released her, Viola took a deep breath and smiled at her cousin.

"Where have you been? Kingsley was worried half to death. I swear he came by nearly every day asking if we had seen you. It is a wonder his hair has not turned prematurely gray the way he has been carrying on about you."

Viola was heartened by Marcus's show of concern and she could not prevent the small smile that appeared on her face.

Margaret was quick to notice it and she commented wryly, "Something tells me your relationship with the duke has been progressing rather quickly."

Viola thought of lying, but since she would be staying at her cousin's, she knew there was no way she would be able to hide her feelings for Marcus. Her words came out in an excited rush as she told Margaret all that had happened during the last month. Margaret listened with wide eyes and as Viola finished her tale, she smiled brightly and hugged her once again.

"I just knew it would work out. Anybody could tell just by looking at you two that you were still madly in love with each other. I am so happy for you."

"Now the only problem is he wants to marry

me. What am I going to do, Margaret?" Viola moved to a settee and slowly sank down.

"Do you not want to marry him?" A small frown appeared between Margaret's eyebrows as she sat down beside her cousin.

"Yes, but what if it all ends terribly? Just like last time. I could not handle it if I lost him again."

"You have to have faith all will end well." Margaret sympathetically smiled. "That's what love is after all, a blind leap of faith. He loves you and wants to marry you, doesn't he?"

Viola frowned. Marcus had not actually said he still loved her. Sure, he lusted after her and claimed to want to marry her, but what if he was just doing that because he had shared her bed? Viola did not relish the thought of a loveless marriage and she would never consent to it just because Marcus felt honor bound to marry her. If there was a child, she would have to marry him but she hoped it didn't come to that. Her mind made up, she decided the next time she saw Marcus she would make sure he knew her feelings on the matter.

No sooner had the thought crossed her mind when the front door opened and in walked Taylor and Marcus. Margaret smiled when she saw her husband and nearly flew across the room in a rush to greet him. They shared a quick kiss and when they broke apart, the heated look they gave one another was evidence of their feelings for one another. Viola and Marcus politely averted their eyes as the married couple kissed a second time.

When she looked back toward the door, Viola saw that Marcus was watching her with a hooded look. Now they were in the presence of others, she was unsure how to act around him. Though they were nearly engaged, she was not completely certain if he would want to announce their relationship. The question was quickly answered as he strolled forward and leisurely reached out to put an arm around her waist and give her a dutiful peck on the cheek. She returned his embrace stiffly and lifted her hand to touch his arm.

"Marcus, we really need to talk."

"What about?" All trace of levity had left his eyes and he regarded her seriously.

"I would rather discuss it in private, if you do not mind." Viola pointedly tilted her head in Margaret and Taylor's direction, who had finally stopped kissing and were watching them curiously.

Marcus nodded and inclined his head toward Taylor and Margaret. "Please excuse us. My betrothed has something she would like to say to me in private."

Taylor and Margaret beamed at them, while Viola resisted the urge to kick Marcus in the shin. From the tone of his voice, he had made it sound like Viola wanted privacy for something other than conversation. She followed him quietly as he led the way to the library, but as soon as the door closed behind them, she began to berate him.

"Did you have to make it sound like that?" Viola glared at him.

"Like what?" Marcus strolled over to an armchair and sat down with a heavy thud. He crossed his booted feet at the ankles and motioned for her to come closer.

"Like I wanted you alone so that I could seduce you," Viola ignored his beckoning gesture and crossed her arms across her chest.

"What does it matter? We are going to be married shortly. Surely you know they expect us to want privacy now and again?"

"I am glad you brought up the subject of our marriage. I have been thinking about it and I am not sure it is a good idea."

She watched as Marcus's mouth tightened into a scowl and he glared at her from beneath lowered eyebrows. She ignored his reaction and began to pace the room while listing all the reasons they should not wed.

"I do not want you to marry me just because you feel honor bound to do so. I had quite abandoned any thought of marriage and I am not sure I want to give up my independence. And neither one of us particularly wants children, and what is marriage except an excuse to have heirs, so I see no reason we should get married." She fibbed a little on the last. In truth, she loved children, but she knew Marcus's aversion to pregnancy, which was understandable.

Marcus, who had remained utterly silent throughout her speech, stood and crossed the room to her. His long legs covered the distance quickly until he was standing right in front of her.

"First of all, you are insane if you think I am only marrying you because we had sex. Secondly, I will not make you give up anything. Your independent nature is one of the things I love the most about you. As for children, I have given it much thought and I would dearly love to have a daughter who looks just like her mother, but only if you want one also. I am warning you though, I will probably be unbearable to live with the entire time you are pregnant. Of course, you may already be pregnant. In which case, we are certainly getting married. So if you do not have any other objections, I suggest you get used to the idea of marrying me because we are doing it as soon as it can be arranged."

"Why do you really want to marry me then, Marcus? If not for any of the reasons I listed, then why?" Viola focused on Marcus's face as she waited for an answer.

"Because I have never stopped loving you and I will go crazy if you do not cease this nonsense and say you will be my wife."

"Do you truly mean it?" Viola's eyes widened at his admission. He certainly looked as if he meant it, but she knew appearances could be deceiving. Marcus's serious expression faded and a tender smile crossed his face as he reached out to her.

"I have loved you since you were seventeen and four years is too long to wait for something that should've happened years ago." Marcus walked closer to her and pressed his forehead against hers. He whispered achingly against her lips. "So are you going to marry me and put me out of my misery now?"

Instead of hesitating, as she normally would have, Viola threw caution to the wind and answered quickly. She had been miserable without him all these years and she planned to grab this second chance at happiness before it disappeared.

"Yes, Marcus. I will marry you." Viola closed the distance and pressed her lips to his. Their kiss was tender and hinted at a future life filled with happiness. Marcus pulled away first and leaned back to look in her eyes.

"Is there something you would like to say to me?"

Viola smiled widely and wrapped her arms around his shoulders as she brought his head back down for another kiss. "I love you, Marcus."

"Stubborn woman," Marcus mumbled against her lips. "One of these days I am going to make you say it first."

Viola laughed and pulled her lips away from him and glanced up with a mischievous twinkle in her eyes. "I love you, Marcus."

"I love you, too. Now be quiet and let me kiss you properly."

*****

The tiny ring glimmered as he turned it in his hands and held it closer to the light.

"Are you sure Viola will like it?"

Margaret abandoned her perusal of the rings on display to laugh and look over at Marcus with a teasing expression. She looked so much like Viola just then that Marcus had to blink to confirm it was still her cousin standing beside him.

"She will adore it almost as much as she adores you." Margaret bent over to peer at the ring. "It is absolutely gorgeous."

Marcus looked down at the ring in his hands once more before handing it to the jeweler to be wrapped. He had finally settled on a pear shaped diamond surrounded by dozens of tiny emeralds. Unlike the first ring he had given Viola, which had been a family heirloom, he wanted to give her a new piece of jewelry to signify their new start. Since announcing their engagement earlier in the week, Viola had been caught up in planning the wedding, but Marcus's mind was still heavily weighted by thoughts of Greenley. His men had yet to trace his half-brother's whereabouts though Marcus was relieved Viola had not received any more threatening letters.

"I hope this ring will please the young lady, Your Grace. It is an excellent choice." The jeweler removed his monocle as he deftly wrapped the box in paper and tied it with a small piece of string.

"A truly excellent choice," Margaret added as she sighed over the exquisite diamond once more. "If she changes her mind and decides to not marry you, consider me available."

"I do believe your husband would have something to say about that." Marcus winked at his fiancée's cousin.

Margaret laughed and turned away to look at the various rings still on display on the counter. The jeweler handed over the wrapped package and Marcus thanked him before taking Margaret's arm and escorting her from the shop.

"Thank you for coming with me this afternoon."

"You are welcome." Margaret answered as he led her to her carriage and helped her in. "You men are so hopeless at choosing jewelry. Who knows what you would have chosen had I not been here?"

Marcus waited until she settled her skirts before reaching to close the door to the carriage. Margaret held out her hand and sent him a questioning look.

"Are you sure you would not like a ride home?"

"No, I still have several things to do in town. It should not take more than a couple of hours. Please let Viola know I should be there long before the ball is supposed to begin."

"I can send a carriage back for you, if you would like," Margaret amended.

"Not necessary, but I thank you for the offer."

"If you are sure, then I had better be on my way. We still have a hundred things to do before the ball tonight."

Marcus rapped on the carriage and stepped back as it began to pull away from the curb. Margaret stuck her head out of the window and raised her hand to get his attention.

"Do not be late. The ball starts promptly at eight and everyone will want to greet the future groom of the unforgettable Viola Haversham."

Marcus laughed and waved back at her. "I would not miss it for the world."

Once the carriage was out of sight, he turned and began to stroll down the street, happily whistling under his breath. If he received any odd looks, he was oblivious. It was not often that Londoners saw a duke walking unescorted down the streets appearing as happy as he appeared to be. He was recognized by several of the passerby and he happily greeted all of them.

"Good God, Marcus! Is that you?"

At the sound of his name, Marcus stopped to greet a former schoolmate and in doing so almost missed seeing the man watching him from across the street. The man looked vaguely familiar. As he talked to his old friend, he kept his eyes trained on the man.

The man in the dark cloak and hat noticed Marcus staring and he abruptly turned away and began to hurry down the street. Marcus cut his conversation with his former schoolmate short and dashed off with a brief apology. Marcus suddenly knew without a doubt the identity of the man across the street.

Greenley.

Greenley realized he was being followed and turned off into an alleyway. Marcus was right on his heels and dashed in after him. He lunged forward and managed to grab hold of his cape, but he untied it and Marcus was left empty handed. Cursing under his breath, Marcus dropped the cape and chased his half-brother for at least another block before finally getting close enough to latch onto his arm.

Marcus yanked Greenley to a halt and swung him up against a wall viciously. His chest heaved with labored breathing as he looked into the face of his half-brother, a face which was remarkably similar to his own. Marcus wondered why he had never noticed it all those years ago.

"Why have you been threatening me?" Marcus asked harshly as he recalled the reason he had been chasing Greenley in the first place. His father's words echoed through his head, but why had he ran from him if he was not guilty?

Greenley's pale face turned even paler as he looked at the rage in Marcus's eyes. He swallowed nervously and cast an anxious look over his shoulder. For the first time, Marcus noticed the lines of strain around the viscount's eyes and mouth.

"What are you talking about? I have not threatened anyone. Why did you kidnap me?"

"What?" Marcus tightened his grip on him. "My men have not been able to find you for months. Why do you think I would kidnap you?"

Greenley's eyes darted from side to side nervously. "I was at an opera in Paris when I was set upon by a group of ruffians who tossed a sack over my head and loaded me into a cart. They said you ordered it."

"I can assure I did no such thing," Marcus said with the beginnings of real unease. If what Greenley said was true, then he had been chasing the wrong person. Someone was also trying to frame him for abducting the viscount. It all made no sense and Marcus struggled to make heads or tails out of it. "My fiancée has been receiving threatening letters for a month now. I have also been shot. Are you saying you had nothing to do with it?"

"Me? Are you insane? Why would I want to harm you?"

"Maybe you are jealous because I have Viola's affection. Or maybe you harbor hatred for me because I'm our father's illegitimate son."

Greenley gave him a surprised look. "You know?"

"I know you are my brother. My father told

me everything before he died."

At Marcus's words, Greenley's face paled even further and he fell limply against the wall. "Our father is dead?"

Marcus nodded grimly and swallowed past the lump of pain in his throat. "Yes, he is. He wanted me to find you and give you a chance to explain about the mask."

"The mask?" Greenley's face was blank.

Marcus began to imagine the viscount might honestly be as innocent as his father had suspected. "Yes, the mask. The one you bought to be an exact replica of the one I had given Viola so I would confuse her with Agnes."

Greenley shook his head in alarm. "No, I did not buy any mask."

"Then why were you so anxious for Viola to find us that night in the garden?"

For the first time, Greenley began to show some guilt. "I must admit when I saw you with Agnes, I wanted Viola to catch you with her. It was my hope she would turn to me, but it was always you she wanted. You have to believe I had nothing further to do with it."

For some odd reason, Marcus believed him and he began to loosen his death grip. "If this is true, then I must owe you an apology. I have suspected you of several very foul deeds."

Greenley waved off his apology with one of his own. "I am sorry for all the trouble I caused you with Viola. If I had not taken her to the garden, perhaps you would be happily married now."

"It would not have changed things." Marcus

would have had to marry Agnes regardless of whether or not Viola had caught him in the garden. "Agnes became pregnant and I would have married her anyway. It is not your fault my betrothal with Viola fell apart." He was struck by a sudden thought. "You say you were kidnapped. How did you escape?"

"My bonds were loosened so I could eat. I used the fork they provided on my guard."

Marcus winced, imagining the scenario. "I'm glad you escaped unharmed."

Greenley let out a relieved sigh. "Thank you for believing me even though I have not given you much cause for faith."

"Do not worry about it. We are brothers after all," Marcus returned with a guarded smile. His mind raced as he tried to imagine a person who would want his betrothal with Viola broken. A sudden suspicion hit him as he realized the motive was not merely to break his betrothal, but possibly to create a new one with Agnes. He cursed silently to himself as a revelation occurred. He suddenly knew with blinding clarity exactly who was behind the threats.

At the sound of applause, both men turned and realized with dawning horror they had just been trapped. Greenley's equally shocked look confirmed he was truly innocent of all knowledge of who had written those notes and Marcus's sudden suspicion was proved correct. His eyes narrowed as he looked at the pistol aimed at his head and beyond it to the maniacal look in the eyes of the person holding the gun.

"A touching reunion," a cruel voice remarked. "I hate to cut it short, but I must insist you do as you are told and get into my conveyance immediately."

*****

"Where is he?"

Viola paced her room and gave another worried look at the clock standing in the corner. She turned and pierced Margaret with a pained expression. "You do not suppose he has changed his mind about marrying me, do you?"

"Do not be ridiculous. Marcus would cut off his right arm before he would do that," Margaret was quick to reassure her cousin.

"Well you are not saying much being that Marcus is left handed."

"Oh, well then. He would cut off his left arm before he would do that," Margaret corrected herself. "Come and sit down before you wear a hole in my lovely Aubusson." She patted the space on the bed next to her and Viola plopped down beside her with a huff.

"He had better be lying in an alley somewhere to do this to me," Viola muttered under her breath.

Margaret smothered a horrified laugh. "You do not mean that. He probably got held up at one of his meetings and lost all track of time." She looked over at the door as Taylor knocked and poked his head inside. "Any sign of him?" She asked her husband, who shook his head quietly.

"Guests are already starting to arrive," Taylor informed his wife. "Would you care to come down and greet them?"

Margaret glanced over at Viola, who made a shooing motion with both of her hands. "Go ahead. I will be down in just a moment."

Margaret and Taylor left the room and Viola was left alone with her worried thoughts. What if Marcus had truly decided not to marry her? The last week had been one of the happiest in her life and she would be devastated if she lost him again. A glance at the clock confirmed it was already ten minutes past eight, way past the time Marcus had promised to escort her downstairs.

Viola ran a hand over her pale silk skirts and fought the urge to wail. Her hands shook, so she wrapped them into fists and pressed them against her churning stomach. If Marcus did not appear soon, she would personally set out in search of him.

At thirty minutes past eight, Viola knew she would have to make her appearance at the ball alone. As she descended the stairs, her mind raced with several scenarios for what could be keeping Marcus. Her father, who was standing at the bottom of the stairs waiting to escort her in, looked nearly as worried as she felt and Viola's heart began beating triple time. Taylor appeared beside her father and she searched his face for any sign.

"Do you think he is in danger?" she whispered to Taylor as she reached the bottom of the stairs and took her father's offered arm.

Taylor tried to smile reassuringly, but the dark look in his eyes hinted at his suspicion. "If he is not here in thirty minutes, I will send out a search party, but for now we must smile and look happy since all the eyes of society are on us."

Viola's lips widened in a grim parody of a smile as she looked around the crowded ballroom. A few of the guests looked genuinely pleased to see her, but mostly she was conscious of the curious looks sent her way for appearing at a ball to celebrate her betrothal without the groom in sight. At the knowing looks, Viola wanted to scream at everyone to mind their own business, but her father squeezed her arm and sent her a warning look.

"I know you are frustrated with waiting, but please remain calm for Marcus's sake. It would not do to cause undue alarm." Taylor spoke calmly from her side.

Viola tilted her head and faced the room with calm eyes. She was quickly approached by several of society's matrons and the next half hour was spent in meaningless conversation. Her worry increased when Marcus did not make an appearance by nine o'clock. Something had to be wrong. There was absolutely no reason he would miss their betrothal party.

Viola moved around the room, but she was aware of when Taylor excused himself from his wife and left the ballroom. She was dancing with a young lord, but she made her apologies and quickly hurried to Margaret's side.

"Where is Taylor? Has there been any news of Marcus?"

Margaret's green eyes were filled with concern as she took her cousin's arm and led her to a deserted area of the ballroom. "He and your father have gone to organize a search party. Do you have any idea where Marcus may have gone? Did he mention he had to meet anyone?"

"No." Viola shook her head violently. "He was to be here at precisely eight o'clock."

Face pale, she swayed on her feet and Margaret hastily reached out a hand to steady her and lead her to a deserted chair.

"What if he is hurt? Someone may have kidnapped him. Oh God! What if the person who wrote those notes got him?" Viola buried her face in her hands and tried to take deep, calming breaths. Marcus would not want her to panic. Besides a clear head was what she needed if she intended to find Marcus herself.

Taylor reappeared and from his pinched expression, Viola knew there was still no word from Marcus. Gathering Margaret to his side, he bent down and quickly whispered something to which Margaret nodded before giving Viola a concerned glance. Taylor smiled reassuringly at Viola before turning to leave the room once more. On shaky knees, Viola stood and reached out to grasp her cousin's arm.

"What is it?"

Margaret seemed to be weighing her words before speaking. With a large sigh, she began to explain what Taylor had discovered. "I was with Marcus earlier in the afternoon at the jewelers. After I left him, some people on the street saw him chase a gentleman into an alley. After that, no one can recall seeing him emerge."

Viola, who had already gone pale with worry, went even paler and swayed on her feet. "This is all my fault. If I had not been so determined to come to

London, it would never have happened. He would still be safe at the Hall."

"Viola, look at me!" Margaret gave her cousin a little shake. "This is not your fault. Marcus would follow you wherever you go, regardless of his safety. He knew the risks when he came here, so do not blame yourself."

Viola straightened her shoulders and gave Margaret a fierce look. "I am going to find him."

"Do not be ridiculous. Taylor has men scouring the city as we speak. What good will you do anyone if you put yourself in danger?"

"If I stay here, I will go out of my mind with worry. I cannot just sit here and do nothing."

"Yes you can and you will." Margaret led Viola from the ballroom and into the private study. She shut the door behind them with a resounding bang and gave Viola a fierce look.

"If I have to chain you to this desk myself, I will. Marcus will never forgive me if I let you out of my sight."

Viola threaded her fingers with her cousin's and sent her an imploring look. "What would you do if this happened to Taylor? Would knowing that men were looking for him let you rest any easier?"

"Of course it would not!"

At the sound of a familiar voice, both women turned and gave the Dowager Duchess of Bradford a quizzical look. The elderly lady tottered in and shut the door behind her with another resounding bang.

"Lady Bradford, would you not be more comfortable in the ballroom?" Margaret tried to politely rid them of the dowager to no avail.

"What? And miss the most excitement I have seen in years?" The dowager fluffed the bodice of her gown and took a moment to preen. "Besides I know where your young man was taken."

Viola came to immediate attention. "Where is he?"

The dowager held up her hand and shook her head. "Only if you allow me to assist you in his rescue."

"Of course." Viola crossed the room to take the dowager's hand. "Where is he?"

"You cannot be serious? Viola, think what you are doing!"

Viola ignored her cousin's protest and held the dowager's gaze. "Please, if you know anything, tell me now."

"The old biddy took him." The dowager's mouth curled with contempt. "I always knew something was not quite right in the head with that one."

"A woman? Marcus left with a woman?" Viola's stomach lurched at the upsetting news. She could not take it if he had tossed her aside for another woman again.

"Calm yourself." The dowager lightly slapped Viola's wrists. "It is not what you think. The Countess of Weatherington and her hired men abducted the duke."

"The countess?" Viola asked in disbelief.

"Yes. I saw it with my own two eyes. She and her thugs took the duke and viscount right off the street."

"The viscount?" Margaret had been silent for

most of the exchange, but suddenly spoke.

"Is there an echo in here?" The dowager said with a disgusted snort. "Yes, the viscount."

"We have to go after them." Viola gave her cousin a meaningful glance. "You have to let me go."

At Margaret's expression, Viola knew she was making headway. She came forward and took both of Margaret's hands in hers.

"I am not asking for you to accompany me, but I have to do this. Marcus is obviously in danger and I cannot afford to waste another minute arguing with you."

Margaret bit her lip and gave Viola a concerned look. "If you are going to attempt to rescue him, I must insist you accept my help."

"Do not be ridiculous. You have Catherine to care for and this ball to look after. Besides, I do not want Taylor's ire directed at me if you come to harm."

Margaret did not look reassured, but she nodded finally. "What do you plan to do?"

"The question is not what she plans to do," the dowager stated emphatically, "But what do *we* plan to do."

Chapter Twenty

Marcus pulled furiously at the ropes which restrained his hands behind his back. His shoulders felt like they had been popped out of socket and his fingers were beginning to grow numb. As far as he could tell, he and Greenley had been trussed up and tossed in the back of a hay wagon before being covered with a burlap sack.

Marcus heard a groan and he tilted his head toward the sound. A gag was shoved in his mouth and he tried to use his tongue to dislodge it. Failing miserably, he pivoted his body and peered through the worn cloth of the sack toward where Greenley was lying in a crumpled heap.

When they had been ambushed, Greenley had resisted, causing their assailant to deliver a firm cosh to his head with the butt of the pistol. He had sunk like a stone and Marcus was worried he might never awaken.

"Greenley?" Marcus managed to mumble around the wad of material shoved in his mouth. It came out as a garbled mess, but Marcus was rewarded by another groan. Obviously he was finally coming around.

With a sigh of relief, Marcus settled back against the hard planks of the wagon and digested the fact that they had been abducted by the last person he ever would have imagined before his encounter with Greenley in the alleyway. He was so caught up in imagining the man guilty he had not given a lot of thought to other possibilities. As he thought about all which had transpired, it made perfect sense. In a warped version of the truth, he could see why his abductor would have cause to hate him. Greenley had clearly been used as a scapegoat and had unfortunately been at the wrong place at the wrong time.

The swaying of the wagon finally halted and Marcus blinked as the burlap sack was tossed aside and a rough pair of hands pulled him to the ground. Greenley received similar treatment and Marcus was relieved to see except a slight gash over his temple, he appeared unharmed. Greenley's eyes were wide with astonishment as he watched their assailant come forward and eye them speculatively.

"Take them into the house," a feminine voice commanded as she stepped back to let her hired men follow her order. "Be quick about it, you dolts. We do not want everyone in London to see what we are about."

Marcus was lifted from under his armpits and his shoulders screamed in protest. His muscles were cramping and if he ever escaped, he doubted he would be able to use his arms properly. Moving his fingers to get the blood flowing, the bonds around his wrists seemed to be loosening. With a little luck, he might be able to get them undone in time to save himself and his brother.

As they entered the familiar townhouse, Marcus was grateful he knew the layout of the place. He and Agnes had only visited a few times, but it was enough so that he recognized his surroundings. It would come in handy when he and Greenley made their escape.

"Where do you want us to put them, your ladyship?" the thug carrying Marcus asked.

The countess turned and the gleam in her eye chilled Marcus straight to the bones. She would not be satisfied until he was dead, of that he had no doubt.

"Upstairs. First door on the left."

Agnes's room.

*****

Dressed in a pair of breeches filched from Taylor's closet and with a dark cap hiding her hair, Viola leaned out of the carriage and cursed for the tenth time.

"Can this bloody carriage go any faster?"

The dowager, in similar garb, shook her head and tapped her cane against the floor. "The driver is already going as fast as he can. If we have an accident, how do you expect to help the duke?"

"You have a point." Viola once more looked out of the carriage which took her closer to the countess's townhouse. The street was nearly deserted and Viola shivered uncontrollably. As soon as they had left, Viola had no doubt Margaret had sent word to Taylor. Praying they reached Marcus in time, she crossed her arms and bit her lip until she nearly drew blood.

The dowager leaned out of the window and used the tip of her cane to rap on the ceiling of the carriage. "Halt!"

At Viola's questioning look, the dowager spoke as if explaining things to an addled youth. "We cannot arrive at the front door, can we? I believe this situation calls for more stealth."

"Of course." Viola cursed herself for not thinking of something so obvious. The dowager may be old, but she was clearly a useful person to have around. Reaching for the handle to the door, Viola climbed down and turned around to assist the dowager.

The dowager jumped from the carriage in a remarkably agile movement and took a moment to get her bearings. She used her cane to point to a house at the end of the street.

"There is the countess's residence, the huge mausoleum on the corner. I suggest we circle around the back and try to find a way inside."

Viola's lips twitched in amusement even though she was deathly worried for Marcus. "Why do I get the feeling you have done this before?"

The dowager shrugged and gave her a blank look. "Some things are better left unsaid. Now do you want to rescue your young man or not? Follow me and try not to make any noise."

With that prod, Viola followed the dowager as she crept past the line of darkened houses. They circled slowly around the house and the dowager once again used her cane to point toward a door. She held a finger to her lips and approached the door cautiously. When the door opened, Viola exhaled in silent relief as the dowager stepped back to let her pass through.

"I cannot believe it was unlocked," Viola whispered as she walked inside the dark kitchen.

The dowager snorted and rolled her eyes. "Some people do not realize times are changing and the days of unlocked doors are long over.

Nevertheless, it certainly was fortunate for us I did not have to waste time picking a lock."

Viola looked at the dowager in amazement. "Do you really know how?"

"Of course I do." The dowager shrugged aside Viola's surprise. "A child could do it."

"Who exactly are you?"

The dowager lifted an eyebrow in amusement. "Some other time I might tell you, but for now we need to concentrate on finding Kingsley." She lifted her finger to her lips and motioned for silence, which Viola quickly obeyed.

"Where do you think they are?" Viola mouthed the words to the dowager, who pointed upstairs.

Flattening against the wall, they crept toward the front of the house and began to creep up the stairs. It was slow going since the stairs were prone to squeakiness and Viola was grateful for all the times she had sneaked out of the house as a young girl. Her training would definitely come in handy now.

As they neared the top of the stairs, Viola heard voices raised in anger. She cut her eyes to the dowager and shared a meaningful glance with the older woman. The dowager nodded and tilted her head in the direction of the voices. Holding out one arm, the dowager forced Viola to a halt and proceeded ahead of her.

Viola felt in her pocket for her gun and her cold fingers wrapped around the handle of the pistol she had stowed there. Pulling it out, she cocked the gun as silently as possible and held it at the ready. Noticing the weapon, the dowager's eyes widened in approval. The older lady pressed a discreet button on her cane. Part of it retracted and revealed a slim blade.

The dowager was full of surprises. If they made it out alive, no one would ever believe her tale. She and the dowager pressed their backs against the wall and listened to the voices for several moments. The thick walls made it difficult to make out words, but the voice was feminine and definitely angered.

Viola's hands clenched into fists. If that woman harmed so much as a hair on Marcus's head, she would tear her limb from limb.

When the door beside them suddenly opened, Viola nearly jumped out of her skin. The door closed and a brawny man stepped into the hallway. He noticed the two of them and he opened his mouth to speak when the dowager suddenly sprang forward and caught him about the neck. With a fierce hold against his throat, the thug was unable to say a word and merely crumpled to the floor in a disgraceful heap.

The dowager dusted off her hands and once more took up her blade. She motioned for the gape-mouthed Viola to follow her as she cracked open the door and strode boldly inside.

Voices trailed to a halt as four pairs of incredulous eyes swung to meet them. Greenley was blatantly surprised and Viola had to hold back a gasp at the sight of a nasty looking gash on his forehead. The countess appeared irritated and her eyes narrowed at the interruption. Marcus's eyes locked with hers and Viola shivered at the look on his face.

Marcus was the first to speak.

"Damn it, Viola. What are you doing here?"

*****

At the sight of Viola standing in the doorway, Marcus's heart plummeted to his stomach. If he got out of this alive, he would make sure she never did something so foolhardy again. He noticed the Dowager Duchess of Bradford standing protectively near Viola and barely kept from groaning. Now he not only had to save himself and his brother, but his troublesome fiancée and an old woman as well.

The Countess turned several shades of red when she spotted the unexpected visitors. "What are you doing here?"

"The same could be asked of you." The dowager motioned to the corner where Marcus and Greenley were trussed up. "I would suggest you release those two young men before something unfortunate happens."

The Countess of Weatherington threw back her head and laughed. "Who is going to make me? You, old hag? Or that whore?"

"Whore? How dare you!" Viola's fingers curved into talons and she launched herself at the countess.

The dowager snagged her neatly around the waist and spun her around. "Let me handle this, Viola."

Viola strained against the dowager's surprisingly strong hold. "But she called me a whore!"

"For the love of God, Viola! Be careful!" Marcus shouted as he saw the countess motion for one of her thugs. The large man held up a pistol and aimed it right at Viola.   Marcus's heart stopped beating and he struggled anew against the ropes binding him. Greenley similarly struggled.

Viola's eyes widened as she stared motionless at the barrel aimed at her heart. Marcus broke free of the bonds just as the room erupted in chaos.

He lunged for the thug, tackling him to the ground and knocking him senseless with one punch. He looked up just as Greenley also escaped his bonds and used the ropes to tie the thug's hands and feet together. Marcus let out a sigh of relief and looked across the room at Viola.

She watched wide-eyed and he stood to walk toward her. He was roughly hauled back and a knife pressed to his neck.

"Oh no, you don't! You are going to suffer for killing my daughter if it's the last thing I do."

The countess held a cold blade to his throat and Marcus could not even swallow without drawing blood. He tried reasoning with the woman.

"She died in childbirth. You can hardly fault me."

"Yes I can. If not for you, my darling girl would still be alive instead of suffering so horribly."

"If not for your conniving, she would not have been pregnant in the first place." At her gasp, he continued. "Did you think I would not discover you were the one to set us up? If you are going to point blame at anyone, you should look toward yourself."

"I never meant for it to go as far as it did. I only wanted you to kiss Agnes."

"And you wanted Viola to witness it so she would leave me and I would be free to marry your daughter?"

The countess made a strangled sound and her grip on the knife tightened. Marcus saw Viola creep forward and he sent her a look that should have stopped her from approaching.

Unfortunately, she ignored his silent warning.

"Let him go!" Viola held up a pistol. "Or I swear to God I will shoot you where you stand."

Marcus closed his eyes in dismay. With her aim, Viola would probably end up killing him instead.

"Maybe you should try to reason with her?" Marcus winced as the knife blade pressed harder against his neck.

"Like it worked so well for you?" The dowager pointed out from across the room. Her statement drew the countess's attention, which Marcus could see was the plan since Greenley began to move.

From the corner of his eye, Marcus watched as his half-brother snuck up on the countess from behind. She seemed to have forgotten about him in the last few minutes. A fact for which Marcus was sincerely grateful.

At just the right moment, Greenley darted forward and wrestled the knife away from the countess. Viola ran to Marcus and hurriedly tugged him out of the way of the struggle. The dowager, no longer content to stay out of the action, joined the fray and succeeded in gaining a slash to the upper arm as she pushed the viscount aside.

"You cut me!" The dowager eyed the countess with disbelief. Shoving Greenley aside, the two women faced off in challenge. If it were not so serious, Marcus would have found the scene of two old women fighting quite amusing.

"It is the least you deserve, you meddling old biddy!" The countess shrieked as she made a vicious lunge with the knife.

The dowager stepped easily aside as the countess lunged. Since the lady was already off balance, it was easy for the dowager to draw back her arm and punch her squarely in the face. The countess went down like a ton of bricks and the dowager stepped back to appreciate the crumpled form.

"I do not suppose anyone wants to wait around until these three wake up, do they?" The dowager said as she glanced at the shocked faces of the three young people in the room. Pressing a hand against her arm to stem the flow of blood, she turned and began to walk out of the room. "My work here is done. I will trust you to see to their disposal."

With that statement, the dowager left and the sounds of her retreat echoed down the stairs until finally the front door slammed shut.

Marcus glanced at Greenley and Viola before finally bursting into laughter. "Remind me to never upset the dowager."

"My God, I never knew an old lady could move so fast." A grin split Greenley's face. He aimed a curious glance at Viola. "Was she a spy or something?"

"How would I know? I am just glad she was here to offer her assistance." Viola leaned her head against Marcus's broad chest. His arms encircled her and he pressed a kiss to her forehead. She glanced up to see his face and winced at the anger that was banked in his eyes. "Yes, Marcus. I know you are angry but I could not sit there and do nothing. Besides, it all ended well."

"It hardly makes any difference," Marcus began to argue, but Viola hushed him with a finger to his lips.

The sound of approaching carriages drew their attention and Viola raised an amused eyebrow. "That would be Taylor. A little belated, I might add."

Footsteps pounded into the house and up the stairs before coming to a halt in the doorway. Taylor surveyed the room hurriedly. His eyes lingered on the unconscious countess and he gave a puzzled frown.

"Marcus, my God! Are you hurt? There is a trail of blood down the hallway."

"No, the blood belongs to the Dowager Duchess of Bradford." Marcus remarked as he took Viola's hand and led her from the room. "Please do something with them, will you?" He nodded his head toward the thugs' and the countess's crumpled forms.

"The dowager?" Taylor echoed in confusion. "She was here? Why would she be bleeding?"

"It's a long story," Greenley said as he followed Marcus and Viola into the hall. He clamped a hand on Taylor's shoulder and shook his head dismissively. "You would not believe it if I told you."

Taylor put his hands on his hips and blew out an aggravated breath. "Will anyone tell me what the hell happened here?"

*****

In the end, Marcus and Viola finally got their

betrothal ball. If the bride and groom-to-be appeared a little disheveled, no one was crude enough to remark upon it, although the appearance of the dowager duchess with a bandage wrapped around her arm was enough to begin a stir of rumors. When Greenley, with his injured forehead, appeared moments later the gossip began anew.

After giving Viola's father and Margaret a brief retelling of the rescue, Marcus and Viola walked to the dance floor to begin the first waltz.

As he took her in his arms and began dancing, Viola looked up at Marcus and smiled brightly. "I am so happy he was innocent. You have a brother now. Can you believe it?"

Marcus pressed a soft kiss to her forehead. "It's good to know I will be part of a family again. If you marry me, that is. You are going to marry me, aren't you?"

"Of course. You do not even need to ask." Viola wrapped one hand around his neck to pull him back for a longer kiss.

"Just making certain," Marcus mumbled against her lips as he wrapped an arm around her shoulders and kissed her soundly.

"Ahem," the dowager appeared at their side to cough and tapped Marcus on the arm. "Kindly remember you two are in public."

"Pardon us," Viola laughed and reached out to embrace the older lady. "Have I mentioned how grateful I am to you, by the way?"

"No you have not," the dowager answered and gave a coy look to Marcus. "I have been thinking of a way you could repay me for my assistance."

"And what would that be?" Marcus tried not to laugh at the fluttering of eyelashes the dowager gave him. He shared an amused glance with Viola, who covered her mouth with one hand to hide a grin. "We could name our first born after you."

"Oh, piffle!" The dowager dismissively waved her hand. "Who wants to saddle a child with a name like Ignacia?"

"Your first name is Ignacia?" Viola asked with a look of horror at the thought that her future daughter may be called such a horrible name.

"You can relax, Viola. I am not going to make you name your children after me."

"Then what do you want?" Viola waited for the dowager to answer. "You can have anything you desire."

"Anything?" the dowager asked with a gleam in her eye.

"Anything," Marcus agreed solemnly.

"In that case, come here, you handsome devil." With a wink, the dowager reached forward and drew Marcus's face to hers for a quick kiss. The shock on Marcus's face as the dowager kissed him had Viola giggling. The entire ball came to a halt as the guests watched the unlikely sight.

When she released Marcus, the dowager thumped Viola on the arm and nodded quickly. "He is definitely a keeper, my girl."

"Yes he is," Viola affirmed before the dowager turned and walked away. She glanced up at Marcus and laughed at the bemused expression on his face.

Several of the guests snickered and Marcus's

cheeks flamed in embarrassment. "You owe me for that one," he said to Viola out of the corner of his mouth.

"Oh, do I? And how do you plan on me repaying you?"

"How does giving me forever sound?"

"It sounds like you have a deal." Viola leaned closer. "Now how about you give me something else?"

Marcus grinned at her wicked smile. "And what would that be?"

Her eyes dropped meaningfully to his cock. "You."

"Now?" His voice echoed his surprise.

She nodded solemnly. "Now."

With stealth worthy of the dowager, Marcus arranged it so they escaped the ball without notice. Hand in hand, they sneaked to the nearest room, which just happened to the library. When the door closed behind them and Marcus's finger nimbly undid the back of her gown, Viola hesitated briefly. "What if we are caught?"

Marcus pulled her back to him. "You started this, remember?"

"I didn't actually think you would take me up on it."

Marcus pushed her gown past her hips and lowered his head to her breasts. "You'll soon learn the dangers of tempting a rake."

She moaned as his teeth teased her nipples. "But you're no longer a rake."

"True, but we can pretend I am."

Muted voices came to her through the door,

but Viola ignored them and focused all her attention on Marcus and the pleasure to be had in his arms. When his fingers crept under her skirts and touched her slit, she cried out.

"Shush. They'll hear you," Marcus teased.

"I don't care." She touched his wrist and directed him in the movements which gave her the most pleasure. She smiled with satisfaction. "You'll soon learn the dangers of tempting a woman in love." She quickly undid his breeches and reached for his cock. "And no pretending will be needed."

He moved his fingers in a way guaranteed to drive her wild. "Have you been pretending so far?"

"No." She tugged lightly on him and seductively licked her lips. "I don't hear anyone outside the door at the moment."

"Shall we take advantage of the situation?"

She laughed throatily, the sound reverberating against his chest. "I thought we already were?"

He put a hand under her thigh and slid her toward him, impaling her in one sure stroke. "Now we are."

She rolled her hips, barely able to keep her balance with just one foot on the floor. He slid forward and back with swift movements, knowing they could be found at any time. No sooner had she had the thought than a knock sounded at the door. Then she heard her cousin's voice.

"Vi! You're needed out here. Now!"

Viola's eyes flew open at the sound of Margaret's voice. "What should we do?"

Marcus barely stopped moving. "Finish in a

hurry."

She curled her fingers into his waist and urged him to move faster. "Sounds like a plan to me."

"No wonder I love you. "

"Why? My daringness?"

"Among many others."

She felt the beginnings of an orgasm. "We'll be right there," she belatedly yelled to her cousin an instant before she exploded. She sank against Marcus and pressed a kiss to the side of his neck. "Please tell me we can do this the rest of our lives."

"I wouldn't have it any other way." He gently pushed her back so he could look her in the eyes. "But in future, let's try to keep things a little less dangerous."

She nodded in agreement. "I cannot make any promises, but we can try."